ACKNOWLEDGEMENTS

As always, my first reader and hubby, Robert "Mad Dog" Schwartz, is my first line of defense. His unflagging patience with the techie stuff that has me screaming at my computer is priceless.

Holly Whitman has been the editor of every one of my books, and she keeps me out of the ditch when my story heads there. Thanks, Holly, once again for your wise input.

Also, I have beta readers! Thanks so much, Mary Jordan and Barbara Novak.

And then there is Donna Rich, who has the final, final, say. And very sharp eyes.

W0006437

Just Needs Killin'
Published by Jinx Schwartz
Copyright 2014
Book 6: Hetta Coffey series
All rights reserved.

JUST NEEDS KILLIN'
by
Jinx Schwartz

CHAPTER ONE

A friend in need is a pest.—Hetta Coffey

My VHF radio crackled to life and a familiar, if tremulous, voice carried throughout the cabin. "*Raymond Johnson, Raymond Johnson,* this is Jan. I'm at the marina office. Can you please, please, come get me?"

That quaver spoke volumes—volumes of ca-ca.

Not that I wasn't happy to hear from my best friend, but Jan turning up unannounced at Puerto Escondido, coupled with the telling timbre of the call, was a dead-on harbinger of an impending pity party. Or worse.

Her pitiful plea was, unfortunately, broadcast throughout the cruising community for miles around. I envisioned boaters lunging for their radios, poised to switch to whichever channel I chose in order to answer Jan's call. Dashing their hopes of "reading the mail" and listening in on what promised to be a titillating conversation, I answered with a simple, "I'll be right there," followed by a smug, "Ha!" after I let go of the transmit key and gleefully imagined a collective sigh of disappointment wafting my way on a light breeze. We boaters are so easily titillated.

Wondering, however, whether the last laugh might be on me, I let loose a sigh of my own, and said, "Po Thang, let us go fetch your po Auntie Jan and see what manner of well-known substance has hit the friggin' propeller."

CHAPTER TWO

Po Thang, a golden retriever I rescued from a treacherous stretch of Baja's Highway One, or Mex 1 as we call it, was doing his version of a point—paw raised, whole body atremble, staring down the boat's radio— from the moment he heard Jan's voice. When I put down the mic and headed aft, he bumped me out of his way in an effort to ensure I didn't leave him on *Raymond Johnson*. Scrambling down onto the swim platform, he effortlessly bounded into the bow of *Se Vende*, a dilapidated-looking panga I use as a dingy.

Dilapidated-*looking* is a proper description for my old twenty-two-foot panga, a fishing skiff like thousands of others plying Mexican waters. To discourage thieves, I've never repaired her banged-up gunwales, nor repainted the peeling layers of bygone colors from years of hard service. I even retained the name, obviously lettered by an amateur with a sense of humor; *Se Vende* means FOR SALE. And even though she sports a brand new 60-horsepower Evinrude outboard, I bought a very used model Johnson held together with baling wire and duct tape, and switched the housings. Why pirate my piece of crap panga or ancient motor when other cruisers have nice fancy Zodiacs with shiny new engines to plunder?

Po Thang and I putted slowly toward the marina to avoid throwing a wake in the harbor, so by the time we arrived Jan had collected a dock load of admirers: single-handers and deckhands for the most part, drawn to the tall blonde like sharks to chum. Not that man-bait is always bad; goodness knows I've used her as such myself more than once. Okay, a lot.

On the way to pick up Jan, I mulled myriad possibilities of why she was here. Had she left Chino, her sig-other, yet *again*? If so, she wasn't in for a whole lot of sympathy on my part, for Dr. Brigido Comacho Yee, a.k.a. Chino, is a handsome, world-renowned Mexican marine biologist with enough letters after his name to put Vanna White on roller skates, and he has done everything in his power to keep Jan in his camp. No really, it is a camp—a fish camp located on a lonely stretch of sand on the Pacific side of the Baja—but he's done what he can to make it comfortable for the love of his life. Unfortunately the *amor de* Chino's *vida* has a bug up her cute butt about being twelve years older than he, but I thought they'd worked that out. So, what now?

Jan had a Mexican plastic carry-all in hand, but dropped it, and her designer handbag, to hug Po Thang after he made the leap from panga to dock while we were still three feet out. I'd secretly vowed to someday throw the boat into reverse at just the right moment and dump him into the drink, but today was his lucky day. I sidled up alongside the dinghy landing and one of the cruisers reluctantly stopped ogling Jan's long, beautifully tanned legs just long enough to snag my painter. One eye still on Jan, he haphazardly secured the line to a dock cleat.

Jan wore the oversized sunglasses we both favor, but I could tell by the set of her mouth she was more than a little disquieted. When you've been friends with someone for over twenty years, their very body language is a 'tell,' and Jan's fairly screamed "knickers in a twist!" Breaking off her love fest with Po Thang, she tossed her bags into my panga, followed them, and ordered, "Let's go."

"Sure thing, Blondie, but I gotta charge ya extra for that pooch," I grumbled in what I considered a fairly good imitation of a New York cabbie.

She had the good grace to give me an apologetic lip twitch. "Sorry, Hetta. I'm a little on the distracted side. I'll explain when we get to the boat."

We motored away, much to the dismay of Jan's admirers. Po Thang moved to the bow again, barking at the occasional gull, pelican, or fish. Jan clammed up, for she knows full well how sound carries across water, and that talking over an outboard's whine is a surefire way of sharing your business with everyone in the harbor.

Rather than go directly to the boat, I coasted up to an isolated strip of beach nearby so Po Thang could do his doodie, thus saving me another trip ashore later. I'd pick up his leavings the next day, for

Po Thang, being a creature of habit, always goes for his favorite six square feet of dumping ground.

Cutting the engine after the dog leapt onto the sand and started nosing around for the perfect spot, I turned to Jan, who had removed her sunglasses and was dabbing tears from her cheeks with the back of her hand. Those big blue peepers I envied so much were bloodshot and swollen, which might have given me a moment of guilty glee had I not known whatever her problem was, it was most likely about to become mine as well.

A friend in need is, indeed, a pest.

CHAPTER THREE

There is something magical about anchoring out, swaying on the hook at the whim of breeze and tide, surrounded by magnificent views and turquoise water. And my boat is no garbage scow, either. *Raymond Johnson* is a forty-five foot powerboat with all the accoutrements of an upscale condo. By some boater's standards, I live in the lap of luxury, but hanging out for long stretches by myself at anchor is nevertheless a solitary business.

Not that I'm totally alone in my almost-empty corner of the harbor. I have Po Thang for company, but that has its good and bad points, as well. Po Thang is a rescue dog in a literal sense of the term; I rescued him, stranded and starving, from a barren six-foot piece of real estate next to Baja's Highway One, aptly named *La Cuesta del Infierno*, or Hill of Hell. This charming two-lane stretch of Mex 1 is carved from towering volcanic mountainsides, and snakes through turns, switchbacks, and blind curves without benefit of guardrails, shoulders, or turnouts.

The dog was skinny, filthy, and his future grim, until a friend and I risked our own futures to snag him. Dubbed Po Thang by Jan, once he was scrubbed and then fattened up, he turned out to be a beautiful young golden retriever with a propensity for eating me out of house and boat.

I wasn't exactly thinking ahead when I nabbed him, and had I known I'd be stuck at anchor with the ungrateful little turd, I might have considered leaving him for coyote food. But now here we were, in Puerto Escondido, just us two, until that day Jan showed up. At least ferrying Po Thang ashore a couple of times a day and taking him on long walks filled up time, which I had plenty of while waiting for Jenks—my long-distance boyfriend—to return from Dubai.

Choosing Puerto Escondido for my new digs made sense. It's a safe harbor in all but really ugly hurricanes, and has a large Gringo community, mostly living on boats or in RVs, in case something goes wrong and I need help. I was wait-listed for a slip soon in the small marina, but for now I swung on my own anchor, and had opted for the far northeastern end of the harbor because there is a window, or low berm, between the hills forming the harbor. Through that slot I have a direct line of sight to a cell tower between Puerto Escondido and Loreto, the nearest town to the north. Near that older tower, Carlos Slim, owner of Telmex, and the richest man in Mexico (and sometimes the world, if Bill Gates is having an off day), has recently bought into a development with a golf course. Rumor has it 5G is just around the corner, but just around the corner in Mexico is on par with mañana, which doesn't mean tomorrow, as many think, but instead it means not today.

I received both cellphone and Internet service via Telcel's supposedly 4G *banda ancha*—in actuality more like 3G, but better than nothing—and therefore a way of keeping in touch (and killing even more time on Facebook) without firing up my bajillion-peso-a-moment satellite system. Cell service in Baja is still spotty on most of the peninsula, so finding a spot with even marginal service is a bonus, although it does relegate me to the nether reaches of the large harbor.

Puerto Escondido was also a logical choice because of my semi-employed status. I am Hetta Coffey, SI (my little phonetic joke for Civil Engineer), Chief Executive Officer, Chief Financial Officer, and sole employee of a consulting firm specializing in Materials Management for offbeat—some might even say shady—projects.

I was recently given the boot as Acting Project Manager at a Baja copper mine when they found someone who is actually qualified for the job. However, they pay me a retainer as a consultant, and as such I'm on call to drive the hundred miles or so north for a couple of meetings a month, for which I gouge them properly. I could have stayed at a marina in a town much closer to the mine, but if Puerto Escondido is a little on the lonely side, Santa Rosalia, a blue-collar Mexican town, is almost devoid of other *Gringos*, and social life for a single *Gringa* is nil to none.

Stuck at anchor with only a demanding dog, daily mundane chores required to keep afloat on the hook, and the occasional visitor or beach party invite to enliven my days, Jan showing up like she did would have been a bonus had I not sensed an impending eff-up with every bone in my somewhat ample body.

"Okay, Chica, what's up?" I asked her as we sat in *Se Vende* waiting for Po Thang to pee upon every bush on the beach while in search of the perfect place to dump his load. My dog can multitask, but every so often gets distracted by a possibly tasty critter, like a lizard, to run to ground, gobble down, and then barf up, before getting back to the business at hand. He always faces south while piling poo, a doggy feng shui kinda thing he picked up from a Shih Tzu play pal that lives on a beach nearby.

As we watched Po Thang sniff around for south, Jan drew a ragged breath and blew it up into her bangs. "I think I've screwed up, and since you do that so much, I thought you could help me out."

"Well, gosh, since you put it that way."

"I meant, Hetta, with your uh…background, and all."

I'll admit I've sewn enough wild oats to end world hunger, but what did she mean by my *background*?

"My background as what?"

"You know, a woman of the world. And you *did* live in Tokyo."

"And that qualifies me for mind reading?"

She gave me a crooked smile. "It's a long story, but we don't have much time. We gotta be there by six."

"Not Japan, I assume? And by the way *we* don't gotta be anywhere by *any* time, much less six."

"There's gonna be lots of great food and free booze."

"Well, phooey, and me without a thing to wear. Po Thang, get your furry ass back into this boat, your Auntie Jan and I have places to go."

Back on *Raymond Johnson,* I poured us both a glass of wine and we moved to the aft sundeck where she gave me the lowdown. When she finished talking I remained speechless, something I'm not known for.

"Hetta, shut your mouth. You've got flies checking it out."

I snapped my lips shut, ran my tongue around inside my mouth checking for insects to spit, found none, and then quaffed my wine. "Let me see if I have this straight. You agreed to meet some Japanese guy at a ritzy resort tonight, and attend a party with him in return for him funding your boyfriend's treasure expedition in Magdalena Bay?"

She nodded.

"And Chino, the would-be treasure hunter, has no idea what you've gotten yourself into on his behalf?"

"Of course not. What kind of man do you think he is?"

"I think he's going to be one pissed off significant other when he finds out you're off for a tryst with Mr. Japanese dude, while *Mrs.* Japanese dude and his three little sushi crunchers are back at his whale camp communing with wildlife."

"It's not a tryst. Ishi just wants a, uh, well...someone by his side, like, you know, a hostess."

"Oh, it's *Ishi*, is it? How very chummy."

"It's what he asked me to call him at the party. So his friends know that we're friends."

I snorted, and rolled my eyes. This Ishi's friends were going to know exactly what Jan was. Or what he wanted them to *think* she was. Having worked in Japan, I know the ways of the men. Jan, although younger than I, is, at thirty-eight-ish, a little long in the tooth by Japanese standards. She nevertheless has assets they prize: 5'11" height, big blue eyes, and blonde hair. Prime *Gaijin* eye candy. And while it *is* true the men are willing to pay great sums for impressive arm decor, they almost always expect payback. My friend was extremely naive if she thought this guy was going to shell out big yen without a roll in the futon.

Jan's reaction to my cynical snort surprised me. Instead of being insulted, she laughed. "See, I *knew* you'd know what to do."

"I didn't say anything."

"I know, but you understand, right? Anyhow, I was headed for the resort when it hit me maybe I was making a big mistake, and that I'd better talk to you first. My original plan was to call you from the hotel and ask you to cover for me tonight, in case Chino called, then I got all rattled, thinkin' about what Chino would do if he found out—"

"So you cleverly deduced he just might possibly take offense at the love of his life selling herself?" I know, that sounded harsh, but what Jan was contemplating was even beyond the limits of *my* nonnormative moral map.

"You're just being a pill, Hetta. For your information, Ishi has arranged for me to have my own room at the hotel, and told me all I have to do is attend a cocktail party in his suite at six, a luau later, and have brunch by the pool the next morning."

"And no hanky panky?" I ask, doubt evident in my tone.

"Nope."

"And just how much of a donation is Ishi prepared to bestow upon Chino's expedition for the platonic pleasure of parading you around like a prized race horse?"

"You make it sound so ugly. But if you must know, a hundred thou."

I choked on my wine. "Dollars?"

Jan gave me a Cheshire cat grin. "Well, it ain't no stinkin' pesos. So, you comin'? You can stay in my room, be my chaperone...you know, make sure I'm safe. Or, go to the luau if you want. Ishi asked if I had any girlfriends who might like to party."

"Uh, I don't think he meant dress up and sip cocktails, you dork. And you don't suppose old Ishi-san might expect a little *shābetto* between the luau and brunch, whether I'm there or not?"

"Well...no. Uh, what shab...whatever?"

"Sherbet. As a palate cleanser between courses, so to speak."

"Oh, come on, I betcha Japanese people don't even eat sorbet."

"Yes, they do, and they also want what they pay for."

"Exactly, smarty pants. Which is why I flat turned down the rest of the deal."

"What rest of the deal?"

"The, uh, other fifty thou if I…you know."

I didn't have any wine left to spew, darn it. "He offered you *fifty thousand dollars* to sleep with him?" I was shocked, and that ain't easy to do.

She sat up straight, tilted her cute little nose righteously into the air, and said, "Yes, but I turned him down."

"Well, hell, Jan. Ya think he'd consider me instead?"

CHAPTER FOUR

Within an hour, we'd moved *Raymond Johnson* to a mooring near the docks, cadged a ride to shore with another boater so *Se Vende* remained chained to my boat, stashed a pouting Po Thang with beach-dwelling friends nearby, and steered my red Ford Ranger toward a fun night on some rich dude's tab.

We took my pickup because it has a few things Jan's jeep doesn't: air conditioning, windows, and a roof. During the drive to the resort we discussed everything *except* what Chino and my always-somewhere-else boyfriend, Jenks, would think about what we were up to. *This* time.

Since the resort, only eight miles or so to the south, was almost within visual distance from Puerto Escondido, we could have taken *Raymond Johnson*, but what the heck, we had a paid-for room in a luxury hotel, and parties to attend. I was already warming to the idea of Jan's new profession as a paid escort.

And even better yet, since the parties were luau/beachy affairs, we even had something to wear. In Jan's case it was a teeny fuchsia bikini with a small, sheer, scarf. And mine? A lot more suit and larger opaque wrap. I couldn't do much, on such short notice, about the extra ten pounds—okay, fifteen—setting off my zaftig-ness. However, I'd just had my pixie-cut hair re-reddened and my toenails lacquered Dior 438, Mango, which Jan said set off my hair.

We decided Ishi-san need not know about me bunking with Jan. I'd wander down during the luau and get myself invited to join the festivities, which shouldn't be much of a problem since my friends say I can talk myself past a Buckingham Palace guard. This way, if Ishi later tried storming Jan's door, so to speak, I'd be there to whack him one. Okay, that might be an unfortunate choice of words, but you get the gist. And if he later reneged on his promise of funding Chino's expedition to find a sunken Manila galleon in Magdalena Bay, I'd bear witness Jan kept her end of the deal.

We turned off Mex 1 and immediately dove into a rocky wash.

"Dirt?" Jan exclaimed as we bounced a couple of times. "They build a multi-million buck resort and don't pave the road into it? Look at this mess. If it rains they're gonna have to take their guests to the airport by boat, cuz this baby's going to flood."

"For sure. They need themselves a bridge, but with the size of this arroyo, it'll cost *mucho dinero*, which is probably why they haven't done it yet. Hurricane season, or even a heavy rain, must pose a serious commute problem."

Once through the *vado*, we climbed a wide gravel road, well-maintained, but still—gravel?

A few dusty miles later, I was patting myself on the back for deciding to bring a vehicle with windows and A/C. We came around a curve and the resort loomed, like a Mexican Xanadu, from the surrounding lunar-like landscape. The turquoise waters of the Sea of Cortez sparkled in sharp surreal contrast to the barren desert. Palm trees and flowering greenery, obviously imported, swayed with the gentle afternoon breeze. I'd seen the hotel from the water, but it was even more impressive when arriving by land, because it was just suddenly *there*.

Since most guests probably arrive via a shuttle from the Loreto airport, we parked right in front, one of the few private vehicles to do so. Three men dressed in light colored shirts and dark pants reminiscent of yacht crew dashed to greet us. While Jan was ushered to the front lobby desk, I dawdled at the pickup so as not to be seen by the office staff, then sauntered into a nearby gift shop. I was, however, close enough to hear her give her name to the clerk: Hetta Coffey.

We'd discuss *that* later.

Our room was touted as a small suite, but was the size of a one-bedroom apartment back home. With a kitchen and dining area, queen sofa bed in the living room, and a king bed in the bedroom, we certainly weren't going to crowd each other. After living on the boat for so long, I was in heaven, space-wise. From the balcony we could have seen the entrance to Puerto Escondido harbor if I'd thought to bring my binoculars.

A large bouquet of flowers, a bowl of fruit, two iced-down bottles of Veuve Clicquot, and an envelope marked "Hetta" sat on the dining table. "So, *Hetta*, looks like you have mail," I snarled.

"Seemed like a good idea at the time. I mean, who knew you'd actually be here?"

"Yeah, who knew?"'

"I might remind you," Jan said, "of all the times you gave *my* business card out in bars to jerks you wanted to get rid of? And when you used my name to rent a car that got burned up? And—"

"Okay, okay. What's the note say?"

"Just a room number and a reminder the cocktail party is at six, which means I gotta get a move on. Will you help me put some of these flowers in my hair?"

I picked out a few huge pink hibiscus blooms and we moved to the master bathroom. I rummaged in her makeup kit for something to fasten them with while she glommed mascara onto her long lashes, and applied a smidgen of blue shadow on those previously swollen eyelids we'd treated with chilled tea bags.

"You know, Jan, I've been thinking. With all the trouble I'm going to here, maybe a little fooling around in a futon might not be all that bad. I'll cover for you and we can split that fifty thou. Just a thought."

"Yeah, well here's a thought for you. No! Now put those flowers in my hair."

Jan wears her hair in a chin-length bob cut shorter in the back, so I braided in the flowers down one side. We added an extra scarf or two over that bikini for the cocktail party.

She whirled on her three-inch espadrilles and vamped. "Whaddya think?"

"Drop-dead gorgeous."

The way our lives had been going for the past few months—okay, years—I should probably be a little more cautious when using the term, dead, but she sure looked capable of causing an up-tick in defibrillator sales.

CHAPTER FIVE

With Jan off to her benefactor's cocktail party, I celebrated our opulent digs by opening some icy champagne. Taking the bottle with me, I swanned (as best as a short, somewhat chunky gal *can* swan) towards an oversized bathtub I'd spiked with lavender bath crystals and had started filling while I was weaving flowers into Jan's hair. Now that I had the place to myself, I lit a couple of candles, turned off the lights, slid into piping hot water, and reveled in the scent and caress of a real bath after so many months of showering on *Raymond Johnson.*

I'd about decided I'd skip the luau altogether and stay submerged in the tub when I heard our room door open and slam shut. Cursing myself for not hanging out the **Favor de no molestar** sign before heading for my bath, I sloshed out of the water and grabbed a big fluffy towel. I was making for the bathroom door lock when the door flew open, almost knocking me on my butt. My towel slithered to the floor as I grabbed the only weapon within reach and held it over my head, prepared to do battle.

Ice-cold, two-hundred-dollar-a-bottle champagne cascaded over my head and into my eyes. Through bubbles I saw a face whiter than my lost towel, and checked my swing just in time. "Jan! What on earth?"

She sank to the floor, settling into a puddle of water, bubble bath, champagne, and flowers that fluttered down from her hair. I flipped on the light, grabbed my towel, wrapped it around me, and sat on the side of the tub. Jan slumped over, her face hidden in her hands, and began to wail. I realized there was still a little bubbly left in the bottle and drained it before saying, "This better be good, Chica. You just screwed up a primo bubble bath."

"Is there more of that?" She pointed to the bottle.

"Yep, but unless you get up off that floor and tell me what's wrong, you ain't gettin' any."

She struggled to her feet, dogged me into the living room and hiccupped little sobs while waiting for me to uncork the second bottle. I filled a flute, she melted into a chair, downed the whole glass in one gulp, and stuck it out for a refill.

I moved the bottle behind me. "No way. Not yet, my friend. Talk!"

The woman who, minutes before left the room looking like a million—or should I say at least fifty-thousand—bucks, now sat in disarray, mascara running down her face a là Alice Cooper, one lone bedraggled flower dipping over a bleary blue eye, and the only reason she wasn't white as a ghost was the blush on her cheeks, some of which was tear-and-eye-makeup smudged. And, dang it, she still looked good. Life is not fair.

She sighed deeply. "You pour, I talk. And Hetta, I'd really, really appreciate it if you put on some clothes."

While she downed another flute and reached for the bottle, I went back to the bathroom and donned a luxuriously soft hotel robe. The moment I returned, she whimpered, "Dead."

"You drank the whole damned bottle?"

"Naw, there's a tad left. *Ishi's* dead."

"So, I guess that means the fifty grand is out?"

"Not funny, Hetta."

"Did *you* kill him?"

"Nah."

"Are you sure?"

"Am I sure he's dead, or that I didn't do it?"

"Either. Both."

"When I got to his suite, the door was open a smidge. I heard music, but no voices, so I peeked inside. To tell the truth, I was a little worried it was a set up. Like, you know, he'd be nekkid or somethin'."

"And?"

"Yup. As the day he was born. But deader than Elvis."

"Some might debate just how dead *that* is."

To lubricate our higher cognitive processes, we were working our way through the minibar. I splashed a mini-bottle of Jose Cuervo over a glass of rocks.

Jan turned from staring out to sea, and squinted puffy eyelids at me. She took a hit of Kahlua straight from the tiny bottle. "Huh?"

"Did you, like, touch him?" I asked.

"Eeewww, no."

"Then how do you know for sure he's even dead?"

"Lemme think. His head is about three feet from his body. That qualify, Detective Coffey?"

I finished off my tequila and selected the next bottle in line: vodka. No rocks. "Yep, that'd about get 'er done. Okay, I gotta think."

"That'd be different."

"Excuse me, Miz Jan, as I recall, you're the one who got us into this debacle. I'm trying to deliberate our way out of it. I'm thinking we get the hell out of this hotel, drive back to the boat, and forget the whole thing."

"You're right. But, doncha think we oughta at least throw a blanket over Ishi or somethin'? Doesn't seem quite right to leave him like that. Butt nekkid an' all."

"Okay, that is totally illogical."

"I'm just thinking of Kayo."

"Kayo? Who the hell is that?"

"Ishi's wife."

"How will she know whether he was covered or not?"

"I dunno, just seems wrong, leaving him like that. I mean, they probably won't find his body until tomorrow morning."

"I doubt that. Isn't he the one throwing the luau? Someone will surely wonder why he isn't at his own party, and go looking for him."

"Yeah, I guess. Oh, hell!"

"What?"

"The front desk. They saw me, and they must know Ishi paid for my room. When they find him—"

"They'll be looking for Hetta Coffey. Thanks a whole hell of a lot."

"Sorry, I just thought it wouldn't be a good idea to use *my* name."

"There a million jillion names in the world. Why mine?"

She shrugged. We sat in silence, each trying to figure out how we'd gotten into yet another mess.

Well, we both knew *that;* it is what we *do.*

Jan screwed the top off a gin bottle. "So, any ideas yet?"

"Yep, but you aren't going to like them."

"Probably not. I never like anything you think up, but somehow I end up going along."

"We gotta put on our big girl panties and go to that luau."

"What? Are you freakin' nuts?" Jan unfolded to her full 5'11"—6'2" in those espadrilles—put her hands on her hips and looked down her nose at me. "No way, no how. And this time I mean it. And besides, I don't have any big panties. That'd be your department."

I let that insult slide. "Sit down and hear me out. For starters, my pickup was logged into the resort, on a one-way-in, one-way-out road, at the guard shack. And there are probably cameras all over the lobby and maybe the hallways. And to make matters worse, you checked in to a room provided by a dead man. We've been *seen.* If we don't show up at that party, we'll be way up on the suspect list when they find both pieces of your boyfriend."

"He's not my boyfriend." After taking a swallow of straight gin that brought tears to her already teary eyes, she nodded. "But, bad as I hate to admit it, you might be right about going to the luau."

"Okay then, let us ice the puff out of those eyes once again, maybe down a cup of strong coffee or two, and get ready to hula."

CHAPTER SIX

The party was in full swing when we arrived, complete with pigs roasting on spits, and hula dancers swaying to some pretty fancy ukulele plucking. Both the dancers and musicians looked suspiciously Mexican, but it's the theme that counts.

Surveying the crowd, I didn't spot any formal security forces checking for invitations and crashers, just a pretty Mexican girl who greeted us with leis. She was, however, flanked by a couple of huge, mean-eyed dudes incongruously garbed in flowered shirts.

Properly lei'd, Jan and I made for a thatch-roofed tiki bar.

"We'll have six triple Mai Tais," I told the Mexican bartender. He grinned and gave us each a huge hurricane glass, complete with umbrella and a bunch of fruit. I stuck the umbrella behind my ear and chewed on a chunk of pineapple while checking out the crowd, most of which, except for staff, entertainers, and what looked like a few local hookers, seemed to be Asian. Jan and I stood out like, well, murder suspects.

"Jan, for God's sake, look innocent. Let's find out who's the big kahuna here. I mean besides your dead kahuna."

Scanning for kahunas, I noticed that one man in particular drew a crowd like remoras to a shark. I elbowed Jan. "*Banzai!* Little wrinkled dude, three o'clock. Follow me."

I led Jan to an elderly Japanese gentleman dressed in impeccable white pants, what looked like a vintage Hawaiian shirt, and draped with at least a dozen orchid leis. We'd only rated one lei each: plumeria.

He spotted us coming his way—or rather, *Jan* coming his way—and said something into the belly button of a towering goon-type Sumo wrestler who was glowering at us. The bodyguard stepped back at his master's command, but reluctantly, judging by his sour puss.

"Aloha," I said with a slight bow to the old man. "Great party. Thanks for inviting us. Actually Ishi-san invited us, but...by the way, where is he?"

With a more formal bow in return, the man said, "You are very welcome. I was told Mr. Ishikawa invited guests, but had no idea how charming they would be."

Charming? Me? Was *he* in for a surprise! Knowing how I react when patronized, Jan quickly, charmingly, ran interference with a smile and a little dip. "Why, thank yew. So kind. We are just delighted to be here." Southern dripped from her voice like moss off a cypress.

"I am Tadashi Fujikawa, but you may call me Tadassan."

"And, Tadassan," I bowed again, a little lower this time, "you may call me anything but late for dinner." See, I can be charming.

He got it and laughed.

On a roll, I set out to grill him like that spitted squealer I planned on devouring later. "So, are you and Ishi-san business associates? And where is he, anyhow?"

Fujikawa didn't miss a beat. "I had supposed he was...detained, but now...." His voice trailed off as he eyed Jan, whom he obviously thought to be the alleged detain*er*, which told me Ishi-jerk had been bragging about his date for the weekend.

"So, he's not here yet? Well, then," I grabbed his arm and led him to a table by the fire pit, "we can get to know *you* better until he turns up." Big ugly dude, whom I decided was more Samoan than Sumo, took a step forward when I strong-armed his boss, but my new best friend waved him off with a subtle hand movement.

Lava Lava clouded up, but acknowledged the order with a wave of his own hand. Which, I noticed as my stomach lurched, was missing a couple of fingers. Oh, crap! "Finger shortening" is an almost sure sign of a Yakuza thug. And the Japanese Yakuza run the largest and most vicious crime organization in the world. I thought it prudent not to mention this to Jan just yet.

I sucked in a deep breath to calm my rattled nerves. "Uh, think your man could get us another drink, Tadassan?" I cooed. I don't coo nearly as well as Jan, but she'd grown uncommonly silent and I hoped it wasn't delayed shock. "Jan, would you like another?"

"Huh?"

"Drink. Want one?"

"Sure."

Our new BFF barked an order at Samoa Boy, who sullenly turned to fetch drinks. But he was smarter than he looked, and collared a waiter for the task. He was back on guard-glower duty way too soon for my druthers.

Oh, well. "So, you're in business with Mr. Ishikawa? Lucky you, he sure knows how to pitch a party."

"We are associates, not partners. We work together on some projects."

"Here in Mexico?"

"At times. Why do you ask?"

"Oh, I just like to know if there are new projects about. Never know when a gal might need a job."

He looked at me closely and cocked his head. "I did not catch your name."

"I didn't throw it. You can call me Hetta-san, or if you prefer, Coffey-san. I answer to almost anything if the money is right."

His eyes did their best to widen as he looked downright alarmed. "Hetta Coffey? Ishikawa's Hetta Coffey?"

I took this as a bad omen.

CHAPTER SEVEN

Oh, *'kuso!'* as they say in Japan.

When Tadassan blew his inscrutable-ness and blurted, "*Ishikawa's* Hetta Coffey?" I experienced a revelation. Actually it was more like an acid reflux attack.

Why I hadn't put *ni* and *ni* together and come up with Ishikawa before, I don't know. Sometimes I can be a little on the slow side. I still decided to play stoopid, which at the moment was pretty easy, since adding two and two got, 'Oh, Crap!' and numbed my brain. Or maybe it was that mini-bar? Anyhow, I somehow managed to squeak out, "Why, yes, I am *a* Hetta Coffey. Have we met?"

Oddly enough my question sent him into a fit of laughter bordering on apoplexy. When he finally got control of himself, his cheeks matched Jan's fuchsia bikini, but at least he was breathing. Once again he waved off Samoa Boy who, like me, probably thought the old dude was gonna croak on us. Two croakers in one night is way over my body count limit.

"Are you all right, Mr. Fujikawa?" Jan, now recovered from her momentary brush with the vapors, asked as we both pounded his back.

Short-fingers handed his boss a drink that looked to be pure whiskey of some kind. He downed it, and wiped his eyes. "Yes, yes, I am fine. I was caught by surprise that Hiro Ishikawa would invite Hetta Coffey to his luau. Or anywhere else, for that matter, what with your, uh, history."

Jan cocked her head, clearly puzzled, so I asked her, "That name, Hiro Ishikawa, ring any bells with you, Miz Jan?"

She scrunched up her face like she does when she thinks. When I do that I look like I have gas. She manages to look cute. A light went off somewhere under that blondeness and her eyebrows shot up under her bangs. "Oh, dear! *That* Ishikawa?"

"Methinks, yes. Who knew?"

"But why would he come here and bring—"

I cut her off to shut her up. "I have no idea why he is here in Mexico. Maybe Tadassan can help us out with that one?"

Our new best friend didn't look all that friendly anymore, and Mount Samoa moved into our circle like a Rottweiler that'd caught a whiff of prime rib.

"Oh, my," I said, holding up my bare wrist, "look at the time. Jan, we'd better go, uh, powder our noses before dinner." I was already backing away, pulling Jan with me, ready to bolt if necessary.

It wasn't necessary. Fujikawa called off his dog as Jan and I beat feet for the lobby, and the little *Mujeres* room. Once inside we stared at each other for a minute, each of us plainly wondering how we could be so dense. *Hiro Ishikawa*, for crap's sake? How did we overlook the obvious?

Okay, so the name, Ishikawa, is Japan's equivalent to Smith in our country, and the last person on earth I'd figure would bring his family to commune with whales was the same guy who, just a few months ago, was planning to can them. Not his family, the whales. *Baby* whales, to boot. And, even though neither of us had ever met him face-to-face, Jan and I were responsible for foiling his whale-packing plot and getting him, and his cohorts, up to their necks in hot sake.

"Okay, that tears it, Jan. We really gotta get out of here. Look for a window or something outta this bathroom."

No luck with windows, but I did, however, find a door with a sign picturing a stick figure man walking through it. He was circled in red with a slash, the international symbol for, DON'T EVEN THINK ABOUT DOING THIS. It read AVISO! SOLO EMPLEADOS!

I tried the knob, but it was locked. Fortunately I always take a credit card with me, even to a luau. I have this little velvet purse I string around my neck to hold lipstick, money, and a credit card—and, back in Arizona, my Ruger LCP—cuz you just never know. Unfortunately, Mexico takes a grim view of an armed citizenry, so only the cartels have guns, and not me, who seriously needs one at all times.

The lock proved no challenge for my Visa card, and once inside the EMPLOYEES ONLY room we discovered cleaning equipment, toilet paper and towels, and lockers with both uniforms and the clothes left by worker bees currently on duty. "Let's suit up, team."

"Okay, but then what, Hetta? We have to get back to our room. Hell, even the car keys are there."

"I know, but both of us don't have to go. Help me tie this scarf over my head. And you, try to look shorter and browner."

My clothing benefactor was obviously a supersize woman, probably a maid, since the lobby staff all looked like Tecate beer models. I cinched in the flowered dress with the extra-large flowered pareo I use as a beach wrap. Jan, on the other hand, actually looks like a Tecate beer drinker's dream, so we picked kitchen staff gear for her; a little ugly-ing up with a black hair net and white hat was the best we could do in her case.

I shoved a load of folded towels into Jan's arms and told her to hold them high enough to obscure her face, hoping kitchen staff sometimes doubled as room maids.

"Take a look at this emergency exit chart. Looks like this door," I tapped on the plastic sign, "leads out the back. Go check out the parking lot and, if the coast if clear, I'll meet you at my pickup." We wanted to make a run for Mex 1 despite the guard post on the hotel's road. Since it was dark by now, our chances of escaping unnoticed from the hotel, and maybe even slipping by the guard, were vastly improved. Not ideal, but better than in broad daylight.

My decision to take the stairs instead of the elevator wasn't one of my best, considering our room was on the fourth floor. By the time I vaulted the stairs two at a time, I was gasping and vowing to embrace a StairMaster in the near future. Evidently taking a dog for a daily two-mile walk on flat roads doesn't do much for the old lung capacity. Surprisingly enough, my legs still felt strong, which wouldn't do me much good when a lung collapsed.

When the room door clicked into OPEN mode, I literally fell through it, catching myself on a chair to prevent splattering my oxygen-starved brain all over the tile floor, which, considering the condition of Ishikawa's room, didn't seem fair to the cleaning staff.

Collapsing into the upholstered chair, I recalled hearing stories about people who passed out because they didn't take the time to cool down after strenuous exercise and this simply was not the time for anything like that. Shoving myself to standing, I swung my arms over my head and did a few arm pumps while running in place, then used my cool down walk to move from room to room, stuffing our belongings—and the remaining contents of the raided mini-fridge—into a hotel pillowcase. I figured they owed Ishi at least one lousy pillowcase, considering what the tab was going to be for that emptied mini-bar. Poor old Ishikawa's bank account was gonna take it in the neck, so to speak, by our bar bill alone.

Scanning the room, I was satisfied we'd left very little to lead anyone directly to us, if you discount about a million fingerprints, enough DNA to create a new person or two, my name on the hotel registration, at least fifty witnesses who saw us at the luau, and my pickup logged in with the gate guard. All circumstantial, in my opinion.

Bad as I wanted to bolt for the parking lot, there was still one more thing I felt I needed to do. My camera in hand, I rushed for Ishikawa's suite. Jan said the door was unlocked, and for some reason I felt the need to document the murder. It was, of course, an unreasonable reason, but just felt right.

His door was indeed still unlocked, and the body—both pieces of it—lay in a brown colored liquid I doubted was Jack Daniels. A combination of best unidentifiable bad smells inside made me reluctant to enter very far into the room, but I zoomed the lens and got off a couple of quick photos, then wiped down the door handle with my skirt, and slid the door closed, locking it from the inside as I did so.

Flying back down the stairs, pumped up with fear and adrenalin, I doubted anyone in authority saw me, since I looked like a bag lady with her entire belongings—or some hotel guest's valuables—slung over her shoulder. Hotel employees are trained to overlook the antics of guests, but someone dressed as I was pushed the limits of normal.

I reached the main floor level and was rushing along the route I hoped led to the parking lot, and Jan, when we almost had a head-on collision.

As we danced around each other to maintain our balance, Jan whispered, "I drew a big fat zero. There are several hotel employees hanging out in the parking lot. Hell, one of them is sitting on your pickup's hood. I think they're waiting for a bus or something."

"Dammit! Okay, back into the locker room. We'll think of something else."

The *Mujeres* room was still luckily devoid of *mujeres*, so we spent a few minutes coming up with a new idea.

"Okay, I think I've got it. Where are our bathing suits?"

Jan waggled a garbage bag at me. We put our suits back on despite the evening chill, left the workers' clothes in a locker in the EMPLOYEES ONLY room, and scooted for the beach using the lush hotel shrubbery for cover. At least now we had money, IDs, and car keys. What we didn't have were a couple of sweaters, which we sorely needed. The sun was gone, a brisk, cool breeze came off the land, and we were trudging down a deserted beach toward a bar we'd spotted from our balcony earlier in the day. A bar with several pangas parked outside.

"Okay, Jan, here's our story and we're sticking to it. We came here from Puerto Escondido with a couple of jerks who got drunk and belligerent. We had a tiff, and they left us. We need a ride back to port."

"Gotcha. Did we come by car or boat?"

"Boat. I saw a couple of speed boats in the harbor this afternoon with a bunch of partiers on board. As for my truck, we'll get it one way or another. Right now we just need a way out of here. Pronto."

Business was a little slow at the Playa Blanca Bar, as it was early yet. We immediately spotted a couple of older Mexicans who might belong to those pangas, so I steered us to a table next to them while ignoring the surfer dude types ogling Jan from the bar. We were the only females in the room.

I ordered two *cuguamas* of Tecate—thirty-two ounce bottles of beer named for sea turtles—and two cheeseburgers with *papas fritas* to keep our strength up.

Turning my attention to the two Mexican men, I said, "*Buenas noches.*"

Obviously startled that a *Gringa* was zeroing in on them, they both nodded and politely replied, "*Buenas noches*" and went back to their conversation.

Our beers arrived, and we'd chugged them by the time the burgers showed up. When the men at the next table scooted their chairs back, I waved a greasy salt-and-ketchup laden fry in their direction. "Say, do you know where we can rent a boat?"

Now I was speaking their language. With a wide grin, one asked, "You wish to go fishing or snorkeling, *señora*?"

"No, we just want to take a boat ride."

"We have good boats." He nodded toward the pangas. "We can take you to the islands." He reached into a back pocket and pulled out a brochure featuring the usual photos of whales, underwater shots of colorful fish, and someone fighting a huge marlin. Handing it to me, he asked, "When do you wish to go?"

"Uh, now?"

They eyed our huge, empty, beer bottles, probably trying to assess just how drunk we were. I noticed the guys at the bar were eavesdropping on our conversation, so I turned to Jan and said, under my breath, "Showtime."

Jan stood, tugged off the scarf tied around her waist, turned those big old baby blues on our prey, and mustered a tear, which I suspect was induced by a salty finger. Dabbing it with the scarf, she wailed, "Can you please help us? We came here with some mean old men who left us. We have to get back to Puerto Escondido. Tonight."

Every man in the room, including the bartender, rushed our table. Jan sniffled while I embellished our sad tale of woe, adding we had money to pay for the panga, but needed to leave immediately. Within ten minutes we were bundled up in loaned surfer-dude windbreakers, and sat mid-panga with our mitts wrapped around two more *cuguamas*.

Since the wind was offshore, our eight-mile ride north was smooth and rapid. Of course, the panga had zero running lights, but with so little traffic on the water, the occasional flick of a flashlight alerted others we were coming. Anyone out there now was probably setting lines and nets, so they could easily hear us anyway.

In no time we were on the dock and waving our saviors a fond farewell. They were all grins, probably because I paid them double what they asked, which was most likely double what they usually charged.

Since I didn't want them connecting us with *Raymond Johnson*, we told them we were staying at the nearby Tripui hotel, thus the dock drop. Now we had to figure out how to get to *my* boat.

Luckily for us, someone left a dinghy at the dinghy dock.

Silly bugger.

CHAPTER EIGHT

By the time we boarded *Raymond Johnson,* Jan and I were frazzled.

It had been a long and stressful day, and it wasn't over by a long shot. My pickup was still at the resort, we had to return the "borrowed" dinghy to the dock, and worry over becoming the prime suspects for a beheading.

I'd figured out how to get the pickup, the dinghy was no problem, but Ishikawa? My vote was to let dead guys lie and hope no one came looking for us in connection with his demise. Then again, I wondered if we shouldn't be lawyering-up.

We tied the borrowed dink to *Se Vende,* returned it to the dock, and then went back to *Raymond Johnson* to contemplate our run back to the resort. We had three choices, all bad in our exhausted condition. We could take *Se Vende,* the fastest method, but that meant a roundtrip in an open boat, and it was already nearing midnight. Taking Jan's Jeep to retrieve my pickup was sensible, but why add yet another identifier to the mix? The guard at the entrance was sure to log in

Jan's vehicle, and it had easily traceable Mexican plates—traceable right back to Jan's boyfriend, Chino. Weighing our options, we decided on taking *Raymond Johnson.*

I started up the engines, Jan threw off the mooring line, and we slowly left port, hopeful not too many people would witness our exit. An hour later, we entered the resort's bay. I had noticed earlier there were two other powerboats and a sailboat anchored there, so I dropped the hook as far out as I could and still be able to catch a piece of bottom without also catching attention from shore. We ran in dark mode, turning off all lights—interior, mast, and running—before we let go the anchor and backed down. To us, the chain playing out sounded like a passing freight train, but the offshore wind carried most of the sound out to sea.

From the flying bridge, my binoculars were powerful enough to see the luau still going strong. An occasional drumbeat drifted our way on the sea breeze, and what looked like a fire dance was in progress. I couldn't make out individuals, but by the size of one, I was pretty sure Samoa was still there. If they'd found Ishikawa's body by now, wouldn't you think they'd stop the party?

"Jan, why don't you grab a nap? I'll wake you when the party's over. I figure it'll go on until at least two, maybe even three o'clock."

"Sounds like a plan. Uh, just what, exactly, happens now?"

"I intend to kill you, just as soon as we're safe. And I've changed my mind; I no longer embrace your new profession as a hooker. I mean, your very first trick ups and dies before you even showed."

I ducked, so the book she launched only nicked me.

The alarm went off at two-thirty. We fed our slight hangovers a sandwich, chased it with a Coca-Light, then bundled up in sweats and donned Jenks's baseball caps so we'd maybe pass for a couple of fishermen. Beaching *Se Vende* on the sand in front of the now-closed Playa Blanca bar, I tucked her in next to the panga we'd ridden in to PE a few hours before. I didn't want to land directly in front of the resort for two reasons; there was a shoal I'd seen waders walking on at low tide when Jenks and I anchored there a couple of months before, and there were almost sure to be guards about.

Under our sweats and caps, we wore tourist garb: Bermuda shorts, sandals, and long tee shirts declaring I HEART BAJA. It was our hope that, should we encounter a guard, he'd just think us a couple of drunken vacationers out for a stagger in the wee hours. But with the exception of a stray dog that woofed once and then fell in step with us, no doubt hoping for a treat, we never saw a living soul, even after we reached the hotel parking lot, and Jan drove away.

As I lurked in the shadows, making certain Jan was not noticed or followed, I heard voices and the sound of footfalls on gravel. Plastering myself to a wall behind an oleander bush, and hoping a scorpion hadn't done the same, I held my breath as the voices grew louder, even though they were practically whispering. One man hissed orders, one whined apologies, and the third just huffed and puffed. If these guys were trying to sneak around, they were doing a crappy job of it. But then again, I hadn't seen any sort of security around.

The three walked right by me, and I had to wonder why they, like Jan and me, were skulking out a back exit like thieves in the night. The answer was soon clear: two of the guys lugged a very large black plastic bag, and the other was the one giving orders and generally harassing the other two.

Hmmm. Ishikawa in a bag? Enquiring minds have to know.

Once again I whipped out the nifty camera Jenks gave me so I could photograph birds at night without making much noise and no flash. I got off two shots of the bag, the luggers, and their tormentor, before following at a safe distance.

Once in the parking lot, the trio made for a Lincoln Navigator, the vehicle of choice for Mexican drug dealers.

With Jan safely long gone, I decided it was in our interest to snoop some before making a run for *Se Vende* and getting out of Dodge. What with tonight's grisly murder, and our possible suspects status, I needed as much on these creeps and their dirty work as possible in case someone came looking for me and Jan. Short of getting a peek into that bag, which I highly doubted contained leftover pig, all I could do was link them to Ishikawa, however circumstantially.

Dodging around behind a few parked cars, I got off a couple more shots of the bag going into the back of the Navigator, and men opening the front doors. What I hoped was the money shot was when the interior lights illuminated the faces of the two men in the front seat, but I wouldn't know for sure until I had a chance to see what I'd captured.

They drove off, I hoofed for my boat, and was underway and heading back to port before my heart quit trying to escape my chest via my throat. The trip back to Puerto Escondido and getting the boat safely re-anchored so I could collect Jan from the dock, seemed to take forever, but was actually only a little over an hour.

We'd agreed Jan would wait for me in my truck, and when I got there she was sound asleep behind the wheel. I considered just crawling into the passenger seat and catching a snooze myself, but we still had work to do.

It is true: there is no rest for the weary. Wicked? Or the weary wicked.

CHAPTER NINE

Because I was single-handing my boat, and it was dark, I had decided to re-anchor *Raymond Johnson* back in my cell tower access spot rather than try to snag that mooring near the marina again. By the time I retrieved Jan from the parking lot, and we got back aboard, it was only about an hour until I could call Jenks back, and lie like a Persian rug about why I wasn't home to take his call the night before. Was it only the night before? Good grief, it felt like a lifetime.

As soon as we were safely back on the boat, we feasted on PB&Js Jan made for us. I'd requested eggs Benedict, but Jan said something rude and shoved a sandwich in my hand. Good help is so hard to find these days.

Jan, revived by peanut butter, had a twinkle in her eye that screamed she was keeping a juicy secret, and I was right.

"So," she finally said, "guess what I've got?"

"Is it treatable with penicillin?"

She laughed, dug into her pocket, withdrew a piece of paper, and waved it in front of me. When I held out my hand, she raised it over her head, out of my reach. "Not so fast, Chica. You owe me a big fat apology."

"For what?"

"You called me a prostitute."

"I did not. I called you a hooker, but I was wrong. I meant to say, more like a high-priced call girl."

"Hey, I turned down the fifty grand."

"I know, dammit. Was he, by any chance, going to pay up front?"

"For me to know, and for you *never* to know. And you're also gonna owe me big time for this little gift." She jiggled the piece of paper. "That's two big fat 'I'm sorrys'."

"What I owe you is a kick in the rear for getting us into this in the first place."

She let down her guard and I jumped up and snatched the paper. I took it to my desk, put on a pair of cheaters, and saw the resort's letterhead at the top of the page. "Holy crap! I take back the kick, and okay, I'm sorry for whatever."

"That was pretty lame, but I'll take it."

"How in the hell did you get the road guard's log sheet?" I peered closely, and sure enough, at 15:45 he'd noted my pickup's license number, description, and my name.

"Let's just say the sweet man was a mite distracted."

"My hero! Okay, lookee what I've got."

I fired up the laptop and downloaded the body and body-snatcher photos from my camera, filling Jan in on the details of the encounter as I did so. I was surprised how well they turned out, considering there was virtually no natural light.

The first photos, of Ishikawa, were shocking, even though we'd both seen the real thing. Jan and I said, in unison, "God rest his soul." We were raised right, no matter how we turned out.

The next few shots were of the bag luggers and their snarky overseer. Much to my surprise, more detail emerged than I could have even hoped for. On a garbage dumpster behind them, the name of the resort was clearly stenciled in bold letters, logo and all. I also captured a brief video clip of the men heaving the plastic bag into that Navigator, and by some miracle, another still of the license plate.

Jan gave me a high five. "Jolly good work, Sherlock. Too bad we can't see their faces."

"Stand by, my dear Watson." I clicked back a couple of shots and up popped the Navigator, interior lights ablaze. The two men in the front seat were facing directly into the lens. I zoomed in on them, and Jan spit peanut butter all over my computer screen.

Back in October, when Jan and I first cruised from Northern California to Magdalena Bay, on the Pacific side of the Baja, we had a serious dustup with a Mexican real estate developer by the name of Ricardo Lujàn, a scuzzbag of the highest order who never builds anything he doesn't plan to later steal. He is what the Mexicans call a *cacique*, after a bird that steals the nests of others. And yes, he richly deserved all the grief we were able to dole out for him after all the crap he pulled on us, but making an enemy of a man of his ilk is never a good thing. Not that that's anything new for me, as I piss people off on a regular basis. It's a gift.

El Señor Lujàn oozed into our lives as our Mag Bay contact for the giant Japanese firm, Tanuki. They'd hired Hetta Coffey, LLC, for a feasibility study for a desalination/salt plant, or so I thought. Turned out that my boss in Tokyo, a Mr. Ishikawa—at that time he still had his head—and this Luján character were conspiring to use the cover of the project to trap, butcher, and can, baby whales.

But even before we uncovered the whale-in-a-can scheme and his other nefarious dealings, Jan and I took an instant dislike to Ricardo Luján. He smarmily told us we could call him Richard, Ricardo, or Rick, but not to call him Dick. So quite naturally we dubbed him Dickless Richard.

Obviously Dickless and his former partner in crime, Ishikawa, had gotten back in cahoots after the Mag Bay debacle, because for them to be accidently at the same resort when one of them literally lost his head is way too much of a coincidence. Potential whale-canner or not, of the two men, Ishikawa was by far my choice to still be breathing.

I paced while Jan wiped peanut butter from my computer screen. We were both still speechless from the shock of Dickless's ugly mug—the one now so justly splattered with peanut butter and spit—popping up. Once in awhile, one of us would start to say something, then not do it. We were too tired, and too appalled by this nasty turn of events in an already nastily eventful evening. Finally, Jan stood and declared, "Stick a fork in me, I'm done," as she headed for her cabin.

Wiping Luján's smarmy face from my computer screen, I sent myself an email with all of the photos attached, then deleted them from My Pictures on my laptop.

My eyes stung with fatigue, and maybe an impending tear or two. I longed for the comfort of a furry rump on my feet, but Po Thang would have to stay put with my friends until after I got a few hours of sleep.

I popped a couple of PMs to give myself half a chance at sleeping, and called Jenks while I waited for them to kick in. I missed his lovely rump, as well. I envisioned his long lanky frame, slightly graying blonde hair, kind bright blue eyes, and his classic Norwegian features as I waited for my call to travel all those miles to Dubai. He picked up on the first ring, and when I heard his deep voice, a tear did escape my burning eyes. "Hey, you're up early."

I made a valiant effort to sound cheerful. "Heck, I've already had breakfast. Jan made it."

"Ah, Jan's there. That explains why you were out and about and not answering your phone. How's Jan?"

I liked the way this was going. No reason for Jenks to wonder if we'd been up to no good, because if Jan was with me it was a given, and he usually just didn't want to know details unless he had to post bail.

"She's going back to the fish camp today. If I had a slip for this boat, I'd go with her, but I'm still on the wait list. I'm actually thinking of taking the boat back up to Santa Rosalia, or maybe down to La Paz. It's starting to warm up in the Sea of Cortez, and before long I'll have to run the air conditioner during the afternoons." *And besides, there's this dead guy, and that rat Luján is involved, and I'm scared, and tired and....*

Jenks's voice cut into my pity party. "Is the generator running okay?"

"Oh, uh, yes. It's just that I hate listening to it. I will, if I have to, but I think I need to maybe move the boat. There's still no electricity at the new small marina here, so no use going there, and I don't have any idea how long it'll be to get into the other marina. Besides, I'm leery of leaving *Raymond Johnson* here this summer anyway. I don't trust that Med-tie situation at the main marina."

Putting out an anchor and backing in to tie the back of the boat to a dock—called a Mediterranean tie—is fine in benign conditions, but Puerto Escondido was hit with a major hurricane a few years ago, and even where my boat was now anchored, there were reportedly one-hundred mile an hour winds, and eight-foot waves crashing into the harbor through the '"windows" between the low hills. Several boats sank, and Puerto Escondido's claim to fame as a hurricane hole sank with them.

"So, you're going to put the boat away and join Jan and Chino on their little treasure hunt?"

Yes, I find it preferable to being beheaded. "Why not? It's much cooler on the Pacific side of the Baja, they have that huge research vessel, and who knows, we might even find Chino's galleon. Beats sitting at a dock in the Sea of Cortez with the air-conditioner droning away twenty-four seven."

"I've heard summers in the Sea are brutal. It ain't gonna be exactly dandy over here, either."

"I'll bet. I read somewhere that Dubai stays over a hundred all summer. Sounds like Vegas. Nothing near that here, but the humidity is fierce. Decisions, decisions. Anyhow, if I put the boat in Santa Rosalia or La Paz and go with Jan and Chino in Mag Bay, I can still drive back for meetings at the mine, I'll have a place to live, and built-in dog sitters. Just sounds like the best thing to do." *Since I prefer to live.*

After we exchanged 'I-love-and-miss-you's', I called Texas, needing the comfort of hearing my mom's drawl. Of course, there is no way I'd let her know I was most likely neck deep in cow patties again, or that I was lonely and scared. Why worry the parents unnecessarily?

"Hetta Honey, I have some bad news for you."

Oh, great, just what I need right now.

"Everything okay with you and Dad?" I asked, which was all I really cared about.

"We're just fine. But your Uncle Fred died."

I rubbed my eyes. The nighty-night pills were starting to kick in. "Uh, I didn't know I *had* an Uncle Fred." We have a large family in Texas, but danged if I could remember an Uncle Fred.

"Well, you do. Or did. He and your aunt Lillian were married a few months back."

"Oh, that uncle. They never last long enough for me to remember their names. The way Lil runs through husbands it's no wonder I don't know who they are. Did she kill him off, like she usually does?"

"Het-*ta*, if you're going to be that way I'm hanging up."

"Sorry, Mom. I know Lil is your big sister, but what number husband is this? Six? And let's face it, she gets them out of what Dad calls the drunk tank at the VA, then they fall into the bottle together. If she'd leave them where they were getting help, they'd probably all still be alive."

"Fred had a weak heart."

"Well, marrying Lil sure as hell couldn't have helped that. Where are they? Last I heard they went to Mazatlan."

"Still are. Well, she is. Fred passed in a hospital there."

"Good thing. If he'd died at home the Feds would have her in custody." Actually the idea of my aunt in a Mexican clink appealed to me, but I didn't share that, and changed the subject. "So what else is happening?"

"Nothin' much. Your father wants to take the RV to Canada this summer, so I guess we'll leave next month. Oh, he just walked in, so here he is."

Dad took the phone and we talked more about their RVing, and my plans to join Jan and Chino on the galleon/treasure hunt for the summer. While we were talking about that, Mom yelled in the background, telling him to tell me to use sunblock and for him to ask me about Jenks. Daddy dutifully did both. My parents really like Jenks and are worried, as I'm wont to do, that I'll scare him off. This latest escapade just might do the trick.

Jan and I were up and about by noon, although still a little fuzzy from too much booze and tension, and not enough rest. I took her to her Jeep and picked up Po Thang, who seemed ecstatic to see me. He circled and whined, telling me just what an old meanie I'd been, but quickly dashed for the pickup to ensure his old meanie didn't leave him again.

It had been a few years since my last dog, RJ, died and I'd forgotten how nice it was to always be greeted by a fluffy critter who didn't give a damn whether you were drunk, or sick, or whatever, just so you are *there*. Po Thang actually seems to *like* morning breath.

RJ, the dearly departed, was also a rescue dog. I got him out of the Oakland pound, where he was deemed basically un-adoptable because of his crappy attitude. I figured we were meant for each other. Unable to come up with a name, I called him Dawg for a few weeks until Jan, deciding Dawg was undignified, named him Raymond Johnson. As in "You can call me Ray, or you can call me Jay, or you can call me Johnny, or you can call me Sonny, or you can call me RayJay, or you can call me RJ, or you can call me RJJ, or you can call me RJJ Jr., but you doesn't have to call me Johnson." Jan was a big fan of that annoying repetitive skit on the old Redd Foxx Show.

Jan also named Po Thang after we'd spotted him on the roadside several times before snagging him. The poor thing was indeed a pitiful sight back then.

But on this morning after I picked him up from exile, his pure joy when we arrived back at the marina and he leaped into *Se Vende's* bow, gladdened my heart and made me forget, for just a moment, this fresh hell Jan and I were into.

For the next few days I scanned the Net, searching for news of a murder in Baja, and found nothing. Then again, the Mexican press is pretty much in league with the tourist bureau, and a beheading at a large luxury resort just ain't good for business. In fact, since the new president took over, even cartel violence has all but disappeared from the headlines. Either The Prez has made some kind of deal with the drug lords, or they finally killed off or terrorized every journalist brave enough to report cartel mayhem.

Days passed without further incident, so Jan and I began to relax a bit. We talked daily, speculating on the what ifs and whys, and hoping Ishikawa was planted next to Jimmy Hoffa.

But why? "What I don't get is why Ishikawa was at the fish camp in the first place. I'm finding it hard to believe he only brought the family for whale viewing. And if it really was just a family outing, why pick *your* camp? Chino doesn't run tours, he's a scientist. How did Ishikawa even contact you in the first place?"

"Lemme think."

"I smell smoke."

"Smart ass. We got an email from a Japanese eco-group saying they wanted to expose Japanese industrialists first hand to whale preservation. Chino didn't really want to get involved, because you know how he feels about a country that kills whales. However, the idea of educating a man who might make a difference was appealing. And, they said that man was willing to pay big time, and we needed the money for the summer expedition."

"Have you checked out this Japanese whale hugger group?"

"Yes. They're legit."

"You say Mrs. Ishikawa and the kids are still at the camp?"

"They have another two weeks."

"Have you asked her where her husband is?"

"No."

"Do it and call me back, okay?"

"She's out with Chino right now, but when they get back I'll figure out a way to ask."

"How about, 'By the way, ma'am, are you aware your husband was beheaded and his body stuffed in a trash bag and hauled off by thugs?' "

"I think I can be a mite more subtle than that."

CHAPTER TEN

"Po Thang, Po Thang, go channel seventeen."

Po Thang practically levitated from a deep slumber. He'd never received a radio call before.

As he ran in excited circles around my legs, I grabbed the mic and switched channels. In my best answering machine voice I said, "Hi. Po Thang can't come to the phone right now, but your message is very important to us. So leave one."

"Cute. Okay, here is the message," I recognized the voice as belonging to Denny, a single-hander who had one of those coveted slips at the main dock. "Tell him the local heat is asking around about his boat mate. And they've commandeered a panga and are loading up to head his way. He might want to take a pee, if you know what I mean."

"Holy…Got it. Gone."

I dropped the mic like a hot tamale, and grabbed my bright orange ditch bag. If you live on a boat, you never know when you are going to have to abandon ship, and my large waterproof satchel contains an EPIRB (emergency position-indicating rescue beacon), a strobe light, flashlight, whistle, a signal mirror, first aid kit, a knife, bottled water, sunblock, a handheld watermaker, a flare gun with extra shells, lots of power bars, and everything one might need to survive a few nights in a raft, or afloat. Into this pack, before I go to bed each night, I always toss in my handheld radio, money, binoculars, and both mine and Po Thang's inflatable life jackets, his with a tether that clips to mine.

Before boarding *Se Vende*, I jammed on an oversized straw hat like the ones favored by local fishermen, then grabbed a fishing pole, which sent Po Thang into a tail-wagging frenzy; he just dearly loves it when I catch a fish.

I hid behind some nearby mangroves, and not a minute too soon, for I first heard, then saw, a panga streaking toward *Raymond Johnson*. It was loaded to the gunwales with six or seven uniformed, armed men. It first circled my boat, then sidled up to the swim platform.

One of them called out something in Spanish, and knocked on the hull, but getting no response, boarded. Finding the boat locked, and no one reacting to their ever more vocal demands, they posted an armed guard on deck. After a discussion of some sort with the others, the rest of the contingent left in the panga, which headed for the other anchorage near the entrance to the harbor, a popular spot called the Waiting Room.

As they disappeared behind a low hill, I figured this was a good opportunity to make a run for my pickup. I opened up the sixty-horse and streaked for the parking lot. The marine standing guard on my boat gave me a glance, but didn't raise a ruckus; he was most likely on the lookout for a *Gringo*'s inflatable, not a beat up old panga like *Se Vende*.

I called Denny on seventeen and he met me at the dinghy dock. He watched the harbor through his binoculars while recounting how this little drama was playing out. "You gotta stay clear of the marina office, there're still some guys up there who are looking for you. They may know you have a red pickup by now, but so far they haven't posted a guard on it. Give me the keys and I'll take it up to the little grocery store. Meet me there. You have any idea what this is all about?"

Oh, boy, did I. I tossed him the keys. "No," I lied, "but I want to be sure I have witnesses around when they catch up to me. Any ideas?"

He shook his head. "No, but you know how things are down here. If it were me, I'd head for the border."

"And leave my boat? No way. I'll meet you at the store, then maybe figure out what to do next. I owe you, big time."

Po Thang and I jogged to the *tienda*, even though I don't jog all that well.

What to do? What to do? Obviously someone finally found both parts of Ishikawa, and zeroed in on me as suspect *numero uno*. At the top of my mental TO DO list was to warn suspect *numero dos*.

The little store has excellent WiFi, and several cruisers and RVers were bent over their computers. One guy I knew was talking on Skype when I arrived, so as soon as he said, "Bye," I asked if I could make an emergency call.

"Jan, the feds are here. I think they're gonna take me in."

Every head in the place turned in my direction.

If I wanted witnesses, I sure had 'em.

The thing about Mexico is they have a really crappy legal system. They got it from the French.

Their judicial swamp is so corrupt and dysfunctional that if you commit a crime in Mexico you only have a two in a hundred chance of getting caught and, if you have money, even less chance of being convicted and punished. I read somewhere that only twelve percent of crimes are even reported, and for good reason: the cops want money to work on the case. Or worse, the person who calls the authorities becomes a suspect. So, lacking a pesky body to deal with at the resort, it was doubtful the staff would report a suspicious bloodstain. So what happened to sic them onto me?

And if nabbed, I'd be deemed guilty until proven innocent—that marvelous Napoleonic Code the French thought up—during which time I'd languish in a Mexican jail. Mexican jails are god-awful hellholes.

I'd just gotten off the Skype call with Jan, telling her to run for the hills, and was considering doing the same, when it was too late. A black and white screeched into the parking lot at the store, followed by a truckload of heavily armed Marines. Almost everyone in the *tienda* started packing up computers and making for the exits. To Denny's credit, he remained sitting at the table with me.

"Miss Coffey?" the biggest cop said. I looked behind me, snagged Po Thang's collar, and pushed him forward. "Uh, this is Miss Coffey. What's he done?"

They were not amused.

When they motioned me toward their car, Denny said he would take Po Thang with him, and keep an eye on my boat. When he asked the head fed when I'd be back, he got a shrug. I took this not to be a good sign.

I was soon alone in the back seat of a souped up Crown Vic, pondering my fate.

Most people will find this hard to believe, but I've never been in jail.

I've been detained, delayed, and interrogated by several international agencies over the years, but never actually locked up.

During the ride into Loreto, a grim future took hold of my thoughts, conjuring pictures of bare cells, mean-looking women, and (probably my worst fear) no privacy or freedom. The cops had the lights whirling, siren howling, and were doing at least a hundred miles an hour. One had to wonder what the big hurry was; after all, they had me, and Ishikawa wasn't gonna get any deader.

And my car mates weren't talking, not that I could hear them over all the noise even if they were.

Trying to think of positives about this mess, I came up with a dismally short list. One, I was not handcuffed. This surely had to mean something good, right? And two, I knew Jan was frantically trying to contact the American Consulates in both Tijuana and Cabo San Lucas, as well as Chino's cousin, a lawyer of some sort in Loreto. Hopefully, my mouthpiece would beat me to the jailhouse. Did they even *have* bail down here? Oh, and three, there was a nice metal mesh grill protecting me from the cops in the front seat.

My head throbbed, but that was no surprise, what with ugly scenarios whizzing around up there, banging against my skull like a pinball machine in overdrive. Oddly enough though, what worried me the very most was Jenks's reaction to all this. Would this be the straw that finally broke Jenks's infinite patience?

Okay, so maybe I have this stupid habit of getting in over my head. It's how I am, and he knows it. But I'd only been in Mexico now for a little over six months, and he's flown back from the Middle East three times when I got into a jam. Maybe I should have thought twice before going off on a lark with Jan? I've heard tell that some people actually look before they leap, but where's the fun in that?

The black and white took a sudden right turn, throwing me against my seat belt and banging my head into my metal mesh protection. A sign flashed by: Aeropuerto Internacional de Loreto.

Oh, hell, I was being deported?

CHAPTER ELEVEN

I have, in the past, been asked to leave a couple of countries, but deported?

Can one be deported without proof of citizenship to the country to which they are being deported? They didn't know I had my passport and Arizona Driver's license with me, and I sure as hell wasn't gonna tell them. Day was that your good word was all that was needed to get into the US, but not now. On the other hand, deportation looked mighty appealing when compared with a possible lifetime in a Mexican jail.

We screeched to a halt in front of the airport entrance, lights and sirens heralding a break in what is most likely a pretty humdrum work day between infrequent flights. Unfortunately, a plane had just landed, so passengers gawked while the driver cop opened both my door and that of his boss. Well, some passengers stared at us. Others seemed fascinated by something else afoot inside the terminal.

The head fed adjusted his pants and gun, growled something at the driver, who hurried to cut the siren and lights. My ears still rang, but not loud enough to overcome a bellow from behind a closed door off the lobby. It was a sound I had hoped to never, ever, hear again.

Curses, screeches, and the thuds of some serious door kicking echoed throughout the terminal.

I turned to the head fed, held out my arms, and begged, "Please, sir, arrest me. I cut off a man's head last week, so you have to take me away."

For the first time he cracked a smile. "I do not think so, Miss Coffey."

It took an hour of talking through the door, and several hits of brandy from the airport bar, for Aunt Lillian to allow me into the room with her, and even then I wasn't so sure she wasn't going to physically attack me. And no, I didn't share the brandy.

With her steely gray hair standing on end, and mean black eyes lasering everything in sight, she would have resembled an angry eagle, had it not been for streaking mascara, and bright red lipstick smeared pretty much all over the bottom half of her face. What she did look like, however, was my worst nightmare: a drunken old hag. Jan and I had discussed at length this possible fate for ourselves, and vowed to kill each other should we ever reach such a state.

Lil was totally out of control, crying one minute and threatening me the next if I didn't get her a drink. I finally did what I knew would work to calm her down: I called Mother and handed the phone to Lil. The minute she heard my mom's voice my aunt morphed from Godzilla to all sugar sweet in a split second. "Hi, baby sister," she cooed. "Yes, I'm here with Hetta. After losing my dear Fred, I decided to come visit family. Why, I'll never know. She had me arrested!"

I jerked the phone from her claw. "Not true, Mom. Best I can figure she got drunk on the plane from Mazatlan and then went bonkers on crew when they wouldn't serve her any more booze. The *federales* locked her in a room until I could get here. They tell me they will release her to me, but I sure as hell don't want her."

"Hetta Honey, she *is* your aunt."

"Yeah, well come get her."

Silence.

"I mean it. Two days, that's it. If you don't come down here I'm throwing her overboard. Tied to an anchor."

"Can't you just send her home?"

"Nope. They won't allow her back on a plane without an escort, and it ain't gonna be me."

"I'll talk to your father and call you back."

I hung up and Lil hissed, "How dare you tell my sister I was drunk. I had a, uh, TIA. That's what must have happened."

"No, you had an FUI: flying under the influence. What the hell is a TIA?"

My aunt is a retired nurse who mixes a goodly amount of prescription drugs and booze, but can always come up with some obscure medical reason to explain away her drunken fits. I think I'd heard this TIA story once before, but it was lost in a long history of her crap.

"Transient ischemic attack, it's like a mini-stroke." Then she went pouty. "I'm lucky to be alive."

Now she was entering the sulky, poor me stage. I'd seen it all before. "You're lucky they didn't search your purse. What do you have in there?"

"Only my mood elevators and, of course, all the other meds I need to stay on this earth. I'm old, you know. And," the expected blubbering commenced, "recently widowed."

I opened the door and the officers jumped back like I was releasing the lions. "Everything's okay now. I'll take her back to the boat with me. Uh, can I borrow those handcuffs?"

Lil has a pattern.

Hungover grouch, then, after a drink, gaily entertaining, at least in her own mind.

Since I wouldn't give her any booze, she went straight into raging at past slights. And, boy, can she hold a grudge. She lambasted me for a time I embarrassed her when I was eight years old, for crying out loud, by not using proper eating etiquette when she took me to some women's club breakfast. "I told you, Hetta, one must tear toast into four equal pieces, then butter each quarter daintily, but only before eating it."

Right after that she wailed, got maudlin, pitiful, and finally, thank the Lord, passed out.

While the old crone slept off her latest TIA, I made a piece of toast, buttered the whole thing, folded it over, and stuffed the entire slice into my mouth. I then removed every drop of alcohol from the boat, loading it into *Se Vende* for pickup by Denny. By the time he left with booze bottles stacked to the gunwales of his dink, it was dark, and I was exhausted.

Po Thang, who had never met Aunt Lil, sniffed her with suspicion, then gave her a wide berth. Po Thang is an excellent judge of character.

I'd already called Jan and told her why the cops picked me up, and asked her to call off the legal and embassy dogs because I wasn't headed for the hoosegow, but was suffering a far worse fate. As soon as I had Lil bedded down, I called Jan again. "Uh, what exactly did you tell the consulate and that lawyer when you called them on my behalf?"

"That for reasons unknown you were rounded up and hauled off by some *federales*. When I called them back, I told 'em everything was okay, and that *this* time you weren't guilty of an international crime spree."

"Gee, thanks. Now I'm really sorry I told those cops you beheaded a Japanese gentleman in his hotel room."

"Very funny. And speaking of," she dropped into a whisper, "Mrs. Ishikawa told me her husband was called back to Japan on urgent business, and that she would like to stay another week before taking the kids back home."

"All right! Wait a minute. He *called* her?"

"Yeah, that's what I asked myself. Nope, turns out his secretary called the missus with the message from the mister. Said he was on a plane or something. Is this getting weird, or what?"

"You want weird? Come over to my world."

"Ya know, Hetta, I kinda like your Aunt Lil."

"I'll have her at your place early tomorrow morning."

"Don't like her that much."

"Some friend you are."

"So, your mom is coming down to fetch Lil?"

"I sure as hell hope so, and the sooner the better. The airlines won't let Aunt Lillian fly without an escort, and that ain't gonna be me."

"When your mom shows up, I'll come over for a visit."

"Good, because if she doesn't get here, like tomorrow, you can help her load her sister's body into my dink."

True to the rollercoaster moods defining her, it was the hungover/grouch Lil who emerged from my guest cabin the next morning. Hungover/grouch, when allowed her first Bloody Mary of the day, usually morphs into Somewhat Tolerable as she explains away her actions, at least those she remembers, of the day, or week, before.

Since there was not a drop of Mary, bloody or otherwise, on *Raymond Johnson*, Lil went immediately to angry/raging aunt.

Po Thang jumped into *Se Vende* and cowered there. If he had an opposable thumb, I think he would have started the motor and escaped to the beach, but lacking that dexterity we humans enjoy, he simply just jumped overboard and swam away.

I didn't even try to call him back, but instead, followed. Yelling over my shoulder as I motored away after my dog, I told Lil there was food in the fridge, and coffee in the pot.

When I caught up to Po Thang, he was on the beach, sniffing and doing his critter-chasing thing with the occasional worried look back at our boat. I cut the motor, and even a quarter mile or so from the boat,

Aunt Lil's yowling echoed across the otherwise peaceful bay. I collected Po Thang, and we motored to the dinghy landing so I could rinse him down.

While he dried in the sun, I sat on the dock and sulked. How was I going to survive the next couple of days until my mother arrived? More importantly, how was Aunt Lil going to survive if I had to live with her?

"Why so glum, Hetta?"

I almost jumped into the water. One of the single-handers had walked up behind me as I contemplated how to off my aunt, and then explain her demise to Mom. "Crap, Robert, you scared me silly."

"Sorry. I, uh, heard about you bein' hauled off by the law. Glad to see you back."

"I wonder if they would consider hauling me off again."

"Boy, must be serious if you'd rather be in Mexican custody."

"You have no idea."

"Try me."

The soft sincerity in his voice got my attention. For the first time since we met, I actually took a good look at him. He was probably in his fifties, dressed in sailboater attire of shorts, tee shirt, and baseball hat. Tall and thin, he sported the mandatory sailor-guy gray beard. Until that moment I'd just lumped him in with all the other men alone on their boats.

I gave him a smile. "You wouldn't happen to be a priest, would you? I need an exorcism performed on my boat."

He laughed. "Don't we all? My watermaker upped and quit."

"No, really. I need someone who can purge evil."

He gave me a wary look. "Hetta, this is none of my business, but are you, like, okay?"

"You mean, like, sane?"

He smiled. "No sane person takes a boat to Mexico. Look, we hardly know each other, but I'd like to help if I can. I'm no priest, but I do have good friends here who helped *me* out when I needed it. I have a few minutes, then I gotta go to a meeting."

"Meeting? Jeez, I thought we came down here to get away from those."

"AA, Hetta."

"The car club?"

CHAPTER TWELVE

Alcoholics Anonymous?

Who knew they had a group in Puerto Escondido, Mexico? And that so many of the fleet attended meetings. Because I had a serious problem brewing, so to speak, on my boat I confided in Robert, telling him of Lil's decades of prescription drug and alcohol abuse, along with failed stays in rehab, and that I'd removed all drugs and booze from my boat.

He frowned and looked as though he was struggling with what to say after I'd unloaded on him. "That might not be the best idea. Going cold turkey for someone of her age, and with her history, might be dangerous. She could die."

"Really?" I tried not to sound hopeful.

He grinned. "I'm sure you don't want that."

"Of course not. If the old sot ups and dies on my boat at anchor, the Mexican police will toss me in jail until after the autopsy."

He shook his head at my flippancy. "Uh, perhaps you might not be the best caregiver for the old lady. I'm detecting a severe lack of empathy here."

"Empathy? This old bat has spent the past...well, her entire life, making everyone as miserable as she is. She's jealous of my mother's good looks, and family. She interferes whenever she can. If she could, I'm sure she'd have broken up my parents' marriage long ago. Luckily my father kept taking jobs overseas, probably to get away from her. Lil is a master manipulator. In Texas we call that a shit disturber. As a matter of fact, I cannot think of one nice thing to say about her."

"Why did she come here? She must know you can't stand her."

"Because I am the one person she hasn't been able to control. I gotta give her credit, though, she never quits trying."

"I think you need medical help here."

"No thanks, I'm a little upset, but feeling okay."

Two hours later, my fondest wish came true. Aunt Lil was off the boat, and en route, thanks to my newest bestest AA buddies, to a small clinic run by nuns in Loreto. I would tell you who my new friends were, but they prefer to remain anonymous.

Lil, who was still raving when I got back to the boat, pitched a *real* hissy when I informed her she was headed somewhere for help, but settled down the minute I hinted they'd probably give her Valium to calm her nerves, which she sure as hell wasn't going to get on my boat, as I was running low.

I also didn't tell her the people taking her into town were voted least likely to stop in a local bar on the way, which I'm sure was at the top of her agenda once she got away from what she called my hell ship.

As soon as I waved bye-bye, I retrieved my bar stock from Denny, and Po Thang and I spent a blessedly peaceful late afternoon swimming, sunning, reading and napping, free of the witch we'd been saddled with. Every once in awhile, Po Thang or I would let loose a contented sigh, just happy to have each other for company. I mixed a Margarita, but fell asleep reading a novel before finishing it. Po Thang took care of it for me, though. What a pal.

The phone woke me just as the sun hovered on the western horizon. "Hetta Honey, I'm afraid I have bad news," my mother drawled.

"Nothing can ruin what has been a delightful afternoon. Lemme have it."

Silence, then, "Have you done something to your aunt? You sound much too…pleased."

"As a matter of fact, I have. She is now staying with friends at a, uh, B&B in Loreto until you get here to take her home."

"What friends? She doesn't know anyone but you down there. What have you done with her?"

"Mom, honestly, do you think I would send her to stay with anyone wishing her harm?"

"She stayed with *you*."

"And now she is in a safer place. Look, just come get her, and this whole hot mess will be over with, okay?"

"Well, that's why I called. I forgot to renew my passport and it's expired. Even with expedited service it'll take a couple of days to get the new one."

"That's okay, no hurry now."

Another pause. "Hetta, have you been drinking?"

"Not really."

"Then why are you sounding so...calm?"

Because Aunt Lil is probably in a straight jacket by now, being beat up on by nuns? "Mother, you have to trust me. Your sister is being taken care of. She's safe and sound. Oh, and by the way, be sure and raid her checking account for some of her cash so you can spring...uh, pay her rooming bill. She says she's broke."

I could practically feel my mother's doubts as to Lil's safety singing through ether, but she said, "I will. I'll call when I have my airline reservations confirmed. I have to connect in Los Angeles for the plane to Loreto, and they don't fly down there every day. And, it's over seven hundred dollars."

"Then take the money from that account she set up for the two of you. Or has she, once again, taken your name off that, and her will?" Everyone in the family had copies of many rescinded wills from Lil, as well as lists of stock certificates and bank accounts she'd put their names on when she wanted something, only to cancel later. I considered it a mark of distinction to be disinherited by her at least once a year.

"I am still able to withdraw funds. And by the way, Lil put you back in her will, so you should be nicer to her."

"She did?" *Hmmm, I wonder if I could cut a deal with those nuns?*

"Just what are you thinking?"

Jeez, she can read my mind over the phone? "Uh, Mom, I hear someone coming. Gotta go. Love you."

I wasn't fibbing to my mother; I really did hear the approaching drone of an outboard, but since Po Thang wasn't raising all kinds of Billy hell, it had to be someone he knew and liked. Sure enough, it was Robert, the Good Samaritan who took Lil off my hands, and he didn't look happy.

No good deed goes unpunished.

"Lemme get this straight, Robert. You've lost Lil?" Fighting to maintain a solemn countenance, and pure glee from my tone, I was also mentally calculating how to offer him some kind of reward for him not to find her again.

"More like she lost us. Gave us the slip when we stopped for gas, and she asked to go to the Ladies'."

"There is a God," slipped out.

"You know, Hetta, not to be judgmental here, but your lack of concern over that little old lady is slightly disturbing."

I barked a scoff. "You think *I'm* disturbing? You haven't seen little old Lil in action. Look, you guys tried to do something generous for her own good, and like everyone else who tries to help her, she's dumped on you. Whereever the hell she is, I wish her as well as I am capable of doing. But, because my mother is going to kill me for losing her big sister, I guess I have to go look for her. Which gas station?"

He told me, I grabbed my backpack, and snagged Po Thang's collar as he made for the door. "Sorry, fur face, not this time. I won't be that long, and I just don't need someone else to watch out for while I'm looking for Aunt Lil."

Po Thang slinked to a spot by the exit, leaned against the door, and gave me a hangdog look. I don't leave him on the boat often, but he'd just have to learn to live with it when I do. After all, I've certainly learned to do so where Jenks is concerned. I have, however, when Jenks is packing, slinked to the exit door, leaned against it, and given him hangdog looks.

I patted Po's head, and told him again how sorry I was.

Leave it to Lil to screw up what had been, for both of us, a great afternoon.

As is usual in Mexico, no one saw anything at the Pemex station, even though it is one of the busiest places in town. And, there are stores and, unfortunately, bars, within easy walking distance. Robert told me Lil left her purse in the van, but I know she keeps stashed cash, uh, elsewhere. As Lil likes to brag, "No one is going to search an old lady's drawers."

I did a perimeter search, starting with the bars, but no Lil. It was dark by the time I got back to the pickup and met up with Robert, who was waiting for me after having canvassed a six-block quadrant, asking everyone is sight if they'd seen an old *Gringa. Nada.*

"You think we should go to the police?" he asked.

"Hell, no. She was released to my custody, and the way the law works down here they'd probably throw me in the clink for letting her escape into the general population."

"Maybe we should check out the pharmacies. She tried to bribe us to stop at a one. Which surprised us, because she also told us she didn't have any money because you took it all. I guess she lied, huh?"

"Lil lied?" I slapped my cheeks and gasped, "I'm shocked! Shocked, I tell you."

He rolled his eyes and grinned. "Yeah, the old saw, 'how can you tell if an alcoholic is lying?'"

"Their lips are moving," we chorused. We shared a laugh and admitted defeat for the moment. We'd been outfoxed for now, so I decided to deal with the latest Lillian fiasco after a good night's sleep.

On the way back to Puerto Escondido we stopped at a taco stand and bought beef tacos as a peace offering for Po Thang. I rarely left him on the boat, and when I did, I almost never locked him inside. Lately, though, he'd taken to jumping off on his own and swimming for shore, and the last thing I wanted this evening was to have to find him in the dark, then give him a bath. One missing person was quite enough for my day.

It was pitch black by the time I reached *Raymond Johnson*, and something didn't look right. My anchor light, solar-powered, shone brightly, so at least finding the boat was easy, but I could have sworn I left a light on inside the cabin. *Just what I need, low batteries.* Well rats, I'd have to start the generator and charge up, when all I wanted was a warm dog, a cold beer, and a taco.

I tied up *Se Vende* and cut the motor. Normally Po Thang would be raising Cain, but all was quiet. I hoped he wasn't busy chewing up my carpet or something. So far he'd been good about that, but Katy bar the door if he'd managed to open the fridge. I'd child-proofed the entire cabin after the first time he emptied out that reefer.

"Hi, honey, I'm home," I yelled.

Nothing.

Scared silly something had happened to him, I dug out my keys while running along the deck, but I didn't need them: the door stood wide open. Crap, two escape artists in one day? After I found him I vowed to eat his entire damned taco right in front of him.

Flipping on a switch, I was surprised when the lights sprang to life. Bright lights. Not a low battery problem. But all that light revealed a much more serious problem. Po Thang had totally trashed my boat?

Then I took a closer look at the mayhem. Since when can a dog, even one as crafty as Po Thang, pull out a drawer and scatter the contents? My heart seized. Po Thang didn't do this, but whoever did must have frightened him off the boat. I grabbed a flashlight and, without much hope, climbed to the flying bridge and turned on my spotlight, figuring if Po saw it, he might swim back.

Heart pounding, I left the spot on and was scrambling back down to the main deck to take *Se Vende* ashore on a dog hunt, when I heard the phone ringing inside the cabin. Doubling back, I snatched it up. "Hello?"

A gravelly voice rumbled into my pounding ear drum. "We have your aunt and your dog. Tell no one.

We will know if you do. We will contact you concerning our terms."

"Hey, you, I—" I realized he'd hung up.

First fury, then terror, turned my kneecaps to jelly. I wobbled to the settee and crumpled onto the cool leather, suddenly overcome with helplessness and self-recrimination. I knew this was all my fault, no matter who was responsible for the dog-and-aunt snatch. I had something they wanted, and whatever their "terms," they could sure as hell have it their way.

I had become quite fond of that dog.

CHAPTER THIRTEEN

After a half-baked attempt to straighten the trashed main saloon, I experienced an anxiety attack. Throwing cushions back onto the settee, I joined them, and curled into a fetal position. Paranoia jangled my nerve ends. Was someone watching the boat? Most likely. The caller said, "Tell no one," and "We will know if you do," so how else would they know what I'm doing unless they were spying on me?

A chill lifted the hair on the back of my neck, and made me want to pull a blankie over my head, but it was quickly dispelled by a wave of white hot anger. I think. At barely forty, surely it wasn't a hot flash? Geez, don't you get a grace period?

Whatever got my blood boiling, it sent me off the couch, and into a frenzy of action. I closed all window shades and began locking hatches and sliders, each one with a little more hostility than the last, as though slamming a door in their lousy faces. Whoever *they* were. Lame, maybe, but it made me feel more in charge.

Once the boat was secured, I kissed my bank account a fond farewell, fired my 8KW generator for some serious power, and set what Jan calls the fancy-schmancy onboard security system Jenks installed on *Raymond Johnson* before I left the States. Feeling empowered, I then activated my bajillion peso-a-minute satellite communications system, which I'd used sparingly except when I had a client who wanted to keep in touch with me enough to pay for it through the wazoo. Ironically that client had been the now-beheaded Ishikawa, and I was certain this was all somehow tied to him.

Back when Jenks—a security expert—and I first met in the San Francisco Bay area, I was being stalked by some nut job, so Jenks installed an Internet-based security system on my then new-to-me boat. It saved my life once back then, but now I was in Mexico without high-speed Internet, and stuck with a 3G system which was, as a Mexican friend of mine once joked, "Slower than a local funeral procession with only one set of jumper cables." For my own sense of security, I needed every tool I had available. Screw the expense.

Cocooned in my little floating fortress, protected by alarmed hatches and motion-activated cameras, I stared forlornly at my empty gun safe. Dammit, the one place where I could use a trusty semi-automatic, and Mexico made me leave them in Arizona, even though their constitution does give one the right to *keep* arms. It's one of those tricky things with the law south of the border; I might be able to keep a gun in a stationary domicile if I jumped through enough legal hoops, but since my domicile moves, the weapon would be deemed as "concealed," and that is a no-no. Anyhow, the penalties for possession are too severe to mess with. Five years in a Mexican jail holds zero appeal, but in this instance even five minutes of helplessness didn't leave me all warm and fuzzy. As my Daddy likes to say, "When seconds count, the cops are only minutes away."

With a deep sigh, I assessed the chaos.

My laptop remained on the desk, which was at least one good thing, and signified, even had I not received the call, that no common thief was responsible for the break-in. It was, however, sitting in a jumble of papers and folders that formerly lived in my IN and OUT trays. The contents of my desk drawers littered the carpet.

All the galley cabinets were open, their stores strewn onto the floor. Ditto the refrigerator. Thawing food oozed onto the laminate. Jeez, where the hell is a perfectly good dog when you really need him?

Thoughts of Po Thang cramped my stomach. When my last dog, RJ, died, I swore I would never put myself through this type of hurt again, so I used the borrow-a-doggie school of canine fixes; I sometimes keep others' pooches when their owners go on vacation. To be honest, life is so much simpler without dogs that go nuts when you even *look* at your car keys, but here I was, once again, aching for a furry critter to clean my galley floor, even though, this time, he wasn't the one who emptied the fridge onto it.

One thing I felt strongly was that Po Thang was alive and hopefully safe for the moment, and I vowed to do everything within my power to get him back.

Oh, yeah, and Aunt Lil, too.

I guess.

It was well past midnight by the time I got the place put back together, and cleaned the galley. I should have been dragging butt, but I was too ticked off to sleep. With nothing else to do, I did what I always do when faced with a crappy situation: make lists.

Grabbing a notepad from my newly reorganized desk, I found a pen and plopped down on the settee. In order to get the complete picture of any story, one needs the five Ws both journalists and police use to get it right: who, what, where, when, and why. I also like to add the H: How?

I headed the page with that ominous telephone warning, "Tell no one. We will know if you do."

Who? I left that blank, although I had some strong suspicions.

What? A filthy dognapper swiped Po Thang, ransacked my boat, and left me a warning not to tell anyone. Oh, yeah, and they took my aunt.

Where? Where did they take my dog? Who knows?

When? Not applicable.

Why? Good question, and I had my suspicions there, as well, but they had mentioned their *terms,* which indicated the possibility we could settle this matter by reaching some kind of agreement. They obviously didn't know me all that well. I am never agreeable with scumbags.

How? Now here is the biggie for now. How will they know if I contact someone?

I tapped the pen tip on the pad. How, indeed? No one can see what I'm doing. All the blinds are closed. Or can they? And if so, *how*?

Looking around the cabin, I wondered if they'd planted a spy camera. I know every inch of the inside of my boat, because at one time or other I've either washed, sanded, painted or cleaned it. I got up and started a search.

An hour later, after going over every bit of the main cabin and finding nothing, I was still at HOW? If they could see me, could they also hear me?

Back when I first got into a problem in Mexico, I discovered that my nemesis, Dickless Lujàn, had a telescope capable of also picking up conversations from a hundred yards away, but it couldn't see through closed blinds.

Lujàn? I put the dirty bugger's name in the WHO column, which led me back to WHY and WHAT. Why did he take my dog, and what do I have that he wants?

Pictures. My camera was in my backpack, still loaded with photos of Ishikawa scattered about his room, Lujàn and his goons loading a body bag into that Lincoln Navigator, and then sitting in the front seat of that same car, and driving away. My best guess is that's what he wanted. Fine, he can have them, but what guarantee did I have that if I gave him the photos, he wouldn't just off me, Jan, and Po Thang? Oh, and Lil.

I made another list: Good News/Bad News, with a line down the middle dividing the pros from the cons. On the good side I scribbled: Nothing missing that I can tell. Bad news? Po Thang and Lil kidnapped. With an evil grin I circled Lil and drew an arrow to the Good

News side and added a smiley face. Okay, juvenile, but everyone needs a stupid smiley face from time to time.

Good News: Nothing tampered with? Note to self: test all equipment and engines on *Raymond Johnson.*

Computer still here, thank God.

That last notation in the GOOD column sent me to my open laptop, which sprang to life when I jiggled the mouse. If I sent an email to Jan, how would they know? I had to warn her, and also get her to call my mother and tell her some story to keep her from coming down for Lillian. The last thing I wanted was for Mom to get snatched, as well.

I was about to chance an email to Jan when I noticed my webcam port was open. I always close the little slider to block it when I finish talking on Skype, mainly because I didn't want Jenks calling and catching me looking natural.

Was someone watching me on my own webcam? Paranoia runs right thick in these veins, and when I see one of those computer hacker warnings on Facebook, I read them. I mean, if it's on Facebook, it must be true, right?

I remembered the alert said you could be hacked if you inadvertently clicked on a shortened URL on Twitter or the like. Had I done that? Nah. But someone was on my boat, and who knows what they did. If they were using my own webcam to keep tabs on me, how could I find out, and then use it to my advantage? If I closed the port, they might figure I was on to them, and besides, me knowing they were watching gave me an edge.

I decided to leave the port open, and assume it was their way of keeping tabs on me. Let them think I'm fat, dumb, and scared, instead of fat, on to them, and royally pissed off.

The Sturm und Drang of the day—hell, several days—finally took their toll, and exhaustion washed through me like a shot of moonshine. I made it to the settee, just out of webcam range, fell onto it, and the next thing I knew, the VHF crackled to life and woke me with a start. Even with the blinds closed I could tell it was daylight out, and my ship's clock confirmed it was eight in the morning.

The call came again. "*Raymond Johnson, Raymond Johnson, Watchfire.*" I considered not answering Denny's call, then decided this was a stellar chance, if someone *was* watching and listening to me on my own webcam, to let them think I was playing by their rules. Well, actually, I was, but I'd most certainly do something really nasty to them later.

"Denny, *RJ* here, switch Zero Five." I like channel five because most boaters don't have it pre-programmed in their radios and they have to take the time to change manually. No use in everyone easily knowing my business.

"So, Hetta, I saw Robert. Any news from your Aunt Lillian yet?"

"Nope. My guess is she hitched a ride out of town, unless she found a spare broom."

"Ha! Maybe, but I still think you might want the local cops to be on the alert. You know, just in case."

"No! Uh, I mean, uh, not yet, okay? She's only been missing for one day, and I'm sure if she got picked up I'd hear from my new best friends with the siren and flashing lights."

"Yeah, I guess. Oh, well, let me know if I can help. You gonna come ashore and take Po Thang for his walk?"

"Ummm, not today. I'm dead on my feet. Not enough sleep."

"Okay. If you change your mind, stop by. Or if you like, I'll bring you out that stack of books I've read, and you can pay me with coffee."

"Can I take a rain check? I think I'll crawl back in bed, and besides I already have a whole TBR list on my Kindle. Thanks, anyway."

We signed off. It was true that I had a backlist of To Be Reads loaded into my Kindle, but I wondered how long I could put him off before he got suspicious that something wasn't right in my end of the harbor.

I reached for my Kindle, not that I could concentrate on a novel, but my conversation with Denny triggered a memory. Something I knew about, I guess, but never utilized. My old Kindle, which I meant to replace soon, was not only loaded with books, it had email capabilities. Yee haw.

CHAPTER FOURTEEN

So, now I had a way to send an email, sort of.

I had never used the keyboard on this Kindle, and had no idea how. Normally I'd go online and read the how, but that was out, because if they could watch me on my own webcam, maybe they'd hacked into my computer, as well? Jeez, where was Jenks, my techie guru, when I needed him?

I feigned restless boredom for the camera, pacing the cabin, then picking up a paperback or two before throwing them down. Then, as if I'd thought of something, I picked up my Kindle and sat at the dining table. Oscar, anyone?

With my Sat system chugging away, I had WiFi throughout the boat, and more importantly, on my Kindle. I cursored to Turn Wireless On, then waited until it showed me some bars. I gave myself an imaginary high five when four lovely bars popped up. I was, as we say in Texas, 'in bidness.' Problem was, I still had no idea how to send an email on this clever little device that I had heretofore only used to read books.

The keyboard keys were so small that I was sure a pen or pencil eraser was called for, and I cursed myself for stubbornly refusing to learn to text message. Something about it, like a typing course I once flunked, ticked me off. I think watching all these people bent over their phones, tapping with their thumbs like monkeys peeling a banana had something to do with it.

If I were four, instead of forty, I probably could have sent a message in seconds, but I was being watched, and I was supposed to be reading. So, I tried to look like I was reading for awhile, all the time trying to figure out how, and what message, to send Jan as a warning. My thumbs were getting a warm up changing pages of an unread novel while I composed an email message in my mind, and figured out how to send it. There was nothing in the menu giving me a damned clue.

I stared at the screen, cursing myself again. When I got the Kindle, Jenks was the one who discovered it was email enabled, but I wasn't interested. After all, I have a computer, who needs anything else? Then I spotted something on the menu: Experimental. Isn't that what Jenks said? It was experimental on this model?

I hit enter and, voila! There it was. Yahoo! I wanted to kiss fellow Texan, Jeff Bezos's shiny head, then do a happy dance. The dance could wait, however. No use entertaining the freakin' peeping Tomases on the other end of my webcam.

Okay, now I had Yahoo. Yahoo MX. Crappola, everything was in Spanish.

I realized I was hunched over, not at all the vision of one enjoying a good bodice ripper. I made a cheese sandwich, opened a beer, picked up my Kindle, and boldly walked out the door to the back sundeck, and out of camera range. Settling in, I experienced a moment of triumph, hoping my actions made *them* sweat for a change.

My cellphone rang back in the cabin. Should I answer it? What if it was them? They had my cell number, obviously. Maybe, if it was someone else, I could further convince the kidnappers that I was going along, and buy some time to figure out the Kindle? I was desperate to send that message to Jan without endangering Po Thang.

I made it to the phone on the fourth ring. "Hello?"

"There you are. No email this morning?" Jenks's voice brought tears to my eyes. I turned away from the webcam.

"Oh, hi, Jenks. Sorry about missing my morning email. Uh, Tel Mex went down for a few hours. I guess it's fixed now, huh?"

"I guess, since we're talking on it. What are you and Po Thang up to today?"

"The usual."

"Is everything all right? You sound…strange."

"Sorry, I was reading and got caught up in it. You know how I am when I'm engrossed in a really good book."

"Yeah, I do. Okay, just wanted to check on you. I gotta run. Love you, bye."

I wanted to bawl, but whispered, "Love you too. Bye."

Well, that was depressing, but at least I got another chance to make the bastards believe I was following orders. I took the phone with me back on deck, just to jerk their chain, and was tempted to call Jan, but decided to give the email thing on Kindle a chance.

You're an engineer, Hetta. Figure it out!

And I did. Sort of.

My first challenge was putting in Jan's email address. I liberally cursed the entire country of Mexico while doing so. Because I had to figure out how to do numbers, find @ signs and the like, it was a chore, but made more so by Jan's email address, which included caps, numbers and then, instead of something simple, like yahoo.com, I had to conjure up the prodigy.net.mx. After a harrowing, sweaty, hour of struggling with a tiny keyboard that any ten-year-old would master in five seconds, I was pretty sure I sent Jan an email reading: **danger dog and aunt kidnapped being watched one eight hundred got bads question mark msg hetta trouble call mom tell her not to come to Mexico we will bring aunt home.**

It would have to do, since I used up all my patience with numbers and caps on the damned email address. And forget punctuation. I've always found it overrated anyway. Jan's a smart cookie, I told myself. She'd figure it out, right?

Right. And if things went the way I hoped—which they rarely do, but hope springs eternal—a cavalry charge would soon be coming my way.

His name is Nacho.

Okay, so Nacho is not the cavalry, and I'm really not sure what he is, but he gets me out of jams.

He also proclaims to have the hots for me, but the first time I met him he was on the verge of killing me and Jenks for a can of gas, so I guess he can be a mite on the unpredictable side. Since that time Nacho has kidnapped me, embroiled me in a plot to blow up a meth lab, and the last time I saw him he took off with a girlfriend of mine, Topaz Sawyer. Who says romance is dead?

He gave me his card a while back, which I was supposed to burn or eat or whatever, which I didn't do because who could destroy a great card like this?

1-800-got-bads?
We get what's bugging you.

Jan and I think Nacho is handsome, in a criminal sort of way. We don't know who he works for, or what he does, but we've concluded he's either a narco, narc agent, or something in between. He is Hispanic, but goes by Lamont Cranston, a.k.a. The Shadow, which I know because I stole his wallet, along with his off-road pickup, once upon a time. Is it any wonder he's so enamored with a charmer like me?

What I *do* know is that he said if I ever gave out that phone number to anyone, *ANYONE*, he would kill me, so I figure when Jan calls him he'll come running to do the job, but maybe liberate my dog first? Oh, and my aunt.

I went back inside, exhausted by my efforts to send a simple email, and plugged my Kindle into the charger. To celebrate I made chocolate chip cookies, then ate the entire batch while they were still warm, chasing them down with a hefty glass or two—okay, a half-bottle—of red wine. All that chocolate and wine was so comforting, I crawled into my bed and slept for ten hours straight. When I woke, someone was pounding on the hull.

"Hetta, Hetta? You in there?" Denny called from the swim platform. I could see his sandaled feet through a porthole near my bed. With my dinghy tied to the boat, he knew I was aboard, so there was no use pretending I wasn't.

"Just a minute. Coming," I yelled, hoping he heard me over the generator's hum. I was still dressed in the rumpled, melted chocolate-festooned clothes I'd passed out in the night before. My mouth tasted like yesterday's red wine, and my hair? I ran my fingers through my bed-head, put a Listerine breath strip on my tongue, and headed to the main saloon. To make certain my watchers didn't think I had a chance to tell Denny anything, I just stuck my head out the door and yelled for him to join me.

I was brewing a pot of coffee when he entered. "Oh, good. Dammit, I forgot to bring you those books. I haven't seen you around, so thought I'd swing by and check on you." He looked around, "Where's Po Thang?"

"Uh, Jan took him with her to the fish camp."

"Really? When? I've been on my boat for a couple of days straight, didn't see either of you at the dock."

Damn! "Well, uh…she called last night and asked me to meet her in Juncalito early this morning. I took him over there in *Se Vende*, just at daybreak, since it was such a beautiful morning."

"Oh." He once again scanned the darkened, gloomy, cabin. "How could you tell?"

"You take sugar, right?"

By the time Denny left, I'd told enough lies to run for Congress.

I stared at my cellphone, anxious for it to ring. I'd even taken it to bed with me the night before, just in case the SOBs called, but they didn't. I cursed the lack of caller ID on my throwaway TelCel phone; I would dearly love to call them back and tell them they could have the whole damned camera, but not before I saw Po Thang safe and sound on my boat. Were they delaying, watching to see if I gave a clue anyone else knew about Ishikawa, Lujàn, and the photos? In this digital age, I could splash those photos all over the Internet in a nanosecond if they didn't have my dog as insurance against it. And by the way, I hadn't been on Facebook for three days now. Were my friends missing me? Or was the cyberworld the same as the real one; out of sight, out of mind?

While I was trying to convince myself that my Facebook BFFs were frantic with worry at my absence, the phone finally rang.

"Hetta!" Aunt Lillian screeched. "If you don't give them what they want, they're going to kill me."

"Really?" I said, striving not to sound too elated with such a grand idea.

"I heard that tone in your voice, young lady. You do what they say, you hear?"

"Is Po Thang with you?"

"Yes, but what do I care about a damned dog. Get me out of here."

"Is there someone there I can talk to?" *Maybe I could cut a deal? Like, they off Lil in exchange for the camera?*

There was the sound of a scuffle, a bark, a curse, and then dead air.

Hearing that bark made my heart sing.

For the webcam's benefit, I yelled into the phone, "Hello? Hello? I'll give you whatever you want, just give me my dog. You can keep the aunt."

CHAPTER FIFTEEN

My generator had been running non-stop for three days, and was already overdue for an oil change. I'd burned through at least a hundred bucks worth of diesel, and running so low on food I was eyeing the Alpo. It sort of looked and smelled like corned beef hash. Maybe with a little ketchup....Worst of all, my wine was now depleted. What in the hell was the hold-up with these guys? Not another word since that lovely chat with dear Aunt Lil.

I spoke with Jenks when he called, both times lying about the Internet being wonky in Mexico, and that's why I hadn't emailed him.

For the benefit of my tormenters, I cooled my jets, seemingly just waiting for them to contact me again. I tried to use the Kindle for incoming mail and failed miserably, then to make matters even worse, I somehow killed my Kindle, along with any chance of sending another email.

So now I was wine-less *and* new-book-less, which for me is a grievous state of affairs. Desperate, I read Pat and John Rains's Mexico Boating Guide, all four hundred pages of it, wishing me, my dog, my boat, and Jenks were in any other place mentioned in the cruising guide but this one.

And, as I was sitting outside, already feeling sorry for myself, a familiar scent rose from the sea, bringing with it memories that moved me first to tears, then bawling out loud. My dad told me many years ago, when we were out fishing and I commented on it, that it was a school of fish we smelled, but couldn't see. It is Jenks's favorite ocean fragrance, and reminds him of fishing with *his* father.

I wanted my daddy.

I wanted Jenks.

I wanted my dog.

Most of all, I wanted to be anywhere but where I was, and out of this situation I had no control over.

When I came unhinged, it took me by surprise.

No big buildup to a Texas hissy fit like normal; one minute I was scrounging in the larder for Velveeta mac and cheese, found none, and suddenly something between a scream and a holler escaped me.

Stomping to my backpack, I yanked out the camera and waved it wildly in front of the webcam, spewing obscenities and spittle. Then, as quickly as the fit hit, it subsided, and I went from loco to deadly calm.

With what I hoped was a Jack Nicholson grin, I slowly and dramatically—exaggerating each move like a silent movie evil dude—waved my camera in front of the webcam, then plugged it into my computer and hissed, "If I don't hear from someone in charge, or get my dog back *today*, I'm going to download these photos onto Facebook, and share them with every newspaper in the world. Your time starts *now*!"

Those guys from AA were certainly right; going cold turkey on my boat is downright dangerous.

The phone rang a little over two hours later. I snatched it up, and completely blowing that deceptive cool I'd managed to portray during the final act of my Oscar-worthy psycho performance, screeched, "Now listen to me you sonsabitches, I am sick and tired of your crap. Give me my damned dog and you can have anything you want."

"*Querida*, you have made my dreams come true. Anything?"

Nacho? Crap, what timing.

"Uh, could you call back later? I'm expecting a very important call."

"Someone more important than me? I am wounded."

"I'm hanging up now."

"Look out your door."

I rushed to the slider and opened it. A panga was alongside, and in it, the most wonderful sight I could imagine.

Po Thang went plumb nuts when he saw me. Barking, whining, and rushing from one end of the panga to the other, he rocked it so much the poor driver, who was standing, almost fell overboard. Po Thang then jumped into the water himself, and dogpaddled to the back of *Raymond Johnson*, where I rushed to meet him. Like a good boy he waited on the swim platform for his normally mandatory rinse off, but right then I couldn't care less about a little salt water on my deck; I had my dog back.

I was nuzzling wet, salty, stinky fur when the panga pulled alongside *Se Vende*.

Crap, I'd sort of hoped I hadn't seen my aunt in it.

"Give the camera to the panga driver," she demanded, "and get me onto that boat of yours. I need a shower and a drink."

Knowing full well she couldn't get on the boat without my help, I left her where she was and went for the camera, blocking Po Thang's entrance into the main saloon with a "no" hand signal. I mean, salty decks are one thing, carpets? Quite another.

Unplugging my camera, I waved it in front of the webcam. "You've got what you want, okay? I'll make you a deal, though. Keep the old lady and I'll put five hundred dollars with the camera." I slid the webcam's port shut and picked up my cellphone, willing it to ring in my hand. I delayed returning aft for a minute or two, in case my tormentors took me up on my offer, but no such luck. Sighing, I went back out and handed over the camera to the panga driver, who looked familiar, and very nervous.

I contemplated starting *Raymond Johnson's* engines and taking off, leaving him stuck with Lil, but his pleading eyes changed my mind. He was just a poor schmuck who was paid a few pesos to deliver the goods, and pick up the camera. Why make *everyone* miserable?

After I yanked auntie aboard, I watched as the panga streaked across the harbor and headed south. It was then I made the connection; the driver was one of the guys who gave me and Jan a ride back to PE from the resort the night of the luau.

Coincidence? You be the judge.

If I had any doubts that Lujàn was involved in the kidnapping of my dog, they disappeared with the panga.

So, we were back to square one, only worse. I was stuck with Lil, and so far as I knew, my mother wasn't even coming to get her. I fired up Skype and called Jan.

"Hetta? Oh, thank God. Are you all right? Po Thang? Lil? I've been worried silly—"

I cut her off. "Everything is fine now. Looks like you got the job done. Standby, I'm going to turn on the camera." I opened the port and suddenly I was looking into Jan's distraught face, which, even distraught, still looked good.

"Can you see me, Jan?"

"Yes. Tell me what happened. After I called Nacho…oh, by the way, he was not pleased to hear from me, you know."

"I could care less if he wasn't pleased. You did your job and he did his. Did you reach my mother?"

"Not yet. I was going to try again in a few minutes. You know how they are."

Boy, did I? I had tried, to no avail, over and over to get my parents to use the answering machine I bought them, or a get phone service that took messages, anything, but they stubbornly maintained that if a caller had something important to say they would call back. And forget email or the Internet; they had only recently caved and signed up for cable television instead of relying on some rickety old roof antennas that picked up three snowy channels. For once, however, their

Luddite ways paid off. "Good, I'll call her. Alas, I got Lil back."

Jan giggled. From behind me Lil squawked, "I heard that. As soon as I get home I'm taking you out of my will."

Oh, that's right. Mom said I was back in the will. Maybe, if I could somehow reach Lujàn, we could still cut a deal?

"Hetta, don't even think about it," Jan warned.

Good grief, can *everyone* read my mind over the phone? "Okay, okay. Can you come to the boat? I need moral support."

"Oh, piddle, Hetta, you ain't got no morals to support."

Gosh, aren't best friends grand?

I called Mother, and miracle of miracles, she not only answered, her passport had arrived and she was booked into Loreto in two days, with a return reservation for herself and her sister two days after that. Four more days of Lil? *One* of us *had* to drink.

Unfortunately for me, Robert's dire warning about the dangers of Lil going cold turkey hadn't panned out, but four days of sobriety had done absolutely nothing for her personality. Faced with four more days of her, I considered turning myself over to those nuns.

What little booze was left on the boat I stashed, along with any prescription drugs, in the engine room, while Lil was in the shower.

Po Thang was already freshly shampooed and sun-dried, and in better luck than Lil; I hadn't been reduced to raiding his food stores yet, and he doesn't imbibe alcohol except on those occasions when I share, or the even rarer times I doze off and leave something in a glass.

I dumped food into Po Thang's bowl and rummaged around until I came up with peanut butter and jelly for me and Lil, but both of them turned up their noses at my offerings. Lillian let me know that their captors fed them better than I, which of course really pissed me off. According to Lil, she and my dog had shared a nice apartment with three squares a day while I was stuck on the boat, worried sick, and scrounging for saltines? Who, exactly, had been the hostage here?

"Jan, sugar," Lil cooed as Jan climbed on board. "Thank goodness you're here. Hetta is starving me. Peanut butter and jelly? I thought we raised her better."

"*We* didn't raise me, Aunt Lillian, my mother and dad did. I suspect you and Mom didn't have the same parents. By the way, how are *your* brothers, you know, Romulus and Remus? Oh wait, I forgot, Rom killed off Rem. How did you escape?"

Sobriety hadn't done much for my disposition, either.

Jan not only arrived with groceries, she also brought big news: Chino, her marine biologist significant other had received an anonymous donation for his Manila galleon hunt. Yep, one-hundred thousand smackeroos. Ishikawa may have lost his head, but somehow kept his end of the deal with Jan. Interesting.

When we escaped the aunt from hell for a trip to the beach, we got a chance to talk about the donation while Po Thang watered the cactus.

"I've been thinking about this Ishikawa and Luján thing. In light of everything that's happened, I find it hard to believe Ishikawa was at Camp Chino by accident. Did you find out exactly how the money came in for Chino?"

"Naw, I asked him for details. All he knows is he got a call from the Mexican National Institute of Anthropology and History telling him his expedition had received a large donation to fund the hunt for the galleon. The actual donor preferred to remain anonymous."

"But they must know something about the benefactor."

"Only that the money came from Japan, for sure, because there are stipulations."

"Like what?"

"They want two Japanese graduate students—divers, by the way—on the expedition, and that they are given official credit for any finds. Something to do with them getting advanced degrees."

"What does Chino think about that?"

She shrugged. "He was so elated I think he'd have taken Godzilla and Mothra on board. He's like a kid with a new bike. He's looking for equipment he didn't dream he'd be able to afford, and arranging to have the boat modernized. The old rust bucket has seen a few year's service, but now he can at least have some decent plumbing and the like installed. And he doesn't give a big bull's behind about fame, as you well know. He just wants to find artifacts and prove the galleon sank in Mag Bay."

"I'll help him out with the equipment as soon as I can. Tell him to email me a list, with specs, and I'll get on it just as soon as mom and Lil leave. If I live through Lil. She's driving me crazy."

"You're already nuts. You *do* know that, don't you?"

"I'm a little eccentric, that's all."

"Oscar Wilde was a little eccentric. You're a flaming lunatic."

"Yeah, but lucky for you, I'm *your* flaming lunatic."

Jan, even though she called me a lunatic, was a godsend.

She ran interference between me and Aunt Lil, thereby saving two lives at once. She played cards with my aunt for hours on end, even though Lil is a well-known cheater. Jan cooked, thereby saving me from Lil's abuse. It was a win-win.

With Lil off my back, I had time to work on Chino's equipment list. I wasn't familiar with the complicated dive gear and stuff he wanted, but with a set of specs and good Internet access, which I now had because Chino's budget was picking up the tab for my Sat system, I can find just about anything worldwide, and get it where it needs to be. It is something I love doing, and quite frankly, I'm good at it. Jan is right when she says I'd rather deal with inanimate objects, what with my sucky people skills.

Aunt Lillian, in true Jeklyll/Hyde mode, transformed into her deceptively sweet persona as soon as my mother arrived. Mom is not stupid, but that sister of hers has a way of conning her, lulling her into a false sense that Lil wouldn't grow fangs and bite her in the butt once again. I guess that blood being thicker than water stuff is true for nice people. Luckily, I am not nice.

Unfortunately, Jan left the day after mom showed up. I hated to see my favorite peacekeeper go, but she and Chino were transitioning from the fish camp to the research vessel in Lopez Mateos, Chino's hometown.

Less than a hundred miles from Puerto Escondido, in the upper reaches of Magdalena Bay, Puerto Lopez Mateos is a small town with not much going for it besides a thriving whale watching industry. It has a population of about two thousand residents most of whom seem to be related to Chino, which is no wonder considering that family legend has them descended from some shipwreck victims over four hundred years ago.

Because the town is on the Pacific, with only a barrier island between it and the ocean, summer temperatures average in the eighties, as opposed to the life-sucking 90s and 100's in the Sea of Cortez.

The channel from Mag Bay into Lopez Mateos teems with some of the friendliest whales in existence during the winter months, but now the whales were headed north, so Chino's family, who made most of their money during tourist season and barely survived the rest of the year, would be involved in the expedition to find the sunken galleon that purportedly stranded their ancestors on the beach.

Ishikawa's money, or maybe whomever he represented's money, was allowing Chino to head up, you should pardon the expression, a one-man war on poverty.

CHAPTER SIXTEEN

If I had resented Lil before, I found her presence almost unbearable when my mother finally arrived.

I hadn't seen Mom in over a year, and wanted to spend time with her, but as always, Lillian spoiled everything. No conversation was held that didn't get high-jacked and turned into some personal beef of my aunt's. Fun shopping trips into Loreto were out, because we couldn't trust Lil if left alone on the boat, and if we took her with us, she'd probably give us the slip and find a bar. The bottom line? Only Lillian was enjoying herself during this little family reunion.

I was, on several occasions, tempted to slip Lil a bottle so she'd eventually pass out and give us a little peace, but I didn't want to put my mother through yet another of her sister's nutso binges.

Finally, after being hounded mercilessly, I agreed to a field trip to Lopez Mateos so Lillian could visit with Chino's grandmother, Abuela Yee. They'd become, much to the dismay of Chino, Internet pals after meeting briefly on my boat last year.

Chino's grandma and Aunt Lillian mostly compared notes on their love life, the thought of which gave everyone, except those two, nightmares. Not *even* wanting to overhear what was said during this little tête-à-tête, I planned to visit the *Nao de Chino* while Grans Yee and Aunt Lillian compared notes on meeting men.

Chino's granny scours the Internet for men via online dating sites, while Lil haunts the hallways of VA Hospitals for her next victim.

It is enough, to paraphrase the Bard of Avon, to 'get *me* to a nunnery.'

The day my mother and Lillian were scheduled to fly out of Mexico was a bittersweet one for me. I would miss Mom, and regretted the regrettable circumstances of our time together while she was on the boat, but getting rid of Lil? Priceless.

The police had happily approved Lil's departure from their country, and Alaska Airlines agreed to take her, so long as mother was with her. I'm sure Alaska was forewarned and wouldn't be serving the old bag any alcoholic beverages in flight, but I did worry whether there was a bar open at the airport. The last thing I wanted was another dust up with the authorities on Lil's behalf.

Because I had a meeting at the mine the same day as their flight, and with my pickup being a little small for four, I had fobbed Po Thang off on Denny for the day. I dropped Mother and Lil two hours early for their flight back to the States, and still had time to make my conference.

What with all the nasty distractions of late, I hadn't had much time to think past the disaster of the day, like getting my dog back and then divesting myself of Lil. Once I dropped her and my mom off, though, I felt a great sense of relief. I popped Willie into the disk player, sighed with deep contentment when hearing his homey voice, and drove along Mex 1 enjoying the music and the lack of Lil.

That contentment lasted about ten minutes as I mulled over the events of the past couple of weeks. Weeks? Only weeks? Seemed like a couple of years.

Rather than dwell on silly things like *why* it all happened, which would have required unwanted introspection I wasn't in any mood to deal with, what with me being in short supply of introspectiveness, I zeroed in on, *what's next*?

Puerto Escondido was fast losing its charm.

I was stuck at anchor, alone, with summer around the corner. Come a month from now, it was going to heat up like the hinges of hell. Even that could be dealt with at a dock with good electricity, and therefore air conditioning, but I'd live the life of a vampire, only emerging at night. And then there was hurricane season, and I'd already lived through one the year before, thank you. I needed a secure dock for my boat, at the very least, and maybe, in light of the Ishikawa/Luján debacle, I should bail myself out of Mexico altogether until at least October, but that would mean losing my only source of income.

My marina choices were limited.

There was the Guaymas/San Carlos area on the mainland, but that posed a problem because I was already sticking it to the copper mine near Santa

Rosalia for meetings like the one I was headed for, and doubted they would spring for airfare and hotel every two weeks. Even if they did, what would I do with Po Thang?

Puerto Escondido, where I had a someday reservation, required that Mediterranean-tie situation. Not great when a hurricane roars up the Sea of Cortez.

La Paz? Great marinas, if pricey, and they took a big hurricane hit several years ago. What were the odds on that happening again? And to boot, there was that long trip up the Baja for meetings twice a month.

Every cruiser in the Sea of Cortez faces the yearly dilemma of what to do with their boat during hurricane season, but most of them leave the country to escape the heat, and I doubted any had to fret over being snagged as a murder suspect.

I was climbing the Hill of Hell, and as I passed by the desolate strip of dirt perched on the side of a cliff where I'd rescued Po Thang a few months before, I realized I'd been driving one of the most treacherous stretches of road in Mexico on autopilot. If I kept this up I wouldn't have to worry about another summer *any*where.

Seeing Po Thang's former slice of Hell did make one decision for me; I was going to call my friend Craig, a veterinarian in Arizona, and arrange to get that pooch chipped with one of his Doc Washington GPS trackers.

The meeting was a no-brainer, a good thing since indecision kept mine ricocheting around like a bullet in a rain barrel, or going as dead as a, well, beheaded Japanese.

On the way back to Puerto Escondido I made the mandatory, for me, pit stop at Saul Davis's grocery store in Mulege to see what Gringo goodies lurked on his shelves and in his cooler. Score! Velveeta cheese, Polska kielbasa, a case of Alpo, a case of caffeine free Diet Coke for a mere twenty-two dollars, and best of all, beautiful thin asparagus. It's the little things that count.

Back on my blessedly Lillian-free boat just before dark, I broke out a kilo of carnitas I bought in Santa Rosalia for me and Po Thang. He even let me have three tacos worth.

Washing it down with an ice-cold Tecate—my first in almost a week—I wiped pig grease from both our snouts, fired up the generator again, and Skyped Craigosaurus, a.k.a. Doctor Craig Washington, DVM.

Craig and I were friends back in the Bay Area, when he was a hundred pounds heavier. We both love dogs, struggle with our weight, and have a lousy history with men, so our friendship went deep.

Craig, highly successful monetarily, as well as tall, black and gay, should have been in high cotton in the San Francisco Bay Area, but his weight and kind nature made him a target for pretty boys looking to break his heart and bank account. His nickname back then, Craigosaurus, no longer pertains.

After being pushed too far by one of those crappy opportunists, he hired my former personal trainer who, through no fault of her own had failed miserably with me. He then moved to Arizona, met the cowboy of his dreams, and they live on a vast cattle ranch outside of Bisbee. Their popular big animal clinic services both sides of the border and not that either of them need it, they make scads of money implanting GPS tracking chips into livestock. Four-wheeling cowpokes can cut their roundup time, and hired hands, in half. Rumor has it quarter horses and cowpunchers are lawyering-up.

His partner, Roger, is a fourth generation Arizona rancher, and neither man is anxious, even in the first town in Arizona to condone same-sex marriage, to out their relationship to their elderly, very conservative, parents. They still do not live together, but instead have two separate houses on the same bajillion acres. To see them together, few would ever guess they were anything other than good old boys—albeit one of them being a *black* good old boy—sharing a business partnership and, on occasion, a beer or two at the local golf club.

Jan and I are now Arizona residents, using Craig's address as our legal abode. So, as far as anyone knows, Craig and Hetta and Roger and Jan all live happily together.

"Hi, honey, miss me?" I chirped when Craig answered. He turned on his camera and I noticed he was even more svelte and chiseled than the last time I saw him at my fortieth—there, I said it without stuttering!—birthday party in Conception Bay a few weeks before.

"Hetta! Great to talk to you. I've enjoyed your emails, but it's not the same as seeing you and dishing some dirt. What are you up to? How's Jan? Jenks? Po Thang?"

"Jan and Jenks are fine, but Po Thang is one of the reasons I called. He has taken up a bad habit or two."

"What can you expect, Hetta? He learns from his master, or mistress in your case. You have stopped giving him people food, right?"

I looked over at Po Thang, who was licking pig leavings from a plate. Pig is not really people food, right?

"Sure. The problem is, he's taken to jumping ship and swimming for shore. Are those GPS microchip doodads you make waterproof?"

"Waterproof, yes. Don't know how they'd hold up underwater for long periods, though. I'll give one a test. You want to bring him up for a fitting?"

"Can't, even though I would love to. How're my guns."

"Locked up safe and sound. Please don't tell me you need them. Again."

"Naw. Just kinda miss 'em. Anyhow, could Chino do the implant? He is a veterinarian, even if he does spend all his time with whales. I know he puts tracking devices on some of them."

"Probably with a harpoon. He'll need a little more finesse with Po Thang."

"But he can do it?"

"Sure. I've been teaching ranchers to do it themselves."

"They chip themselves?"

He laughed. "Very funny. I miss your sense of humor. When *are* you coming home?"

"Maybe soon. I can't decide what to do when I grow up. Say, could you arrange for someone to implant a chip in Texas?"

"That'd take a pretty big chip."

"Very funny, yourself. Someone *in* Texas."

"No problem."

"Great. Well, you've met my Aunt Lillian...."

Turns out the chip's tracking distance is only five miles, and I didn't want to be within a hundred miles of my aunt. Oh, well, it would have been nice to have some kind of alarm go off if she ever headed my way again.

But, for Po Thang, five miles would be better than nothing.

Since I had Skype up and running, I called Jenks, even though it was five a.m. in Dubai. He gets up at four anyhow. He picked up on the third ring. There was a loud roar in the background.

"Hello? Hello? Hetta, I can't really hear you. I'll call back when I can." Just before the line went dead, I heard him yell, "Oh, hell, we're going down...."

CHAPTER SEVENTEEN

Jenks is a pilot, and when an aviator says, "Oh, hell, we're going down," it can only mean one thing.

I went cold with fear. It took me forty years to find, stalk, and snare the world's greatest guy, and now he's crashing into some godforsaken desert? "No!" I screamed.

Po Thang jumped to his feet and looked guilty.

I reached out and gave him an ear rub. "Sorry. You haven't done anything that deserves an N-O, sweetie," I told him, spelling the dreaded word so as not to upset him further. He looked relieved and licked my hand. Poor thing already thinks his second name is, "Sit-and stay."

I tried calling Jenks back, got nowhere, grabbed a glass of wine and went out on deck to wash down my fears. What seemed like an hour, but was probably only ten minutes later, my cellphone rang.

"Hetta. Sorry about that. The prince and I are out practicing with his RC helicopter, and something went wrong."

"What? Oh, my god, you *did* crash. Are you and Prince Faoud all right?"

"What? Of course we are."

"Thank goodness. You scared the hell out of me. What are you doing flying the prince's helicopter?"

There was a pause, then Jenks started laughing, which pissed me off. First he scares the poop out of me, and then laughs about it? What kind of nut case had he turned into over there?

"Okay you s.o.b., I'm hanging up now. You can take your helicopter and shove it—"

"Wait, Hetta, I'm sorry. It's a radio controlled helicopter. You know, a model airplane."

"Oh."

I was relieved Jenks was still alive. Honest. But as I tossed in my lonely bed—okay, maybe not so lonely, now that a golden retriever manages to take over way more than half of it—I became annoyed.

Jenks was living as a guest of Prince Faoud in Dubai. A Saudi prince who, by the way, was *my* friend first. Jan and I met him during the aftermath of a hurricane in Magdalena Bay the year before, a doozy of a storm that threatened both our boats, if you can call *Golden Odyssey*, the prince's two hundred and fifty foot yacht, a boat. Hell, the "little" boat he trails behind his yacht, just in case he wants to go big game fishing, is almost as large as *Raymond Johnson*.

So, here I was stuck at anchor in a Baja backwater while the two men yucked it up in the lap of luxury, and flew model airplanes that, knowing the prince's extravagant tastes and limitless pocketbook, cost more than my boat.

I stewed all night, then called Jan the next morning to vent. After listening to my rant, she drawled, "Lemme get this straight. You've got your panties in a twist because Jenks is letting you do what you want to do, instead of what *he* wants you to do, which is go live with him in Dubai in the most luxurious hotel in the world?"

After I hung up on all that logic, I decided to take Po Thang out for a beach party, so we could both cool off. I took a snorkel and fins, along with my light-weight Lycra neck-to-ankle, form-fitting, sea-critter-keeper-offer, bodysuit. It isn't the most flattering piece of clothing I own, and I rarely wear it without a tee shirt to cover up some less than lovely bumps, but Po Thang doesn't notice. He's too happy splashing around and trying to drown me on the occasional pass by putting his front feet on my shoulders and pushing me under. Luckily I'm able to fin him off.

I am the original chicken of the sea, but I love to putter around in shallow water and spy on fish and stuff. Unfortunately, I've been stung, bitten, and generally terrorized by more than one salty threat, and for some reason I think that sheathing myself in a thin layer of Lycra protects me from harm. Not logical, of course, but it works for me.

The water was clear and seventy-eight degrees, just the way I like it. My chosen reef, which actually more of a pile of rocks, harbors myriad brightly-colored fish, some of them just tiny bright blue streaks, others multi-hued and larger. Itsy bitsy baby octopi, no larger than a fingernail, abound. I was hoping for a seahorse, but didn't get that lucky. Before I knew it, two hours passed and by the time I got back to the boat my outlook had lightened immensely.

I gave both myself and Po Thang a fresh water rinse off, poured a glass of wine, and went out on the sundeck to let my hair air-dry while I determined my next move.

Jan was right: Jenks *had* invited me to join him in Dubai, but I stubbornly refused because I am stubborn. He says my independence is one of the things that attracted him to me in the first place, although I think he may have rethought that a time or two.

I called Jan back. "I'm pissed off because I'm stupid, and that is really hard to fix."

"So fix it anyhow. Get that boat into a slip, jump a plane, and go."

"I just might. But the truth is, I'd worry about you. After all, there is still that Ishikawa/Lujàn thing."

"I'm touched. Okay, I'll come with you."

"What? You can't. You have to keep my dog. And speaking of which—" I went on to tell her about the GPS tracker chip Craig was shipping for Chino to implant in Po Thang. Somehow Po Thang sensed we were discussing him, and not in a good way, and frowned at me.

I told Jan and she giggled. "I swear, Hetta, that dog understands everything we say."

"Then why doesn't he mind better?"

"Cuz he takes after you."

Spaghetti and meatballs were on the dinner menu, along with a salad, and heated garlic bread. Po Thang gave the salad a sniff and a miss.

We ate out on deck, as the evening was uncommonly warm, a reminder that summer was coming on fast and I had to make a decision on what I was going to do with mine.

My contract at the mine ran out in late summer or early fall. That meant attending at least two meetings a month in Santa Rosalia. I could move the boat to the marina there, and still sign on as a cook or whatever for Chino's Manila Galleon/treasure hunt in Mag Bay, where it is nice and cool all summer long. From there I'd drive to the mine site for those meetings and spend the night on my own boat. Po Thang'd have built in baby-sitters aboard *Nao de Chino*.

It was the perfect solution with one ragged snag: Lujàn.

My spirits plunged.

I was starting to feel like a sitting duck.

A victim.

A wuss.

Coward.

Shrinking violet.

Everything I hate in a woman.

Something I *really* hate in me.

It was that last bit that had me pulling Po Thang close for a comforting hug. Comforting for me; he was comfortably asleep when I grabbed him. After a little grumbling he gave me a nose lick, and I smelled sweet doggy breath with a hint of garlic.

He depended on me to feed him and keep him safe. Mostly from himself, but he didn't know that. I had let him down, but he didn't know that either. He'd been held hostage with my mean old aunt, and wasn't very pleased about it, but it was *why* he was held with her that stuck in my craw.

Lujàn.

Once again on the verge of tears, I wrapped my arms around Po Thang's warmth and fell asleep on the carpet. My last thought was that for someone who rarely cries, there was way too much of it lately.

When I awoke at midnight, I was stiff. And I heard music.

Disoriented, I sat up and listened. The music was in my head.

A team of buglers played an eerie rendition of a song that sends a chill down the spine of any Texan: *The Deguello.*

Most people have only heard it at bullfights. It is what they play when the matador receives his killing, throat-cutting, sword. And it is what the men at the Alamo awoke to the morning of that battle; Mexican president Santa Anna's musical message that he would give no quarter.

Drawing a mental line in the sand, I conjured up an adoring roar from the bullring fans, executed a theatrical sideways stance, swooped a throw around my body, and held it up dramatically. Snapping the blankie in front of my dog, I challenged, "*¡Toro! Aqui!*"

Po Thang scooted backwards so fast he tripped over himself, landed in a heap, regained his dignity with a mighty shake, and gave me a dirty look.

I dropped my cape and gave him a hug. "I'm so sorry sweetie. Trust me, it ain't you who ain't gonna get no quarter. Okay, I think that was a double negative, but you know what I mean. That filthy dog-snatching coward, Lujàn, is on notice from this day forward. How *dare* he kidnap you?"

He snorted in agreement, and I added, "And to make matters worse, he gave Lillian back."

CHAPTER EIGHTEEN

I'd call it Plan B, but since I never had a Plan A, I guess it was just a plan.

The definition of a plan is: A series of steps to be carried out or goals to be accomplished.

Okay, then, let us start with goals to be accomplished.

Ultimate goal: Take down Lujàn, once and for all. Note to self: define "take down."

Steps to accomplish feat? I have no freaking idea.

Accomplishing lofty goals is kind of like playing pinball for me. For instance, I'm an engineer, but it wasn't a bar I set for myself. I just ricocheted through several schools in several countries until I found one that kept my interest, which is why it took me *for*ever to graduate. However, reaching a goal by bouncing around barriers, or sometimes right through them, usually gets the job done for me these days, although, at times, leaves me, and everyone around me, somewhat the worse for wear. But, hey, why mess with a working system?

Every plan needs an accomplice. Preferably an unsuspecting one.

"Jan, wanna take a boat ride?"

"Sure. Where we goin'?"

"La Paz. Gonna put the boat in a nice safe marina for the summer, and join you and Chino on the treasure hunt in Magdalena Bay."

"Cool. But didn't a couple of marinas in La Paz get wiped out in a hurricane a few years back."

"Yeah, that's why I'm going there. What are the odds of that happening again?"

"In your case? I'd say pretty darned good."

"Look, hurricane season is a long time from now, so I've decided to come spend the summer with you guys if you want me. Much cooler during the summer at Mag Bay, and besides, you'll have the privilege of dog sitting when I drive up to Santa Rosalia a couple of times a month."

"Sounds very reasonable. Which means you're up to no good. You are never reasonable. What gives?"

Sigh. The woman knows me all too well. "I'll tell you on the way to La Paz."

"When do we leave?"

"ASAP. Have Chino and a couple of his electronically talented cousins bring you over. And ask them to bring an extra truck. I see no reason to leave a perfectly good Sat system on my boat when we can use it on *Nao de Chino*. That way we'll have fast Internet and even television. Plug more airtime into the expedition budget, okay? It won't be cheap, but at least Chino won't have to spring for that new communications system he wants for the summer, right?"

"So, Missy Generous, how much are you gonna gouge him for renting your system?"

"You wound me."

"Yeah, yeah. How much?"

"Half the price of a new one."

"Piracy!"

"Aargh, matey."

Not convinced I wasn't still being watched, or somehow bugged, even though I gave those lowlife-dog-napping-so-and-sos my camera, I inspected my boat, over and over again, with the scrutiny of the paranoiac I am, and found nothing, but was still taking no chances. I drove into Loreto, bought a cellphone from Telcel, then found an Internet café and used their computer to send out an email with the new number to Jenks, or anyone who might want to call me on a Mexican number.

I dropped into the port captain's office and told them my VHF radio was acting up, but I was leaving Puerto Escondido for La Paz, and might not be able to call them when I exited port.

At the marina office in PE, I cancelled myself from the slip waiting list because I was leaving for La Paz.

The next day I drove to Mulege, dropped Po Thang off with friends there, telling them I was leaving for La Paz with the boat, but would pick him up in a few days. He wasn't happy getting saddled with a couple of Dalmatians for company, but it was for his own good.

Jan and the wrecking crew arrived, and we carefully dismantled the Sat system, with me diagramming and tagging each and every part and wire. I also made sure Chino's cousins knew we were leaving for La Paz before they took off for home. By the next day, thanks to the cousin's chinwagging ways, everyone in the Mag Bay area would know where we were headed.

We said our goodbyes to the fleet at PE during the morning net, telling everyone we were going to take maybe ten days cruising down to La Paz, then we headed south. We passed the resort where this whole disaster started, made a sharp left, went out to sea for five miles, then turned north, and made a beeline for Santa Rosalia.

If Lujàn and his spies were keeping tabs on me, they wouldn't be able to locate my boat for days, thereby giving me time to sneak up on him and knock his Dickless self in the dirt.

Sometimes I am absolutely brilliant.

"Ya know, Hetta, this is plumb dumb."

So much for my brilliance. "Why?"

"Lujàn has about a bajillion people in the Baja who feed him info for a few hundred pesos. He gets wind of properties in dispute and moves in to snatch them. When permits are applied for, he knows, and can buy up the property next door, stuff like that. He'll know we're in Santa Rosalia an hour after we get there."

We were about fifteen miles southeast of Santa Rosalia, where I'd planned a late arrival so no one in the marina office, or the port captain's, would know about us until mid-morning the next day, when I had to check in. "But, we'll catch the bus to Puerto Escondido, get my pickup and Po Thang, head for Lopez Mateos, and join Chino on the research vessel. No one will know where I went."

"And then what?"

"I figure, what with Chino's family's deep roots in the Baja, maybe they'll know where that pig, Lujàn, is lurking."

"And then?"

"How about we hire *American Hoggers*, have them round him up, and grind him into sausage?"

Jan got a dreamy look on her face. "I love that show." She shook her head to clear what I knew were fond memories of her days as a goat roper. Of course, roping goats is a far cry from those two Texas gals—Jan's heroes—on *American Hoggers*. Those tough women crash through snake-infested underbrush hot on the tails of baying hounds, and then pounce on two-hundred-pound porkers sporting six inch tusks, hog-tie them, and haul them off to a local sausage factory.

"But," she said, "won't work down here. You're right, though, we need to remove the dog-stealing, beheading bastard from our lives. Don't you just hope he had to deal with Lil himself while they had her?"

"He didn't. Lil didn't tell me much, but she did say she and Po Thang were together in a nice apartment, and the food was better than mine. The only person she saw was the kid who brought meals. She bribed him to sneak in hooch."

"She told you that?"

"Naw, but I know her. She called him 'a polite young man whose manners belied his station in life.' That means he brought her booze."

Jan smiled. "Underwear money, right?"

As the sun lowered toward the horizon, we were running on a glassy sea, with a slight southerly behind us. The air was so clear we could see the tip of the Tetakawi peaks in Sonora, seventy miles away. Under these ideal conditions, we'd spotted several whales, lots of dolphins that ran with us for awhile, a giant manta ray, and even a shark. Had we not been on the run, it would be an ideal cruise.

Five miles from Santa Rosalia, Jan decided it was all right for us to have a drink. Docking was going to be a breeze, even after the sun set. The port was fairly well lit, the entrance clearly marked with working—always a miracle in the Sea of Cortez—entry lights. If my old dock was available, I'd glide in there. Piece of cake.

But, as Jan had asked, then what?

I sorted options. They were not great. To successfully get lost, we really needed to hide a forty-five foot yacht, and David Copperfield is all booked up in Vegas.

I spotted a light on the horizon, grabbed binoculars, and identified the Santa Rosalia/Guaymas ferry heading across to Sonora. "Jan, you remember that guy we met in San Carlos."

"You mean in Mag Bay?"

"No, over on the other side. San Carlos, Sonora. We met him in a bar."

She gave me a look. "Can you, like narrow that down? I can think of maybe a hundred off the top of my head. Did we sleep with him?"

"Very funny. No, but he was telling us about a free marina in Guaymas. I drove out there one day. No electricity, no water, no nothing. But what it does have is no employees. Only a guard."

"So?"

"So, we stash the boat there and ask our new best bar buddy to watch it for me. What do you think?"

She drained her drink. "I think it's gonna be a long night."

We arrived in Guaymas early the next morning after tailing the ferry all night. I have to admit it was kind of comforting to keep another boat in sight, even if I did have to kick my boat's engines in the butt to keep up.

Jan and I didn't take formal watches, but we spelled each other. Neither of us really got more than a couple of hours of sleep, but we slid into the free marina without fanfare, parking behind *Island Lady*. Bart heard us coming in and helped with our lines. He remembered Jan, of course.

I didn't know this guy from Adam, but since he was Canadian, I trusted him. I mean, everyone knows there is no crime in Canada, right? I'd bet those Mounties have nothing to do but look good.

Anyhow, Bart jumped at the chance of earning three hundred a month to keep an eye on *Raymond Johnson,* so long as I got back before July, when he went home for the summer.

There was no cell signal in the tiny cove, and my Sat system was being installed on *Nao de Chino*, so Bart drove us into Guaymas to buy airline tickets, then I called Jenks on my Mexican cellphone. I'd read that

Carlos Slim slipped to second place in the Forbes Richest People in the World list, and figured calling Dubai via Telcel might help him out in the ratings.

After we bought Bart lunch, dinner, and some gas for his car, he agreed to take us to the airport the next morning. It would have been so much cheaper for Jan to sleep with him, but she balked. I think I liked her better as a hooker.

When I called Jenks, I'd told him *Raymond Johnson* was safely at a dock in Guaymas, and I was returning to the Baja to work on what I now dubbed the Great Galleon Hunt. He didn't seem surprised that I'd changed my destination to Guaymas, although he did lamely grouse a little about me and Jan crossing the sea by ourselves. Again. I guess he's used to my whims by now. Or maybe he was just relieved I'd be occupied and out of trouble for the summer. He had no idea I had a killin' in mind.

At O-dark-thirty the next morning, we packed up, secured the boat, left all kinds of written instructions and contact numbers for Bart, and headed for the airport.

The airline insisted we be at the airport one hour prior to our departure time. As expected, the only person in the terminal was a security guard. While we waited for anyone else to show up, like the guy who sells coffee, or any airline employees at all, Jan and I contemplated DO IN DICKLESS possibilities.

I printed, in large block letters: FIND HIM. KILL HIM.

When I wrote down the 'kill' part on my notepad, Jan frowned. "Ya know, Hetta, I think I'm a witness to what might be legally considered premeditated conspiracy to commit murder. And, in Mexico, I don't suppose you could claim insanity or self-protection, like you normally do."

"Those cases never went to court."

"And this one better not, either. Mexico doesn't have a death penalty. They figure their prisons are a much more severe form of punishment."

I tore the note into tiny pieces. "Here, eat this. No paper trail." I glanced at my unplugged computer. I was pretty sure my watchers were no longer able to see or hear what I did, but was taking no chances with that mini-cam. Jan had run a scan and rooted out the dastardly virus planted by Luján's guys, but I was still antsy.

"And no witnesses," Jan added, with a TAKE THAT! look at the now debugged computer.

"So that means I have to off you? Dang, you were growing on me."

"Nope, I am signing up for this one. If I'm going to live in Mexico like, forever, I want that piece of crap either in prison, or dead. Preferably dead. Now, there you go, I am no longer a witness, but a full fledged co-conspirator."

I gave her a high-five. "Thelma and Louise!"

"Butch Cassidy and the Sundance Kid!"

"Bonnie and Clyde!"

Jan lost her wide grin. "Uh, Hetta. Didn't all of them, like, die?"

"We all die."

"Yabbut, they died young."

"See, we have nothing to worry about."

She swatted me. "Get serious. It just ain't all that easy to off someone and get away with it."

"We're talking *Mexico* here, for crying out loud. You know, the country where over sixty *thousand* people have been murdered by the cartels, and not one person prosecuted? Jeez, it's worse than Chicago."

"That's because the prosecutors and judges prefer to live? But we don't have buckets of money like the druggers do. We only have our brains."

"Damn."

Fifteen minutes before departure time, airline personnel and Customs showed up. They gave our bags a perfunctory rummage, opened my computer case, and we were sent into the secure area. The minute we settled into plastic chairs, and were forbidden to return to the lobby, the coffee guy showed up out there.

Five minutes before the plane landed from Hermosillo and coughed out a couple of people, Mexican passengers for our flight stormed into the airport.

We were herded out to a single engine Cessna 208, which was so fully booked someone had to sit in the copilot's seat. And, gee, guess who the pilot chose?

While I stuffed myself into the undersized seat in the cramped passenger compartment, Jan was strapped in next to the beaming pilot. And, before I figured out how to fasten my own seatbelt, we were taxiing down the runway.

Our departure was right on time.

When we landed in Santa Rosalia a little over half an hour later, all passengers deplaned. The pilot, who by now had Jan's phone number, would backtrack to Hermosillo, via Guaymas, minutes later. This type of efficiency is just downright un-Mexican.

Continuing with our charade to throw off anyone tracking me, we took the airline courtesy van to Santa Rosalia, called Denny, and were waiting for him just outside the marina parking lot when he arrived in my pickup. From where we met, he couldn't get a gander at the docks, and especially the absence of *Raymond Johnson* in one of the slips.

Po Thang had bonded with the Dalmatians, or so it seemed, because he didn't exactly go nuts when we showed up. Turns out his new BFF—that second F is for Fidos—Dal-pals and he were feasting on hamburger steak three times a day, so he was less than ready to leave with me and Jan.

Fickle little turd-dropper.

CHAPTER NINETEEN

Chino's dream of finding the wreck site of a galleon that stranded his ancestors on the shores of Magdalena Bay goes back to when he was a small boy, and first able to grasp the meaning of the old folks' stories.

Unlike many who have to resort to Ancestry.com to unearth their roots, his family was documented generation by generation. Someone, a couple of grands back, had the foresight to gather everything and log it in a large volume reminiscent of the family Bible, and as soon as Chino was old enough—and in his case that was pretty danged young—he drew a flow chart/family tree. I'd seen this work of art, complete with a painting of the legendary galleon, *San Carlos*, hanging on his Abuela Yee's living room wall in Lopez Mateos. The chart kicked off in 1600 with the two original men who washed up on Baja's shores: Yee and Comacho.

The family also possessed a written account by Gómez Pérez Comacho, telling of a harrowing voyage from the Philippines, bound for Acapulco, but shipwrecked in Magdalena Bay. Comacho was a rich merchant moving his family and business to Mexico, and Yee, as he was only referred to in the document, was a Chinese jewelry maker in Comacho's employ. The families intermarried after the shipwreck washed away all former social boundaries, and sixteen or so generations later, we have Doctor Brigido Comacho Yee. Chino to his friends.

During a hurricane the year before, my boat anchor dredged up an astrolabe, an ancient precursor to the modern-day GPS, which dated to around the right date for the *San Carlos*, and Chino was convinced the wrecked galleon bringing his ancestors to Mexico lay on the bottom nearby. The question is, where? Was it outside the bay, in the Pacific Ocean and stuff had just washed in over the centuries, or was the wreck inside the Bay itself? People had been finding pottery shards on the beaches year after year, but as far as anyone knew, no one actually went looking for a galleon. Why, I don't understand, what with the family history, and blue and white Ming Dynasty shards on their beaches.

Oddly enough, Chino's break at finding his roots got even better when I exposed Ishikawa and Luján—and thereby Tanuki Corporation—as connivers in that scheme to trap and can baby whales. Rather than face angry Mexican ecologists, and to obtain their man, Luján, a GET OUT OF JAIL card—even though they vehemently denied any guilt in the whale scheme—Tanuki graciously "donated" a research vessel for the galleon hunt, and then, in another weird turn of fate, Ishikawa recently dropped a hundred grand into the pot. The question is, what interest did Ishikawa and Luján share in this expedition? Or in Luján's case, just what did he plan to steal? The booty Chino found? Not if *I* got to it first.

Chino doubted much gold would have been on the galleon, but *any* gold or jewels would be nothing to sneeze at in today's market. He also knew that in comparison to galleons leaving the east coast of Mexico bound for Spain back in the day, the so-called Acapulco, or Manila Galleons, were carrying chump change. Those east-bound galleons were overloaded with ill-gotten gains, as evidenced by the *Atocha,* discovered off of Florida. That wreck alone has garnered over forty tons (tons!) of silver and gold, with more to come. The Spaniards were probably, until Hitler came along, the most successful treasure thieves in history.

So, here I was, full circle.

I was back in Magdalena Bay, living on the indirect largess of Tanuki, and the major players were back in the mix. Of course, this time I wasn't on my own boat, and I was gunning for Lujàn while working, for free I might add, on the *Nao de Chino* in the search of a lost galleon.

The manila galleons were called Nao de la China, because even though they sailed from Manila, most of their cargo originated in China. Chino cleverly used a play on words to name his research vessel.

I was dubbed the logistics and materials management officer, which is a fancy title for gopher. My job was to help identify everything needed to keep the boat afloat, feed and house the crew, and order and get delivered all of the above.

As the crew assembled, I gathered wish lists from everyone, and made a few of my own. I also assigned cabins, other than the master, which went to

Chino and Jan. In doing so, I made up a plan that was certain to piss everyone off equally.

I took the captain's cabin, just behind the bridge. It was small, with two bunk beds; one for me and one for Po Thang, Ship's Dog. His list was short: food. I added doggie shampoo and a life vest.

The two Japanese crew, stipulated in Ishikawa's requirements to get the hundred grand, were graduate students working on PhD's in marine archaeology, and seemed awed by Chino. They had both been on previous searches for sunken ships off the coast of Japan and the Marianas. Mostly for WWII wrecks. Japan was on a kick to find all those sunken vessels and account for the lost crew. I learned from them that two Japanese subs had been found on the bottom in Magdalena Bay. I felt that subject was best left in my "no comment" column, since I knew a little about that incident.

The Japanese divers, Kazuto Fukoda and Mototada Hashimoto, whom we'd quickly dubbed Kazoo and Moto, had few requests, other than diving supplies, fresh fish, seaweed, and rice. They brought their own rice cooker with them, much to the chagrin of Rosa, Chino's cousin and Ship's Cook, who takes great pride in her Arroz Mexicana. She warmed slightly toward them when they gave high praise to her seafood *ceviche*.

Enrique, Ship's Mechanic, and Javier, Ship's Deckhand, were Chino's relatives of some sort. They, and Rosa, were the only paid help, so far.

We had only one itsy bitsy problem. We needed a professional Mexican boat captain, as neither Chino nor I were qualified to skipper a research vessel in

Mexican   waters.

CHAPTER TWENTY

"Miss Coffey, as I recall, the last thing I said to you in Cabo was, 'Should you ever need another *capitán*? *Por favor*, do not call me.' "

"It's not for me, Fabio, it's for Chino."

"Ah, the galleon hunt. Will you be aboard? If so, I shall have to charge extra. You have a way of getting people thrown into jail."

"That was all because of Lujàn, whom, I recently heard from credible sources, was run out of town, along with that cousin of his from the port captain's office. And we can actually pay you some decent money, because Chino got a big donation for the expedition." *From a guy who is now dead*, but I didn't think mentioning that to an already leery Fabio was a great idea.

"How long?"

"Three months, more or less. You are the most qualified captain we know, and Chino would love to have you."

"So, *you* would be working for *me*? I'll take it."

"You're not going to go all Captain Bligh on me, are you, Desi?" I asked, using the nickname I'd given him when he was on my payroll from California to Mag Bay the past fall. His contrived lapses into Spanglish earned him the moniker.

"No, Loocy, of course not. I shall see you in…five days."

Chino was delighted I'd snagged Fabio. They'd grown close during their brief incarceration in a Mag Bay hoosegow. Unlike Fabio, Chino didn't hold me personally accountable for that little stay. Or if he did, he kept it to himself because of Jan's loyalty to me.

"Yep, said he'd be here *pronto*. He didn't even ask what we paid. Has the ship's mistress, uh, I mean the ship's bean counter figured out what that might be?"

"I heard that," Jan yelled from the main saloon, where she was making spreadsheets of budgets based on our schedule, built-in costs, and the like. The cook, mechanic, deck hand, and Fabio were the only paid staff. On this bare-bones project, the rest of us were fed, and supplied with other expedition-required gear.

We joined Jan around a large dining table that one of Chino's cousins built. It was really the only place for the crew to eat, meet, and watch movies or television. There were also many built-in shelves and niches harboring scientific equipment throughout the saloon. This was no pleasure craft, but a working boat with every inch of space designated for a purpose.

Sleeping arrangements were bunks, but in deference to three months living together, walls were erected, dividing the sleeping area below decks into eight small cabins, each containing two bunks, a desk, a hanging locker and a sink. There were four toilets, or heads, and three showers in the crew area, so Jan and I made up WOMEN ONLY signs and claimed one shower and one toilet, which made Rosa, the cook, a happy woman. It is always a good idea to schmooze the cook.

Fabio was entitled to the captain's quarters on the bridge that I had previously laid dibs on, darn it. His cabin wasn't much larger than the others, but it had a private shower and head. I was still trying to figure out how to glom onto it for me and Po Thang, but couldn't come up with a legitimate reason.

However, the cabin I did take was previously some kind of storage area, and had a hidden hatch leading into the engine room one deck below. Having an extra exit, even if it did lead down to the bowels of the ship, satisfied my somewhat claustrophobic bent. All of the occupied cabins had a porthole; a fairly small porthole that I estimated to be about three inches smaller than my derriere. I swiped a jug of olive oil from the galley, just in case I had to slither out when the boat sank or caught on fire or any of those other things that give me the heebie-jeebies. I guess I've watched one too many disaster movie.

For someone who lives alone most of the time, bivouacking in close quarters with other humans was worrisome for me. I've never even had roommates, and when my boat or apartment or house gets more than one visitor at a time, I can turn even more fractious than normal. Jan said maybe this could be a growth experience for me. I told her if I wanted to broaden my horizons, I'd prefer to do it on the *MS Queen Elizabeth*.

However, I had to focus on my main goal for the summer: Do in Dickless.

Oh, and if somehow a portion of that treasure we were after happens to find its way into my bank account, so be it.

Jan and I decided making a provisions run to the Costco store in Cabo san Lucas was in order. Local grocery stores carried some basics, but they were not *our* basics, like several cases of Argentinean Malbec, a ton or two of Velveeta cheese, Wolf Brand Chili (no beans), and feta cheese. Chino at first protested what he considered the undue expense, but the ship's mistress stuck out her cute bottom lip, so he lamely handed her his credit card and requested a few cans of SPAM.

We left early, intending to make the five-hundred-mile round trip in one day, and in daylight hours. This was a highly ambitious schedule, even with the new four-lane highway between La Paz and Cabo, but doable. By the time we skirted La Paz, our PB&J breakfasts were running on empty, but we pushed on to Todos Santos, one of our favorite places, for lunch.

Todos Santos is one of those towns where artsy folks have settled, taken over, and rocketed real estate prices into the ozone layer. Only an hour north of Cabo, this small coastal village has blossomed into a tourist center boasting such things as film festivals, jazz festivals, and all the uppity stuff that comes with being a cultural center for a bunch of foreigners. And, as will happen, Gringos have caused sprawl in their desire for an ocean view. Where ranches and sugarcane plantations once were, foreigners build homes. Rumor has it a huge complex is in the offing. Seems like no one learned the lessons of the once charming, and now plumb-ruirnt, village of Cabo San Lucas.

We found a small outdoor restaurant and settled in for fish tacos.

Across the street, a boutique owner was hanging out jewel-toned gauzy tops, skirts and pants. Jan was eyeing the clothing like Po Thang eyeballs a steak.

Taking a sip of my Tecate, I asked, "Say, Jan, when was the last time we actually went shopping for anything besides food and boat parts?"

"We went to Walmart in Arizona and bought some tee shirts. Oh, and you purchased yon pickup." She pointed to my red Ford with her glass of wine.

"Ya know, that pickup has been giving me trouble. I think it just broke down. Call Chino and tell him we'll be home tomorrow."

We checked into the Hotel California, took the penthouse suite, and hit the bar for a giant, very tangy, Bloody Mary. Or two.

Naps were then in order, after which we showered, put on what makeup Jan carried in her purse, donned our new, highly overpriced, Mexican gauze outfits, and went down for a sumptuous dinner by the pool.

And the rest, as they say, is history.

"So, Hetta, ya think that guy was a real bull fighter?"

"I dunno. Hey, where did you learn the flamenco? You looked pretty good up there on that table."

"Don't remind me. My ankles hurt."

"Didn't do a lot for the table, either. Wanna get more coffee before we hit Costco?"

"Oh, yes."

When we got back to Lopez Mateos, the entire expedition crew was finally on board *Nao de Chino*.

A deckhand—okay, *the* deckhand—helped us unload my pickup and ferried us out to the boat in one of the ship's pangas.

Captain Fabulous was checking out the engine room with our ship's mechanic, and Rosa began stowing our Costco goodies into the large pantry and walk-in refrigerator/freezer unit attached to the galley.

Jan and I were giving Rosa a hand when Fabio entered the galley and demanded, "What. Is. That?" He jabbed an accusative forefinger at several cases of wine we were stacking in the pantry.

"Malbec. And two Sauvignon Blanc."

"Miss Coffey, this is a working ship. No wine."

"No wine, no work, Captain Bligh." I crossed my arms in front of my chest and struck a pose. Jan did likewise.

Fabio looked to Chino for support, but only got a helpless shrug. After a thirty-minute wrangle, we agreed on a compromise. The wine would be stored on Fabio's extra bunk, and he'd issue a couple of bottles for dinner each night. Jan and I asked what the others were going to drink, but only received a glower.

Luckily, Jan and I had already stashed two cases in an empty cabin next to mine before taking the rest to the galley.

Oh, and I had a key to Fabio's cabin.

Don't mess with Texas.

Or their wine.

Surprisingly enough, Fabio named me First Mate.

I was flattered until I learned he did so because no one else on board knew how to operate a large vessel, or were as familiar as I was with most of the operating systems. And when I Googled a First Mate's duties, I found my job less than glamorous, except the part where I keep the ship off the rocks when the captain ups and dies. It turns out I was not at all qualified as a real First Mate, as that requires a real license. When I pointed this out to Fabio, he shrugged and told me he intended to run a fairly loose ship, and who better to do that than me?

Doncha just hate it when someone learns sarcasm from the master, and then turns it on her?

CHAPTER TWENTY-ONE

With provisions on board, the crew settled in, and most of our equipment either on the way or being installed, it was time to turn my attention to my main mission for the summer: Get Dickless.

One of the best things about living amongst so many of Chino's relatives is their penchant for nosiness. It is a trait I value, being a natural born snoop myself. In this part of the Baja, if you want to keep track of someone, this respected family is a primary source of info. And to make matters even better, Dickless's nefarious ways had put the family in direct conflict with him a time or two, including his involvement in having their favorite marine biologist, Chino, tossed into the slammer. The family doesn't have a lot of money or political clout, which is probably the only reason Luján never actually tried to steal anything from them. What they do have is connections.

I started the search for Dickless with Grandmother Yee, or Abuela Yee, as the family calls her. Jan and I had somewhat rescued her from an iffy situation earlier in the year, so she was my new best friend. Jan, she had doubts about. She liked her, but wasn't sure Jan was right for her darling, Chino. I heartily agreed, for Chino's sake.

Abuela tossed a stone into her far-reaching gossip pool and got a ripple. She imparted her news when I stopped in for a visit at her home in Lopez Mateos, and I couldn't decide whether it was good or bad news.

"He's *here*?" Jan squawked when I told her what Grans Yee learned. We were in my cabin, polishing off a bottle of wine after dinner. Po Thang lounged on the top bunk, a place I thought impossible for him to get to until I stashed a bag of Fritos there earlier in the day. He was sawing logs and sharing loud, corn-scented snores with us.

"Not *here*, here. His ticket's been punched in Mag Bay. But she told me the vegetable guy told her that the tamale woman's aunt's cousin rented him a house in Constitución."

"Which is practically next door."

"Yep. Ain't that grand? Now we can off him at will."

"Oh, sure, Sherlock. We do him in, and before the body cools the tamale woman's aunt's cousin will tell the police Granny Yee was looking for him, and then they will come looking for *you*, because you two have history, and Chino's cop cousin knows it. You'll be convicted of murder and I'll be stuck down here for the rest of my natural life in order to make sure you get proper food and medicine."

"That should make Chino happy, at least. Crap, why can't you just be the dumb blonde you resemble?

And why do I go to prison alone? You're in this up to your shapely eyebrows. By the way, I've been meaning to ask you if you had those done around here."

"Eyebrow gal in town, but it's hard to get in; it's that Frida Kahlo thing with Mexican women. And, Hetta, *one* of us has to stay out of jail to feed the other."

"I'm feeling all warm and fuzzy here."

"It's those eyebrows. I'll get you an appointment."

Jan was annoyingly right, my eyebrows were bushy, and terminating Lujàn outright was out of the question unless I could pull off a drive-by shooting, which would be difficult without a gun.

We had to hire someone.

Someone in low places.

Someone who kills people all the time.

Someone like…Nacho.

Who was not returning my calls.

I put Dickless on the back burner for now, because first things first: We had sunken treasure to unearth.

Our first tactical meeting was held in the dining/computer/movie room, with all hands in attendance.

Chino greeted each member of the team, gave their title and a summation of duties, then said, "As you all know, we are looking for the Manila galleon *San Carlos*, known to have sailed from the Philippines near the end of the 1590's, bound for Acapulco. I said *known* only because of my family's historical account, because there is no actual record of this ship in the Spanish archives."

That was news to me, and by the looks on the others' faces, to them.

I was the first to verbalize our shock. "Say what? I thought the Spaniards were meticulous record keepers. They sure as hell recorded deporting my family from Spanish Texas in 1811."

Everyone except the Japanese guys laughed. They just look confused, but the laughter lightened the up-until-then somewhat tense atmosphere.

Still grinning, Chino quipped, "For circumventing the King's tax system, no doubt. Actually, that is exactly what happened during the galleon trade era. Before 1600, ships sailed with fake or no manifest, but were loaded with merchandise belonging to rich merchants who did not care to share their wealth with Spain's tax collectors. This ship could have been one of those. Like I said, the only way we know about *San Carlos* is through a family historical account passed down through the generations."

"So how did you get a permit to search for it?" Fabio asked. I suppose the last thing he wanted was being chief officer on an illicit treasure hunt. His license was at stake.

"Fabio, you were there when the evidence surfaced. The astrolabe we dredged up with Hetta's anchor last year. After testing, the Mexican National Institute of Anthropology and History experts feel it is from a galleon, and that allowed the permit."

"And," I added, "Hetta is still waiting for her payoff for said astrolabe."

"Which brings me to another point everyone on this ship should be aware of. There is no payoff. Everything we find belongs to the Mexican government."

"What if Spain wants it?" Jan asked. "I've read lately the Spaniards got a bunch of gold brought up by a British salver because it was from a sunken Spanish ship."

Chino shook his head. "Only because that was a ship sunk by the British in an act of war. No, Spain would play bloody hell getting an international court to award them plundered Mexican gold and silver, even if it is in the form of Spanish coinage. Or jewelry fashioned in the Far East for Spanish royalty.

"And bye the bye," Chino added, dredging up the Queen's English left over from his days at University there, "chances of finding much gold are slim. These merchant galleons bound for Acapulco were sometimes carrying as much as two and a half million pesos in treasure, but that described the entire cargo, because a peso wasn't a coin, but a monetary unit equaling one and an eighth ounce troy of silver. In other words, that was what would be called insurance value these days."

"I guess finding a piece of the galleon is out of the question, right?" Fabio asked.

"Four hundred years in salt water? Not a chance the wood could survive, although there was one instance, in Sweden, where a sunken vessel was found almost intact after almost as long."

I waved my hand in the air in a 'Me! Me!' gesture. Chino nodded. "Let me guess, Hetta, you have something to add?"

"I have visited the Wasa museum in Stockholm, and the only reason that ship was so well-preserved was it sank into heavily polluted, highly toxic water. The little buggers that eat wood and break it down couldn't live."

"Very good. You are simply a font of trivial knowledge. Point well taken. I doubt a sliver of wood still exists, but we'll be dragging a magnetometer and, with any luck, the San Carlos's cannons were not bronze, as it will only detect ferrous metals."

"Like cannon balls?" Jan asked.

"Does anyone at all besides Fabio, Hetta and Jan have anything to say?"

Chino's cousin, the deckhand, spoke up. "The bay is not so large, and not so deep. Why have we never found this ship?"

"Very good question, and I have a theory. We know bits of pottery have been found on the beaches for years, and then there is our astrolabe. I think maybe everything is covered in tons of sand and silt. We have had many storms in four hundred years, and the bottom has shifted. For all we know, the artifacts could be under one of the dunes." He pointed to the high sand dunes nearby.

"Clive Cussler. *Sahara,*" I said, referring to the book about a submarine buried in the desert.

"Fiction. But based on a like-theory. Anyway, our job is really to mark any promising sites for later exploration by someone allowed to vacuum up the bottom. Our permit only allows diving, detecting and recording. Unless, of course, we find visible artifacts, and then I will call in the Mexican Ministry."

That pretty much put a damper on the meeting. It looked as though we were all in for a long, tedious, boring summer with little to show for it. Sensing our gloom, Chino said, with a twinkle in his eye, "But then again, if we find a bronze cannon from this period, and it is well-decorated and preserved, it will be worth at least thirty-or-forty-thousand dollars, and there might be as many as twenty-five or thirty of them."

There was a moment of silence as we all tried to do the mental math. Chino, reading our minds, grinned. "Over a million dollars, U.S. I said earlier there was no payback in order, but the truth is, we are entitled to a ten percent finders fee for non-gold and silver items. Divided by we nine, it could come to at least ten thousand each. Not bad for a few month's work."

The Japanese men finally smiled.

"Uh, that's divided by ten," I said.

Everyone looked at me. "Ship's dog: Po Thang."

Later in our cabin I told Po Thang, "Hey, buddy, I tried to get you your share, but only got soundly booed for my efforts."

Po Thang whined and curled up on the top bunk. Someday I was going to catch him getting up there, but for now I had no idea how he did it.

I made a note to order an animal cam.

CHAPTER TWENTY-TWO

Still no word on Ishikawa, dead *or* alive.

Nacho would not return my calls.

I went into Constitución and drove by the address I was given for Dickless, but the place looked deserted. How was I gonna punch his lights if he wouldn't stay home?

Meanwhile, I was working my butt off. Considering the fact that I was not being paid, I began to rethink this treasure hunt thing. I mentioned this to Jan and she reminded me I was staying rent free, meals provided, and had a chance to get a share of a possible cannon find. "Think of it as a kind of summer sea camp. Besides, Hetta, what else you got to do all summer?"

"Besides doing in Dickless?"

"How we gonna do that, by the way?"

"I was kinda hoping Nacho would take care of him."

"And how is that working out for you?" she sneered.

"Not well at all, Doctor Phil. He won't call me back."

"And you find this unusual in a man? Might have something to do with you giving me his number when he told you, in no uncertain terms, not to give it to *any*body."

"It was an emergency. Beside you aren't anybody."

"Thanks."

"You know what I mean. He knows you. I guess I really pissed him off, huh?"

"It was only a matter of time."

"I don't piss off everyone I meet."

"Name one."

"Well, uh, you?"

"Don't even go there."

"Okay, okay, point made. So, any ideas on how to do the dirty deed?"

"You're asking me? Hell, you're the one determined to plant the bastard. I'm in, but don't count on me to come up with some idiotic plan. That's your job."

"Remember *The Equalizer*?"

"The one with Denzel Washington? Haven't seen it yet."

"No, the old television show, with that British guy." I stood and rasped, "Got a problem? Odds against you? Call The Equalizer."

"Robert McCall! I loved that show. We could sure use him."

In my best British accent, I said, "I can equalize the odds."

"He was wonderful. But, he wasn't real. I agree with you that Nacho is our best bet."

I smiled. "In a criminal kind of way."

"And speaking of, I was thinking about that dognapping thing. Doesn't it seem odd that when I called Nacho to ask him for help, he said he was very, and I do mean *very*, upset that you'd given out his number. But the next thing we know, he gives *you* a call. And it seems he was responsible for springing Lil."

"I'll never forgive him."

"What exactly did he say when he called that day?"

"Look out your door."

Jan swiveled in her chair and craned her neck. "What?"

"No, dummy. That's what he said."

"Aha! He *knew* the panga was there, and he was letting you know he knew. He was taking credit!"

"I've never thought otherwise. And if he'd ever return my calls, I'd thank him. Oh, and try to hire him to erase Luján's smarmy face from this universe for us."

She laughed. "Did you ever consider that maybe he was somehow involved *before* I called him?"

"How could that be? Surely he didn't have a hand in nabbing Po Thang? Although, those two have had their moments. Nope, you told him about Lil and my dog, and he fixed it."

"That's just it. I didn't."

"What do you mean?"

"All I said was someone took your dog, and he hung up. Next thing we know, dog and aunt show up, and we know for sure he had something to do with *that* part."

"Which means he knew about the pictures I took?" I sipped wine until Jan flapped her hands impatiently at me. "Just hold ye hardy, mate. I'm concentrating here. Trying to remember how it all went down that day. Okay, first off, I had some kind of nervous fit, and went totally bonkers."

"Nothing new there."

"No, really, *really* nuts. I mean *Jack Nicholson* apeshit. I was screaming like a madwoman—" Jan started to make what was no doubt some smart remark, but I stabbed a warning finger in her direction, "and then suddenly went deadly calm. Waving the camera in front of the webcam, I threatened to share those photos of Ishikawa's body, and Lujan and his goons loading what looked like a stiff into his Navigator, onto my Facebook page. *And* with every newspaper in the world, if I didn't get my dog back that very day."

"And by some miracle, Nacho, who was not *at all* involved in any of that resort debacle, calls just a few hours from your deadline, and tells you to look outside where, by some miracle of presto chango, there's Po Thang, all safe and sound? Okay, we are *way* beyond coincidence here."

"Watson, methinks Nacho has some 'splainin' to do."

"Good luck with that, the man has written you off. Not the first time *that's* happened."

My satellite communications system made life so much easier on the research vessel *Nao de Chino*.

Not only did we have high speed Internet, and phone service, we also received television channels from all over the world. The problem was getting everyone on our little ship of Babel to agree on a program. The official ship's language was English, with a smattering of Spanish and Japanese thrown in for confusion.

Fabio, Rosa, and the other two Mexican crew were addicted to Mexican telenovellas, Chino and Po Thang quite naturally loved *Animal Planet*, Jan and I stuck with the Turner Movie Classics, and the two Japanese grad students were out of luck, as we didn't pick up anything from Japan. They took it with good cheer, saying they wanted to improve their English and learn Spanish.

In a small shop in Puerto San Carlos, I found a DVD of *Tora! Tora! Tora!* with Spanish and Japanese subtitles. We all watched it together. I knew enough Japanese to know that *tora* meant tiger, but the two students explained it was also the code name of the attack on Pearl Harbor. They also commented, as young people do sometimes when looking back on history from a safe distance, that the entire war was a disaster for Japan, but they staunchly defended the bravery of the men who died.

"Did you lose any relatives?" Jan asked.

Both gave a curt nod, a bow, and left for their quarters, leaving us a little embarrassed and somewhat confused, because they seemed to enjoy the movie.

Jan stared at their backs as they left. "Umm, ya think maybe next week we need a comedy?"

"Okay, how about *La Cage aux Folles*? I saw the DVD in town."

"French or American version?"

"Both, if I can get them. *La Cage* marathon night."

"Ya know, the Mexican crew might not appreciate a gay movie."

"Too bad. From now on I'll get something to guarantee someone gets annoyed."

"What will annoy us?"

"*Love Story*. Ali MacGraw was so annoying I couldn't wait for her to die."

"And people say you are no sentimentalist."

After two weeks of intense labor by the entire crew, *Nao de Chino* was finally ready to start the search for our galleon, or rather what the wreck left behind. Because Magdalena Bay is only a little over thirty miles long, and has many shoals, skeptics said there was no way any treasure could have escaped discovery all of these years, but Chino remained optimistic.

Between shopping online for expedition materials and equipment, getting it all shipped via whatever method available, and then dealing with Mexican customs, the time flew by. I talked with Jenks on Skype when I was on the ship, but there were days when I was on the road, and then he called me on my Mexican cell. I didn't have time to worry about Ishikawa, or keep tabs on Luján. A mistake, I learned, when I stopped at the marina in Santa Rosalia after one of my copper mine meetings, to pick up a package flown in from Monterrey on Aero Calafia.

I was acquainted with several of the airline employees because I'd not only kept my boat at the marina, I'd bought airline tickets at their marina office.

"*Hola*, Lupe," I said to the office manager after she greeted me. I asked about her family, work, the usual, then requested a package addressed to Expedición Magdalena.

"Yes, it is here. I did not know you were working with them."

I grew leery. Mexicans are notorious gossips, and have no problem sharing information. "Oh, I don't, really. I'm just picking up the package for my friend, Jan. You remember her?"

"Yes, the beautiful one."

I cringed to think what she called me.

"I did not know where you were, so I told your friend I thought you were still in Puerto Escondido, but when I called the marina there for him, they said you went to La Paz."

"My friend? Which friend?"

She frowned. "He is Mexican."

I wondered if that frown was one of disapproval because she suspected me of diddling the local man-pool. "What did he look like?"

She shrugged. "Mexican."

If I said that I'd catch flak for the *everyone looking alike* thing. "Tall?" I held my hand a foot over my head. Tall in Mexico isn't all that tall. Also, if he was above average height, it might be Nacho who was nosing around. Jeez, all he had to do was call.

She shook her head.

"Old? Young?"

Another shrug. "*Medio*." She then held her hand up, thumb and index finger an inch apart, in the classic *momento* sign, then reached into a desk drawer and pulled out a clipboard. Riffling through a few of the attached forms, she zeroed in on one, and stabbed at a line with a bright purple fingernail. It was a signature next to a shipment number, exactly like the list I'd just signed off on for the expedition package.

I leaned in and squinted, dug into my bag and came up with a pair of cheaters. Focusing again, I saw a name I really, really didn't want to see.

Ricardo Lujàn.

Hey, I was supposed to be stalking *him*.

CHAPTER TWENTY-THREE

"Okay, Hetta, I've thought of one good thing about Dickless," Jan said after I told her about the Santa Rosalia incident.

"I cannot wait to hear this. The only good thing I want to hear about him is he's a goner. And I mean that in the absolutely most permanent way."

"Yeah, that'd be just dandy, and save us a lot of work. But my bit of good is that at least we know, as of last week, he evidently didn't know you were here in Mag Bay. Maybe he wasn't really looking for you. He knew you had been at the marina before, he had to pick up a package, and so he engaged in a little info fishing."

"One can hope he now thinks I'm in La Paz. By the way, I got the address for the package he picked up, and it matched the one Abuela Yee gave us. I took a little detour on the way back, and swung through Constitución for another gander at the house he's supposedly rented."

"And?"

"Didn't see him, but there were signs of life. Before, the place looked uninhabited, but now windows were open and the driveway swept. No car, but still..."

"Field trip?"

"Yep."

Coming up with a legitimate reason for both of us to be away from *Nao de Chino* at night wasn't easy to come by, considering we were now anchored out three miles from Lopez Mateos.

Jan and I decided the optimum time for spying on that house in Constitución was about nine p.m. and it takes about forty or so minutes to drive from Lopez Mateos, which was a fifteen minute panga ride from the dive ship. None of the crew ever did anything like going into town for dinner, so we had to come up with an overnight shopping trip or something. Ideally, we'd get a room in Constitución, do our spying, then very early the next morning head for La Paz, hit Walmart, and get back to the panga landing before dinnertime the next evening.

One of our problems was my bright red pickup with Arizona plates. It practically screams Gringo! Constitución is an agricultural center with, as far as we knew, zero Gringo inhabitants, and few tourists. Skulking around in the Ford Ranger at night, in a residential area, was an invitation to get noticed. Not only that, I was certain that by now Dickless knew my ride.

As for our room, I figured our best bet was a *hotel de paso*, literally a *transit Hotel*, actually a cheap motel resembling what my dad called tourist courts back home, where rooms are rented by the hour for those wishing to not be seen with a person other than with whom they were supposed to be in a hotel.

Your first clue that perhaps you've chosen a *hotel de paso* is there is no lobby, but one checks in via a drive-through à la McDonald's. You never see the attendant's face, nor he yours, because of one way glass. Business is conducted by microphone, paid in cash, with no ID required. Each room has a private garage, with a door into the room, and the price? About thirty-two dollars, for twelve hours.

Since we'd told everyone we were going to La Paz, we had to leave Lopez Mateos by three or so in the afternoon in order to supposedly make the two hundred mile drive to La Paz and arrive before dark. In the Baja, driving over fifty miles an hour is not advisable, and even though we all do it, I use that speed as an estimator of driving time between points.

So, with only forty miles to drive, instead of the two-hundred, that put us into Constitución way too early for a twelve-hour stay. Rule of thumb in Baja: Never, ever, drive at night if you can avoid it. If we planned to scope out Dickless's pad around nine that night, we had some time to kill. Messing around in Constitución all afternoon was too risky; Lujàn or his minions might spot us, or my truck.

A skulkmobile was required.

Abuela Yee is the materfamilias for Chino's kinfolk, and her home the familial epicenter. Her house, located at the edge of Lopez Mateos, is better than average for the area. The cinderblock abode, set on a couple of acres, is painted a tasteful, for Mexico, shade of purple, and is festooned with every color of bougainvillea imaginable. It also boasts a large vegetable and flower garden, which is carefully tended by a cheap labor pool; grand kids.

Most of the family adults have a job of some kind, either in the agricultural business in Constitución, operating small *tiendas* with various services, running whale watching tours in the winter months, and fishing tours or simply fishing for food during the summer. Like so many families in Mexico, they live life on a rocky fiscal plain that would give most Americans ulcers, but they never seem to lose their good cheer, and besides, somehow children are fed and cars get repaired, so why worry?

Because both parents work, Abuela Yee's house is something of a family enterprise. Outside her chain link fence is her taco stand with picnic tables, open from six a.m. until one p.m., and conveniently across the street from a Tecate beer *deposito* run by a nephew, where one can get a cold beer to go with those fabulous tacos made with fresh fish dropped off by some relative every morning.

The house overflows with kids, all of them busily engaged in child labor, like chopping onions, cilantro, tomatoes, and chile peppers for the taco stand, and tending the garden, or doing homework, playing soccer, sewing clothes, and through it all, laughing. It is the laughter that so characterizes the place. These kids are loved, well cared for, proud of their contributions to the family, and have never heard the word, "allowance."

Computer time is limited, as there is only one computer and so many people. And, after all, Granny Yee is still on the search for that perfect man.

Part of the yard is compartmentalized by a run of chainlink fence that keeps her precious house pet, an ill-tempered, overweight goat named Preciosa, out of the veggie garden. Preciosa has the run of the house, and she and Po Thang have had a dustup or two, so I leave him in the car when I visit.

Within the compound are several vehicles in various states of repair, but Grammy Yee's old van is always clean—that child labor thing—and runs like a top, thanks to all the mechanics in the family.

Chino called ahead, so one of the cousins picked us up at the dock, and drove us to Grandma Yee's, where I keep my pickup. On the way over, I groused, "Dang, the taco stand's already closed, but maybe we can raid Abuela's kitchen. There's always something simmering there, and if nothing else, there are those fantastic tortillas she makes."

"Okay, now you've gone and made me hungry. Gotta have something to eat before we hit the road."

"I hope my pickup starts," I said for the sake of our driver. "I kinda worry about driving it to La Paz, what with the way it's been running."

Jan looked puzzled. "I didn't realize—"

I cut her off with a squint. She shrugged, knowing I was up to something.

Jorge, at least I think it was Jorge—I can't keep them straight—said, "You truck no run good? I fix it."

"Thanks, but we have to leave for La Paz soon."

"Is okay, you take Abuela's van."

"You think she would mind?"

"You ask. She let you."

We pulled into the compound, he took a deep sniff in the air and winked at me. "I think she cooking something *muy* good."

Two hours later we were on our way to Constitución, driving Abuela Yee's van.

I was suffering slightly from an overabundance of *birria*, a savory goat stew made with chile peppers and all sorts of spices. It was a Yee specialty, and Abuela made a pot for a clan birthday party later that day.

"Jeez, my ears are still ringing. Where in the hell do all those kids come from?"

"Hetta, do we have to have a little talk about the birds and the bees?"

"Very funny. You do realize, of course, that could be you in forty years?"

"What?" she screeched.

"Think about it. Chino is already looked up to as a sort of family leader, his grandmother will almost certainly leave the house to him, and guess who will have to step in and pick up the slack? Grandma Jan, that's who."

"Oh, goodie. By then you will have turned into your Aunt Lillian, and we can live together."

Well, that is a depressing thought. I had to remember to call Jenks and tell him how much I love him, and that I was never, ever, going to do anything that might piss him off, ever again.

Oh, wait, too late.

Stalking Dickless, while it sounds like the title of a tasteless romcom, really was a dangerous business.

No one knew where Jan and I were, nor what we were up to, so if things went badly, it would be many days before we were tracked down. If at all.

We checked into our love hotel around six and had three hours to kill before our reconnaissance mission. Reconnaissance sounds ever so much more sophisticated than stalking.

I have this quirky travel habit. Whenever possible, I carry my own bed linens and towels. And since we were bedding down in a by-the-hour hotel, this was one of those times. I am especially suspicious of bedspreads and blankets, so at the very least I try to pack a duvet cover. This time, I had it all.

We stripped the king-sized bed—I instinctively knew there would be no twin beds in this kind of establishment—and remade it, plumped our own pillows for backrests, and turned on the television.

Since we were on a mission, we sadly forwent our usual beer while watching movies, which was too bad because the only ones available in English were cleverly entitled Forrest Hump, Hung Frankenstein, and Twelve Horny Monkeys. We watched part of each one, but they were so annoying we really could have used that beer. Giving up on the porn-cinemas, we dug out the cards and played Baja Rummy until time to snoop.

Balaclavas being in short supply in the Baja, we dressed in dark clothes and baseball caps.

I had already scoped out Lujàn's house a couple of times before during daylight hours, so the drive was quick and uneventful. We drove by once, not too fast, not too slow, and saw lights on. Unfortunately, there was about an eight-foot stucco wall hiding the bottom floor of the two-story house from the street.

Fortunately, there was also a metal double-doored gate into the driveway, which stood wide open. The Lincoln Navigator was there.

"Bingo! Jan, that's the car I saw Luján's goons load Ishikawa's body into at the resort."

"We don't know for certain that it wasn't just a sack of garbage."

"What are you, his defense lawyer?"

"Just stating the facts, ma'am. Ya know, maybe driving a white van wasn't such a great idea. Why didn't we just go to Loreto and rent a car?"

"Because the last one we rented got blown up. I'm persona non grata with every car rental agency in Mexico. And so are you."

"Because you used my credit card. That was kinda sneaky."

"You mean, kinda like signing someone else's name on a hotel register?"

"Hetta, stop!"

"Okay, then, I forgive you."

"No. I mean stop the van."

I pulled over. "What?"

"Turn around and drive by again. I saw something that might help us out."

Sure enough, just across the street from the house was a weedy lot with no permanent structure, but hosted a rusting, wrecked, hulk that maybe started life as a school bus. On both sides of the lot were boarded up, unlit houses.

"God I love Mexico. Luján's house looks classy, and across the street you got crap. Works for us." I drove slowly over the crunchy weeds, wincing at what sounded like tiny explosions to us, and parked the van behind the bus, using it for cover.

When I cut the engine, we rolled down the windows and watched and listened, trying to determine if anyone at all had noticed us. Crickets chirped, dogs barked, but otherwise the neighborhood was quiet.

With no street lights, the only thing illuminated on the whole block was Dickless Manor, and it was lit up like a cruise ship. There was no way anyone inside could see anything outside.

I took my key chain from my knapsack, flicked on the attached tiny penlight, then we made our way to the open door of the bus, which luckily was facing the van. I went in first, not real happy with the idea of what might live in there.

Some windows were broken out, giving us an unimpeded view of the house, the Lincoln Navigator, and the street in front. Once in awhile soft music wafted our way from across the street. Willie Nelson? Maybe Luján wasn't at total a-hole?

We cleared a couple of rotting seats, and watched. Nothing. Surveillance is highly overrated in my book.

After a couple of hours, Jan whispered, "Hetta, I gotta pee."

"Me, too. Wanna risk a squat in the weeds?"

"Not no, but *hell* no! Remember the time that asp bit me on the butt?"

I smiled, recalling that evening in Texas. We'd been out drinking beer and shooting the cans with a couple of cowboys when nature first called, then yelled. It was spring, and with it comes a particularly nasty caterpillar we Texans call an asp. Its proper name is pus caterpillar, and if that ain't repugnant enough all by itself, these furry, inch-long critters are venomous. And, they don't have to bite. They hang on bushes and when something, like, say, Jan's butt, brushes against them, they discharge their venom.

That little incident ended our country girl phase—and any alfresco peeing—as if it was the good old boys' fault asps hang out in the pasture.

"Okay, let's call it a night " I said, making a note to self to buy a port a potty if we were going to continue this sleuthing thing. "At least we learned—"

"Hetta, look!" Jan hissed.

We saw movement near the Navigator, then the door opened on the driver's side and someone got in. In the moment before the interior light went out, we clearly made out Lava Lava.

We froze in place and about thirty seconds later, several recognizable men stepped into the driveway lights. Tadashi Fujikawa shook hands with Luján, and got into the back seat. After Lava Lava drove off, one of Luján's goons that I'd photographed lugging a body bag on the night of Ishikawa's murder, held up his hand and aimed it at the gates, closing them with what was evidently a remote control.

Much to our physical distress, we forced ourselves to wait until the outside lights went off before racing through the streets of Constitución for the nearest Pemex station.

CHAPTER TWENTY-FOUR

It was nearing midnight by the time we called our snoopery a night, and our twelve hours at the hotel were up at six a.m. We had to leave by then anyway, in order to get to La Paz, hit Sam's Club and Walmart, drop off Granny's van, and return to *Nao de Chino* before dark.

As tired as we were, we agreed our little night of detective work was well worth losing a couple of hours sleep. We now knew for sure where Luján was, and even though we had suspected it to be so, we'd proven to ourselves without a doubt that there was a definite connection between Ishikawa, Dickless, and old Tadassan. But, what were they up to? And why had they offed Ishi? And, what had they done with his body?

We discussed all of this ad nauseam during our drive, but didn't come up with any definitive answers. When we were almost back to Lopez Mateos, Jan called Chino so he could send in a panga for us. Instead of just saying, "Hi, Horny, I'm home," like she usually does, she stayed on the line and listened to something Chino had to tell her.

After a minute or two she asked, "Well, what are we supposed to do about it? I'm sorry if that sounded pretty unsympathetic, but, really what can we do? And if we *can* do anything, can't it wait until tomorrow? We're freakin' beat."

I guess he said yes, and she ended the call.

"You are not going to believe what Chino just told me."

"Try me. I'm pretty gullible at times."

"Mrs. Ishikawa called Chino with some very bad news. Seems her husband may have died."

"I wondered when that might come up, seeing as how he's been dead for a couple of weeks now."

"Yabbut, get this. The plane he was on disappeared, along with everyone on board. Ring a bell?"

"Lemme guess. Malaysian Airlines?"

"Yep."

"Pretty slick. But how do you add someone to a passenger list after the plane crashes? Or in this case, vanishes?"

"Who the hell knows? But that tells us something. Whoever *they* are, they have connections and power. And *we* are playing with friggin' fire."

"Another fine mess you've gotten us into, Ollie," I said, mimicking to the best of my ability Stan Laurel, from the old Laurel and Hardy skits.

Instead of reminding me, once again, of all the messes I'd gotten the two of us into over the years, she sighed. "I think we're about even now."

Finally back on *Nao de Chino*, I forwent dinner, which in itself should have raised alarms all over the boat, and opted for the peace and quiet of my cabin in order to think about all I'd learned, and what it meant. Po Thang was not at all happy with this lack of consideration on my part, what with him not being able to beg diners for handouts like he usually does, so I gave him half the ham sandwich Rosa brought me. She also reached into her apron pockets and handed me two ice cold Tecates.

Those, I did not share with my dog, even though he gave me the evil eye when I finished off the second one, which he clearly considered his.

By eight I was long since asleep, but sometime in the middle of the night I awoke with a start. Had I heard a noise? Po Thang snored softly on the top bunk, so I discounted any disturbance capable of waking me while not even getting his attention.

I was turning over, hoping to go back out quickly when a thought jolted me wide-awake.

What connection did all of these men have in common?

Japan.

And who, or whom, did we have on this very ship?

Two, count 'em, *two*, *Japanese* scientists.

Coincidence?

You be the judge.

After breakfast the next morning the expedition for exploration and recovery officially began, so we were all busy bees. By early afternoon of the first day, only Fabio, Rosa, Jan, Po Thang, and I remained on board. All the others were out and about in pangas, either diving or mapping. The ship moved slowly around the bay, executing a grid and testing our towed array equipment.

My job was to monitor screens as totally boring underwater footage drifted ever so slowly across them, looking for stacks of gold coins. In my dreams. I was actually making sure the graph on another monitor reflected my visuals. Later on, when Chino compared film against graph, he'd hopefully spot anomalies suggesting something buried under all that sand, but I failed to see how that worked.

The task I was assigned was so stultifying I was seriously considering brushing off my resume and applying for a more exciting job, like maybe an assembly worker in a car factory. Thankfully Jan showed up to relieve me after a couple of hours, and it was the first time I'd had a chance to tell her my thoughts regarding Kazoo and Moto.

"So, let me get this straight, Hetta. Just because these guys are Japanese, you think they might be guilty of something? You ever heard of profiling?"

"Think about it. Who sent them?"

"Well, whoever put up the hundred grand, I guess. I thought it was Ishikawa, but after what we saw in Constitución, maybe you're on to something here. But what?"

"I dunno, but if Ishikawa had lived, you two could have gotten tight and you'd be able to grill him. And, we'd be fifty grand richer. I mean, come on, you'd just be doing what we've been giving away for free since we were twenty-one."

"Sixteen."

"What?"

"I gave it up at sixteen."

"You never told me that."

"Because you were so high and mighty about being a college-graduate virgin."

"That was only because no one tried."

"No surprise there. You scared the crap out of those Texan boys, and evidently a bunch of Europeans."

"Yeah, I guess. Thank goodness Jenks is descended from hearty Norwegian Vikings."

"And, at least he has you worried. Not enough to totally clean up your act, of course, but you're enamored enough with him to worry he might dump you, like all those hundreds did in the past."

"Hey, I—oh, never mind, let's get back to Kazoo and Moto. If they are, in fact, here because of some association with our den of thieves, why? What do they want? Some cannon balls?"

"Chino told us chances of finding any real treasure are slim to none, and even if we do, we're not talking a fortune. Certainly not enough to go to such lengths, including cutting off someone's head, to get it."

I rolled my own head, trying to work out a kink in my neck. "You're right. And why kill Ishi in the first place? What could he have done to make them so mad?"

"I dunno, but I sure don't want to piss 'em off. I like my head right where it is, thank you."

The whole we were talking, we were watching that boring screen, but suddenly it was alive with a school of bright blue fish. We oohed and ahhed for a few minutes, and then they were gone. If spotting a school of fish now and again was the highlight of the day, we were in for one dull summer.

On the other hand, we might break the monotony a bit by running Luján to ground, chopping him up into tiny pieces, and feeding him to Abuela Yee's hogs?

Nah, it would spoil the *carnitas*.

CHAPTER TWENTY-FIVE

Experienced divers will tell you that looking for a sunken ship is exciting, but frightening. Searching for treasure on a monitor? Just plain boring.

As Chino told us, if there was anything to find, it was most likely buried under several feet of sand or mud, and looking for a bump in the bottom of the ocean is right up there with watching paint dry. After the third day of charting a small area, I was so annoyed I almost volunteered to join the dive team.

I say almost, because as I'll readily admit, scuba diving under the best of circumstances scares the crap out of me, and I never underestimate the power of fear. Or my ability to panic. Way too much equipment is involved, and in Mag Bay the water clarity isn't anywhere near my very high standards. I'd been down eighty feet off Aruba, but there, if you sit on the bottom and look up, the boat appears to be floating on glass.

Even then, I made the mistake of looking out to sea, instead of up or down, and it took two instructors to keep me from shooting to the surface in sheer panic.

Nope, my diving skills would only be a liability to the expedition, so I was stuck with monitor duty.

It was on the fifth day of mind-crippling monitor-gazing when a flash of bright blue yanked me out of a near coma. I leaned forward, thinking maybe those cute blue fish were back, but at sixty feet? I'd only seen them in shallower water before, hanging around rocks. We were scanning the smooth, boring, sand in the south bay that seemed to go on forever, like an underwater Sahara Desert, but Chino wanted to start there, because it was where we'd dredged up that astrolabe the year before.

Whatever caught my eye, it was gone in a flash, so I scooted over to another monitor Chino, Kazoo and Moto use in the evenings to review the day's scan. This way we had eight sets of eyes—six of them infinitely more experienced than mine—on the daily watch. I hit playback and blue flashed by again. Freezing the screen I zoomed in and my heart took a leap. I whacked a big red button faster than a *Wheel of Fortune* contestant does when they know the answer to a toss-up round.

Fabio immediately stopped the ship, and within a few minutes the divers—they were working with metal detectors in areas of the bay too shallow for *Nao de Chino* to navigate—heeded Jan's radio call to return. Meanwhile, Fabio had maneuvered the ship back over the exact location where I'd seen something, and was holding position with the engines, as we didn't dare drop an anchor into what might be a treasure trove.

Our divers got ready for the sixty-foot descent, which necessitated all kinds of equipment changes. The tension and excitement on the boat was palpable, and now I fully understood why people spend a lifetime of countless unfulfilling hours, days, even years, in search of treasure.

"Ya know, Hetta, this is kinda like when we were fixin' to go into a brand new bar back in the day."

I nodded, knowing exactly what she meant. We used to love walking into an unknown bar, saddling up on a stool, and giving everyone in there the pleasure of meeting us. And buying us drinks. There was always that anticipation of meeting men, of course (which we rarely did, but hope springs eternal), but also something exciting in the doing. We could have saved a great deal of money and aspirin by taking up something less risky, like, say, ice hockey or skydiving.

We watched, tension building, as Kazoo and Moto, one holding a hand-held metal detector, descended slowly toward the location of my blue find.

"Chino, can they grab it if it looks like a relic?"

He shook his head. "No. Our permit only allows us to locate, photograph, and mark anything that might be from the galleon."

"What if whatever it is isn't from a galleon? I mean, if we don't bring it up, how will we even know what it is, or its origins. And, by the way, who's gonna rat us out if we grab something by mistake?"

"We are on the honor system, so far."

"So far?"

"Yes. When we do report a major find, they will send in an inspection team. In fact, they are allowed to search our vessel with no notice."

"Who the *hell* is they?"

"Mexico City."

"Gonna get a little crowded on here if Mexico City shows up, don't you think? Last I heard *they* had a population of about twenty million people."

Chino smiled, but never took his eyes from the bank of four monitor screens. Two showed views from the divers' head-mounted cameras, another sent back a moving video from the ship's towed digicam—now hovering over my find—and another monitor relayed images from a Remote Operated Video/Vehicle. This nifty little ROV was being controlled by Jan from an iPad. We looked downright National Geographic-like.

The divers reached my find, gave us a thumbs up and moved to the side so Jan could zoom in and capture a closeup. Chino leaned in, then let loose a mighty whoop. "Chinese porcelain? And no shard, either! Maybe even intact, if we're lucky."

"Porcelain?" I asked. "How come we got a reading on the magnetometer? Glass ain't metal."

"I would guess it was once packed in a wooden box held together with iron nails. The wood is gone."

The divers moved in and waved their dive gloves above the find, displacing sand and revealing more and more blue and white, until it became obvious we had a large vase on our hands, and so far, no visible cracks. After a few more minutes, an entire vase lay on the bottom, and Chino declared it might even be from the Ming Dynasty era, which would have put it at the right time to be on a galleon en route to Acapulco.

Much to my disappointment, the divers covered the vase with a steel cage, and began their ascent.

"They're just gonna leave it there?"

Chino nodded. "Have to."

"But, it's my vase. I found it."

"Hetta, you have a lot to learn about underwater exploration, especially when it comes to artifacts."

"I know, I know, you've told us all this stuff. And it even sounded logical until we actually found something!"

He just shook his head, went to a printer, and removed a photo of the vase so he could hopefully identify the dynasty.

Jan came over and patted my hand. "I don't think you were cut out for this kind of bidness. You're used to, you know, kicking ass and taking names. Doesn't work that way on Chino's expedition. You should be happy you'll get credit for spotting the first find."

"As I've said before, I'd rather have credit at the bank." I then feigned nonchalance and added, "Oh, well, it's just an old vase, anyhow."

Jan's eyes narrowed slightly at my sudden change of attitude. "Yeah, just an old vase," she drawled, her suspicion evident.

A Ming Dynasty vase, which the guys measured out at eleven inches tall, could draw millions according to a search I did on the Internet the minute I got back to my cabin. And with a provenance of originating from a Manila Galleon? Katy bar the door!

Our search with the ship now was concentrated on the area of the vase. It wasn't long until the divers marked another piece of pottery, a small bowl they found under a foot of sand, six feet from my vase. We had magnetometer hits all day, but didn't find out what was setting them off. Darkness soon put a stop to our search, and besides, everyone onboard was exhausted.

We moved a quarter mile away from the site to an area where we'd had no hits, and anchored in twenty feet of water for the night.

Tired or not, everyone was in a state of high anticipation as we gathered around the dining table for Rosa's famous *chiles rellenos.* Even Po Thang seemed excited. Probably, however, because Rosa makes a mean *relleno*, and he always begged enough to send him into a near coma right after we ferried him to the beach for his last pee and poo of the day.

When we beached the panga, he took off like a flash, running joyfully into the edge of the water, then up onto the beach and back like a wind-up toy. Being cooped up on the boat all day, he'd slept between begging handouts and occasionally barking at birds, and all that pent up energy was now unleashed. Jan and I finally gave up tracking him with our flashlight.

We heard him crashing around, then stop, crash, and stop. I assumed the stops were dump sites, but had no way of knowing until the next morning, when we would repeat this little foray during daylight, and I could pick up his leavings.

"Here he comes again. Maybe he's done. I hope so, I'm beat," Jan said, yawning and stretching.

"Me too, I—" a loud yelp stopped me. Jan and I both leaped from the panga and ran toward the pitiful howls. Po Thang limped into the flashlight's beam, sat, lifted a paw and howled some more. As I took his foot for inspection, blood ran over my hand. Jan held the flashlight for me as Po Thang, who was obviously in pain, nevertheless allowed me to raise his leg and check the paw further.

"Stingray. He never learns."

We called the boat on our handheld, and by the time we got back, Rosa met us on deck with a large pot of one hundred ten degree water. Po Thang, still whimpering, ran over and put the paw in the water without any coaxing. For some reason he just couldn't learn to leave stingrays alone, but did know that when he put his foot in the water, the pain stopped. Evidently his doggy brain couldn't grasp the concept of cause and effect when it came to stingrays, but got the idea that hot water stopped the pain. Go figure.

Po Thang, now relatively pain-free, dozed off with his foot still in the water, while his humans fretted and watched as the milky venom and more blood leached from the wound—both good things in the treatment process. Rosa added more hot water every so often for the next hour, then finally declared we'd done enough. Chino smeared antibiotic on the wound, and wrapped it in a bandage, which I knew would be chewed off by the next morning.

"Okay, Po Thang, it's Astroturf for you for the next week," I told him as Jan and I walked him back to my cabin. "You just never learn."

"Well, hell, he's your dog. Why shouldn't he mimic his master. Mistress? Whatever?"

"I'm capable of learning," I protested. "I got an engineering degree."

"We're talking life lessons here, and since when has that ever happened?"

"Since, uh, well it *has* happened."

She rolled her eyes and headed for her cabin.

"Well, it *could* happen," I yelled after her.

"In the meanwhile, you and that dawg of yours had better keep the kettle hot, Chica."

CHAPTER TWENTY-SIX

Jan was somewhat correct when she said I never learn, but it's my personal choice not to pay much attention to others' "life lessons." I mean, it's my life, so why should I let someone else have all the fun? However, once in awhile I do learn something from my own adventures. I prefer using the word, "adventure" versus, say, "freakin' catastrophes."

For instance, I've finally fallen for a nice guy, so I must have learned something from those bad boys along the line. Not that they don't still hold some attraction, Nacho being a prime example. My great grandmother lived to ninety-eight, and she still never learned to toe the line. Can I help it if my basic disrespect for what others consider normal is genetic?

I fired up my PC and went online in search of a refresher course in the use of a self-contained underwater breathing apparatus: scuba for short. It had been ten years since I (barely) qualified, but it took only a couple of serious dives to learn—I *can* learn!—it wasn't my cup of salt water.

But that was before I actually had something to dive *for*.

Complaining of eyestrain, I announced at breakfast the next day that my monitor monitoring was over and someone else would have to fill in. Chino promptly assigned Jan to the job, earning me a murderous squint from the ship's mistress.

"But," I added, "I'd like to join the shallow water dive team."

Continuing to work me over with those eyes Jan said, "Hetta, you don't dive. You hate scuba gear. Remember Aruba?"

"I'm willing to give it another shot. Especially now that we have those fancy rebreather thingamajigs, and I don't have to lug around heavy tanks and stuff. One of the things I hated most about diving was running out of air."

With conventional scuba gear, the type I learned on, you have to carry a couple of heavy tanks from which one gets an air supply. The exhaled carbon dioxide goes up in bubbles. These hi-tech rebreather do-dahs allow you to breathe your own air, over and over, with no bubbles. Ruins the hell out of those movie plots where the bad guys follow your bubbles so they can depth charge you, though.

I bought a bunch of these units for the expedition, so I'd snag one of the spares for my very own. If nothing else, Jan could suit up and we'd futz around shallow reefs looking at fish and stuff.

"How shallow?"

"Huh?"

"How shallow do you wish to dive?" This came from Moto and I almost dropped my coffee cup. He'd hardly spoken to me the whole time he'd been on board, preferring to address all questions to Chino. I was annoyed enough by what I considered his male chauvinist attitude to go out of my way in order to force a greeting from him on occasion. I'd cut him off in a hallway, make him look at me to pass, and let loose with a hearty, "*Ohayou*,"—pronounced Ohio—and he'd reluctantly respond with a slight bow and the more formal, "*Ohayou gozaimasu, Cohe-san.*"

I answered him. "Uh, twenty-feet or so is within my comfort zone."

We all looked at Chino, as he was the one who assigned the jobs. He shrugged. "I could use a break from diving, so I'll take over Hetta's monitor watch until we have to make the deeper dives. That way I'll be fresh. But first we'll have to check you out on the equipment, Hetta. I can even re-certify you. Where did you get your certification?"

"Aruba."

"Deepest dive?"

"Eighty feet." *Right before I panicked, almost clobbered a couple of instructors in a frantic attempt to shoot to the surface, and was asked to never darken Aruban waters again.*

Jan, who knew that story, pursed her lips, but remained silent.

"Okay, then," Chino said, "let's go to work. Yesterday's find was pretty exciting, but let's go get the big stuff."

I headed for my cabin, with Po Thang and Jan hot on my heels. Po Thang because I had a piece of bacon in my hand, and Jan because she knows me all too well.

"Okay, just what are you up to?" she demanded.

"*Moi?*"

"Yes, *Tu.*"

"I'm just so done with watching the bottom crawl by. Besides, you know I love to snorkel, and figured since you do, too, we'd have fun with those expensive rebreathers and fancy dry suits I bought. We might go explore a reef or something. And, I'll be weightless."

"You could sure use some of that."

"Hey!"

"I can see us taking a reef dive, but Hetta Coffey, Chickeness of the Sea, *working* underwater?"

"How hard can it be?"

"Holy crap, Jan. What just happened out there?"

"Chino tried to kill us, that's what."

Jan told Chino she, too, wanted to learn how the rebreather works. He'd been after her to get certified in Scuba, but she'd dragged her heels, fearing she'd be forced to jump into the water with purportedly friendly whales the size of eighteen wheelers. However, when I volunteered to join the dive team, her competitive juices rose, so she signed on as well. At the end of the first training day, we wondered if the light at the end of this torture tunnel was indeed an oncoming train.

For the certification process, Chino made us hit the books, studying manuals, familiarizing ourselves with the equipment, and taking all kinds of written tests. After two days, we were actually ready to suit up. Since my less than illustrious scuba career years before, dry suits had come a long way in their comfort level. We headed for the beach in a panga, waded into the shallow water, and the hard part started.

"He says we'll get used to it, but we haven't even actually done anything yet but learn the drills and I feel like I'm training for the Olympics."

Jan nodded. "I guess the good thing is that now we can carbo-load with the other divers."

"Can we call for take out? If I drag myself back to my cabin, I'll probably never leave it again."

"The hell you won't. Our dive master's got us scheduled for two more days of this torment, and I'm not going through it alone."

"Might I remind you, Miz Jan, no one asked you to suit up?"

"You know danged well I can't let you do something like this alone. Besides, I have a feeling you're up to no good, and I want in."

"That's my girl."

A week later, Jan and I were getting the hang of this shallow dive thing, and secretly boning up on what it would take to go down sixty feet, all by our lonelies, with zero backup.

I say no backup, because it was our intent to snag that vase.

"Ya know, if Chino even suspects what we're up to, he'll have a conniption fit."

"You're the ship's mistress, so book him outta here. Think up something only he can do, and send him away to do it. All we need is one night."

"Lemme think on it. Say I do get rid of him, how are we gonna slip off, with our gear and all?"

"I haven't thought that through yet. One thing for sure, though, we have to get Kazoo and Moto to take us with them on one of their nighttime lobster snagging dives."

"Bless their little lobster-lovin' hearts. Problem is they also grab those icky sea cucumbers." Jan gave a visible shiver. Then we both laughed while recalling the hissy Rosa threw when the two men brought several sea cucumbers on board, put them in white plastic buckets, and asked her to change their seawater every twelve hours until they could harvest their gonads. Dried sea cucumber gonad soup is a delicacy where they come from.

"Lobster, she okay. *Pepino del mar, no!*" I said, mimicking Rosa when she dramatically put her foot down. "No in *mi cocina!*"

"I guess we won't see sea pickle tacos on her menu any time soon?"

"I think not. Last I heard, Granny Yee had talked some guy in town into letting them process those slimy critters at his ranch, but you can bet your sweet arse there will be no sea cucumber soup cooked on this ship."

I grinned and nodded. "I kinda feel sorry for those two. The rest of us have so much more in common, even if the language thing gets a little complicated. It's no wonder they put all their energy into their work."

"They haven't taken a single day off since we boarded. Even when the rest of us go somewhere on Sunday, and we do invite them, they stay on board. They gotta be getting a little lonely by now."

"Maybe I'll check into getting some Japanese movies for them. Got to butter them up so they'll take us lobster diving, anyhow." I stretched and yawned. "I am so done for. I'm headed for dreamland."

"Me too."

"Think about how we're gonna send Chino on a wild goose chase. Like I said, all we need is one night."

She stood and headed for the door, then turned. "Okay, say if, by some miracle we get our hands on that vase. Then what?"

"We find the highest bidder. Those Chinese millionaires are buying this stuff up for their private collections."

"Hetta, you ever heard the term, plunder? How the hell do we even sell something like this vase? You have lots of friends in low places, but not the right low places for this kind of thing."

"Never you mind. You help me grab it, and I'll find a fence."

"Fence? Jesus, we're going to jail."

"No we aren't. We look crappy in orange."

"I liked it better when we were only plotting to kill someone."

"Yabbut think how interesting your resume will look with Global Antiquities Thief on it."

"More like, under international experience: Learned fluent Spanish in a Mexican jail."

"They'll never take us alive."

"Gosh, that's reassuring," Jan said, then we both fell into a giggle fit as Jan left for her cabin.

I sent a quick email to Jenks, then climbed into my bunk and read a new novel on my new Kindle for a millisecond before dropping it onto the bridge of my nose.

Kindles are much harder on the old schnozzola than paperbacks.

As I drifted off, I wondered if Amazon has some nefarious plan to branch out into plastic surgery.

CHAPTER TWENTY-SEVEN

Jan and I made our first sixty-foot dive the day Chino got a hit on the ship's side-scan sonar fish, and then, on a second sweep, the ship's magnetometer started pinging. Something was down there, and this was our chance to get trained on a deeper dive. We'd made every-other-day twenty-footers for two weeks, were getting pretty comfortable with our equipment, and gaining confidence with the entire process by the day.

So far our dives had produced a couple of anchors, various fishing equipment, and general trash, but just being down there with all those beautiful fish, shells, and even the occasional turtle, made it worthwhile. Even better, we were burning calories like a furnace, so we got to carbo-load the night before each dive.

When I checked the underwater camera monitor before suiting up, I was pleased to find the water particularly clear, which helped assuage that old fear factor. And even better, Chino decided to go down with us. I think he really just wanted to keep an eye on her preciousness, but having him, as well as Kazoo and Moto—three expert divers—along just might keep me from doing something stupid. But then, they are only mortals.

Both Jan and I confessed to sleeplessness the night before, and when I had finally dropped off, I awoke in a cold sweat during a nightmare involving toothy great whites. Maybe I yelled, because Po Thang left his upper-berth perch and snuggled up to me, evidently picking up on my need for comfort.

I finally gave up getting any more sleep, got a cup of coffee from the galley, then sent an email to Jenks that I hoped didn't come off as my last will and testament.

Chino insisted on overseeing the refilling of our breather mixture tanks. He was adamant that we use all fresh CO_2 absorbent for each dive after he caught Kazoo and Moto mixing previously used stuff with new. Turns out this is a fairly common practice— potentially a deadly one—used by many divers using rebreather equipment. If the mixture isn't scrubbing all the CO_2, the diver is breathing it back in, and may not even realize they're in trouble until it is too late, especially on deep dives.

In addition to our rebreathers, we also carried an extra compressed air canister for this dive, and Jan and I had been schooled on how to switch over if need be.

Once in the water, we pulled ourselves down the anchor line, which I held onto like the lifeline it was. Even when we reached the bottom and I saw how good the visibility was, I was loathe to let go until Jan slapped my clenched hands. We trailed Chino, with Kazoo and Moto following close behind.

My fears soon vanished once we started exploring. Schools of curious fish followed us, seemingly unafraid. Jan and I found ourselves poking each other, pointing out neat stuff, and actually having a great time.

Chino, maintaining the lead, carried a hand-held metal detector, as did the two Japanese divers. Jan and I were not confident enough to handle any more equipment, but we had underwater cameras. When Chino suddenly stopped, picked up a broken sand dollar, and started to fan the sand with it, my excitement rose, and I practically forgot I was under sixty feet of water. We all hovered over Chino, anticipation climbing. He'd fan for a few seconds, let the cloud of sand and debris settle, move the detector over the spot, fan again. I dug out my camera and zoomed in on him just as his arm shot up, thumb held high.

The next thirty minutes were magical, as we spread out along the bottom and did our own fanning after the detector picked up a signal. Jan and I worked together, and we were the ones who found what looked to be a cannon ball encrusted in hundreds of years of sea gunk.

Chino found a cannon.

Kazoo and Moto found another.

Ka-ching!

I didn't want to surface. Ever. I could have stayed down there forever, or so I thought. Chino thought otherwise, pointed to his dive watch and computers, and steered us back to the anchor chain, where we reluctantly started our ascent.

A medium sized shark swam by, and I waved!

"Jan, we're gonna be rich! And we don't even have to sneak back down there and steal those cannons." We were in my cabin after dinner, polishing off a bottle of wine and celebrating our success. Both of us were so stoked, it wasn't until about then we realized how tired we were.

Jan yawned. "Like we could. Might I remind you they weigh a ton, and Chino says we'll have to bring them up with that big old winch thingy on the back of the boat."

"Winch thingy? That a new technical term?"

"You know what I mean. So, does this mean we don't have to do that night dive for the vase?"

"Nope. We still gotta have it. I see no reason to let the Mexican government glom on to my find. We'll get a piece of the action on the cannons, but that Ming might bring big bucks. I'll get a bigger boat. You can buy Chino his own whale. Jenks and I can stop working and be together for a change."

"Or, we could go to jail, like, forever."

"Nah. So, when can we get rid of Chino and the gang for a night? Have you come up with any ideas yet? After today I'm sure we'll make that dive just fine all by ourselves."

"Not me. We've never done a night dive."

"I'm gonna remedy that. Moto and Kazoo take off every night for fresh sushi fixin's, and I'm gonna get us an invite. You work on getting everyone off the boat for one night and we'll be golden."

Jan yawned again. "I'll come up with something. I gotta get some sleep. Tomorrow I go back to being a bookkeeper for a day instead of my moment as Jackie Cousteau."

"Speaking of which, how are we doing, financially?"

"Not all that hot. Even with all our free labor, expenses are eating us alive. We spent a lot on equipment, even with your careful shopping. We've blown through almost half of Ishi's money, and Chino was only able to get another twenty-five grand from the Mexican government. At this rate, we'll only last another month and a half."

"I have a little I can throw in, maybe ten grand."

"How generous of you," Jan said sarcastically. "Is that before or after you steal the vase."

"You wound me. Before. I have some bucks put away. How about you? And Chino's family?"

She shook her head. "Chino and I tapped out everything we had to refit the boat into livable shape. Tanuki had gutted the entire living quarters level, evidently planning to retrofit the area into a whale canning factory."

"Just as well. Made for us having much larger cabins. So, I guess I'll have to cut Po Thang's rations?"

"Nah. Abuela Yee is providing meals two days a week so Rosa can have those days off, and Chino's family's contributing what they can, mostly fresh fruit and veggies, but we are definitely a low-budget operation when it comes to treasure hunts."

"We could use some investors, but investors in what? This ain't no *Atocha* we're looking for. Maybe we'll find more cannons, but everything of real value goes to the government. Except my vase, of course."

"And it'll probably take years to get any money out of it."

We'd done some snoopery into selling ill-gotten artifacts, and realized it wasn't quite as easy as listing the vase on eBay. We had to be very careful, or we'd find ourselves in deep ca-ca. "Did you take care of the paperwork?"

"Yep. Somehow that vase find got lost in a morass of Mexican bureaucracy. By the time it gets found, we'll have a lot of gray hair."

We gave each other a high five, then Jan lost her smile. "I feel guilty, though. Chino is so honest and trusting, and here we are...."

"*Dis*honest and *un*trustworthy? Damn right we are. In the end, it's for Chino's own good. You know damned well someone in Mexico City will end up rich on this deal, and Chino won't get squat. So why shouldn't we take out a little insurance?"

"I know you're right. But...."

"No buts. Now, get some sleep and try to come up with something to get everyone off the *Nao de Chino* for one lousy night."

Jan handed me the salt shaker at breakfast and whispered, "Mother's Day."

What is scary is that I knew exactly what she meant. Mother's Day in Mexico is huge, and all the Mexicans on our ship would want to spend time with their mothers, wives, and grandmothers. Jan and I would graciously volunteer to man the boat. All we had to do was get rid of our Japanese buddies, as well, and we'd have *Nao de Chino* all to ourselves long enough to grab the vase.

Maybe even in broad daylight, which was a good thing because no amount of hounding had gained us an invite to join Kazoo and Moto for their nightly dive.

CHAPTER TWENTY-EIGHT

Po Thang's chip, along with the animal cam I'd also requested from Craig, finally arrived. Chino hadn't implanted the chip as yet because Po Thang rarely left the ship, and when he did it was only to roam remote beaches where chances of him getting nabbed again were slim. Also, he now took to swimming with us when we dove, so Chino decided to not do anything right away, fearing even the slight incision might become infected.

We took a dark blue rubber raft with us for Po Thang to climb up on when we were down on a dive, just in case he got tired, but he seemed tireless. He could easily dive down six or seven feet and retrieve a shell or a toy, so sometimes when we surfaced there would be a pile of his treasures on the raft. If we ever found anything of value in shallow water, I decided I'd just send him down and save myself the trip.

I looked into getting him his own scuba equipment, and found it was possible, but extremely expensive. He'd just have to be content with paddling his way through the dog days of summer.

The great Mother's Day heist was fast approaching.

Fabio was taking three days off and going to Ensenada to be with his wife and mother. Chino's family planned a two-day reunion at Abuela Yee's house, so that got rid of him, Rosa, and the two cousins. All we had to do was figure out how to get Moto and Kazoo off the boat for a guaranteed two hours or so while we made the dive and snatched the vase.

Meanwhile, I was still scheming to do in Dickless, but with less enthusiasm since I now felt that, after the summer, I'd take *Raymond Johnson* back to the States, and away from the SOB. Then I'd sell the vase, and hire a hit man to do the deed, since that rat Nacho wasn't returning my calls.

After the cannon and cannon ball finds, we hadn't made anymore discoveries, but had tightened the search area to where we found both them and the vase. The vase was a quarter mile from the other finds, but Chino put that area on hold for the moment, which was fine with me.

Keeps away anyone more dishonest than I.

As it turned out, the Japanese divers already had plans for the weekend. They left in a panga at dawn on Mother's day, taking camping gear, dive tanks, and enough food for a two day campout a few miles south, on the Pacific side of the bay. They'd heard of abalone there, and promised to bring us some.

"Okay," I said to Jan as we waved goodbye to the last crew member, "let's roll."

"Ya know, Hetta, we are about to break every single, solitary, expedition rule."

"And when did we start caring about rules?"

"Like, never?"

Preparing to break rules is hard work. Disregarding Chino's hard and fast policy, NEVER LEAVE THE MOTHERSHIP UNATTENDED, was unavoidable, as I didn't dare move *Nao de Chino* over the vase, then try to move back. Someone was sure to notice.

We spent a couple of hours preparing for our snatch, taking care to load the panga with a net, basket, and line for bringing up the vase, then repacking our rebreathers, and making sure our conventional canisters were full. The dive itself would not take nearly as long as the prep, but that was normal.

Leaving the ship's workhorse—a twenty-foot panga with a 60-hp Johnson outboard—on the surface unattended was also a no-no, so we figured Po Thang left on guard got us around that one.

Chino had carefully photographed the vase, then reburied it, but we knew where it was, and the GPS coordinates told us where to anchor the panga so as not to drop ten pounds of steel smack on top of our future fortune.

"So, the way I figure it, a vase that size, packed with sand, has got to weigh a lot, but with the basket and net, bringing it up should be no problem. I'm not even going to try carrying it to the surface. We'll haul it in with the net's line once we get back into the panga."

"Good plan. You got the package ready?"

"You betcha."

"Okay, then, let's do it."

Po Thang whined and paced when we went over the side, but I told him to stay, and by some miracle, he did. We also attached and floated his raft nearby, just in case his little doggie mind forgot he was supposed to stay put. Getting himself over the water-slicked gunwales of the panga was beyond even his magical canine talents, even though he'd tried over and over, only to slide back into the water.

We just followed the twenty-foot panga's anchor line down, as I was afraid we'd dislodge the anchor if we pulled ourselves to the bottom using the rope. The water was clear, and Jan and I were comfortable by now with the equipment, if not the idea that we were out here on our own for the first time on a sixty-foot dive.

I heard Jan make a noise and turned to see her pointing to a large school of sardines, their silver sides whirling in the blue as if in a kaleidoscope. We hovered and watched for a few seconds before remembering we were international artifact thieves on a mission.

We located the vase site easily, since the small white flag Chino planted was still there. Digging the vase out was harder and took more time than we thought it would, as the sand kept collapsing back into the hole. Finally we managed to run two lines under it, lifted one end and began working the net around the base, one inch at a time.

I was burning air like the amateur diver I am, and if the water hadn't been, according to my dive computer, sixty-eight, I'm sure I'd be filling my suit with sweat. One thing's for certain, I was tiring rapidly, and Jan probably was, as well.

After what seemed like an eternity, but was probably only thirty minutes, the vase was in the net and into the basket. It took another ten minutes to plant the vase I bought at a local store that was blue and white, but otherwise in no way resembled the original except in color and shape. We covered it well, replanted the flag, and pointed to the surface, leaving the basket on the bottom.

We knew we didn't have to do stops on the way up, but we followed the rules set by Chino and only ascended to thirty feet before taking a rest, and catching our breath. Once again, the sardines caught our attention and while my breathing returned to somewhere near normal, I enjoyed the view.

Jan tugged on my hand, grunted, and pointed to our left. A school of dolphin attacked the sardine ball, cutting through and herding them. Then cormorants began diving, rocketing straight down into the melee, and further panicking the sardines. I'd seen these bait boils on the surface many times, but watching it from below was both exhilarating and a little scary. I also knew the commotion up there had to be sending Po Thang into a frenzy.

Sure enough, another burst of bubbles and red fur near the surface announced Po Thang's entry into the kerfuffle. I heard what was probably a giggle from Jan and we headed up.

Po Thang was dog paddling madly toward one sea gull, then another, barking to beat the band. When he saw us, he headed for me and I prepared to fend him off. Being hugged in the water by a large dog is not the best thing for someone trying to stay afloat. I moved the raft between us and he launched himself on it, torn between snagging a bird that sat there, and climbing onto my head.

Jan was already in the panga when I used my last bit of strength to pull myself in and remove my mask. We were right in the middle of the boil now, with frenzied sardines actually launching themselves into the panga. Po Thang managed to snag one in midair, then got the funniest look on his face when he realized he had a mouthful of slimy, wiggling, fish.

As he spit out the sardine, we collapsed into a giggle-fit bordering on hysteria, a combination of fatigue, stress, and excitement. It was then that I saw the large fin headed for Po Thang's flimsy, rocking raft.

"Oh, crap! Jan, look!"

She turned and shrieked, getting Po Thang's attention. He cocked his head, then launched himself from the raft into the panga just as a sailfish the size of a taxi cab broke the surface in pursuit of lunch.

The huge fish went airborne, snagged a sardine, and dove, sending a wall of water over us.

Po Thang yelped and dove under my legs, Jan yelped as well as the big fish's wake rocked the boat. We held on tight as the panga, always seaworthy, settled out. It was then I felt a tug on my wrist. I checked to make sure the line to our vase was still attached.

The sailfish suddenly reversed direction, and came straight at us again in pursuit of more sardines. This time, when he breeched, I saw piece of yellow polypropylene line trailing from his mouth.

"Jan, that big mother has our vase!"

"Holy crap, what are—"

She froze in mid-sentence as her eyes widened and dropped to my wrist.

The wrist I'd wrapped several times with yellow polypropylene line.

CHAPTER TWENTY-NINE

I stared dumbly at the line tightening around my wrist, but Jan sprang into action, reached into her dive scabbard, and slid out a razor-sharp, titanium bladed knife. As she reached for the line, I yelled, "No! If you cut it we'll lose the vase."

"If I don't, you're either going to lose that hand, or go on a water-skiing trip. He'll drown you."

The sailfish's sail appeared on the surface nearby, but he was rapidly swimming away from us. It was only a matter of seconds until he hit the end of his rope, so to speak.

I lunged for the bow of the panga and took a wrap on a cleat with what slack I had left before letting Jan sever the line near my arm. Less than ten seconds later the panga pitched forward so wildly, we were all three thrown into a heap, then the boat settled and the fish pulled us fifty feet, until the anchor did its job.

Jerked backward, he reacted to the hit, and, fighting for his life, once again soared skyward, throwing his huge head and sword-like beak from side-to-side as he jumped. Maybe he'd been hooked before and managed to throw the hook, or maybe it's just what they instinctively do, but one thing was obvious: that basket was lodged somewhere inside him, and it wasn't coming loose easily.

With the line taut, he began circling the panga. Something was gonna have to give. I'd fought a three-hundred-pound marlin once, and remembered the boat captain's instructions for what I should do, and his handling of the boat in order to fight him.

"Jan, cut the anchor loose, and standby for a boat ride! We have to tire him out."

The minute the sailfish felt some slack, he took off like a flash, and we braced ourselves for when he hit the end of the line and started towing us again. If we could wear him down, we might have half a chance of dragging him into shallow water and getting our basket. Okay, so we probably didn't have a chance in hell, but we had to try.

He towed us for a couple of miles without showing any sign of tiring, so I started the outboard and put it in reverse, increasing the critter's drag. Another two miles later, he still didn't lag, and now he was headed for the bay's entrance, and open ocean.

"Hetta, we gotta do something. We can't let him take us out to sea."

"Why not? We have to wear him down somehow."

"And then what? What if he just dies and sinks?"

"Then we'll drag him back in behind us. He's not getting away with our vase."

"Maybe it's...we stopped!"

"Feel the line."

She reached over the bow and grabbed the line. "It's loose."

"Is it hanging straight down?"

She leaned over. "No, it's under us. Hetta! Kill the...."

I reached to shut down the outboard, but it was too late. It ground to a stop, the propeller fouled with yellow rope. "At least we didn't cut the line, thank goodness. But now we'll have to wait this fish out, and when he dies, clear our prop before motoring back inside the bay. Or maybe we'll get lucky and the tide will turn and float us back in." We had oars but paddling a panga is akin to herding cats.

"Uh, we're moving sideways."

The big guy had us bow and stern, and if he pulled us crossways into the waves outside the protection of the bay, we could easily take on water and sink. It was time to face facts and cut him—and my vase—loose.

Jan took her knife out again and was moving to the panga's aft when we heard, "*Ohayo, Cohee*! We come fast!"

Kazoo and Moto were headed our way rapidly, and Jan and I cheered them on. I tried not to think about how much 'splainin' we had in our future.

Our Japanese saviors were so excited about that sailfish, they didn't question that we'd caught him on a piece of polypropylene line. They tied to us and began pulling our panga, and the fish, back into the bay with the powerful dual 100hp motors on their thirty-foot boat. The sailfish, already worn down by us, hardly fought and by the time we were near the beach, gave up the fight completely.

"Can we set him free somehow?" Jan asked.

Not with my vase inside him, we can't. How I was going to get to it, if it was indeed still in the fish, right under the noses of Kazoo and Moto, I had no idea.

Kazoo shook his head. "No, Jan-san, he will not live. He fought bravely, but now he will make delicious sashimi, and soup." As if on cue, the fish gave one last gasp and went still.

I felt a sadness that must have showed, for Moto asked, "Do you wish us to take him now?"

I shook my head. "No, we caught him, we'll take him in. Can you clear my prop and help tie him alongside? We'll meet you at the fishing pier in Puerto San Carlos. You two can clean him there where they have a hoist, and a large concrete cleaning table, okay?"

"As you wish," he said with a bow, and a look that said, "If this crazy broad wants to haul in a nine-foot fish with a twenty-foot boat, so be it."

We still didn't know for sure that the basket and vase were in the fish, but I couldn't check for my treasure until we got rid of Kazoo and Moto. The minute they motored away toward Puerto San Carlos, I pulled all loose yellow line into the boat until it went taut. The rest was still inside the fish, whose beautiful silvery skin was fading, and his large, accusatory, black eye clouding. I tugged on the tight line and took a wrap on a cleat. Jan and I then put our combined weight into pulling on the line, and the fish's head raised.

Peering down into his open mouth, I said, "Okay, Jan, you stick your arm down his throat and see if that vase is still there."

"How about you stick...never mind, no way. You do it."

"Jeez, I have to do everything myself. First though, let's try tugging more on the line, see if something comes loose. Grab your end, and we'll pull on three. One, two—"

We both fell backward into the bow of the boat, but when we did the heavy basket flew out of the fish, bounced on the gunwale and back into the water, but we had, thankfully, tied off the end of the line.

I flinched as the basket hit the solid fiberglass hull, hoping the sand packing the interior protected it from shattering. It took everything we had left in us to hand over hand the net into the boat, and again, when it finally rolled over the gunwale, I was afraid we'd break our hard earned treasure.

We hid the basket under some towels and beat feet for the quay, as promised. A promise I wish I hadn't made, because if left to me, we'd cut the damned fish loose and head for *Nao de Chino*, but it was not to be.

CHAPTER THIRTY

Jan and I were experiencing an Earnest Hemingway kind of day.

By the time we motored into the harbor with that poor fish tied to our panga, word was out—I still don't know how it happens so fast in Mexico—of our catch and a small crowd was gathered, mostly men, as the women were still in church.

Unlike what happened to the unfortunate Santiago in *The Old Man and the Sea*, our catch was not eaten by sharks on the way in. During the entire trip, however, scenes from the movie, with Spencer Tracey fighting off the sharks as they attacked his prize over and over, plagued my mind. I didn't care so much about the fish, but Po Thang's reaction to sharks worried me, so as a precaution I tied him tightly to a cleat.

When we pulled alongside the wharf, a couple of strapping young Mexican men climbed into our panga, fastened our sailfish's tail to a hoist, and others on the dock hauled him up.

He weighed in at eighty nine kilos—around two hundred pounds—and was a little over nine feet in length. One local fisherman said it was close to a record, as far as he could recall. Several residents whipped out their phones and asked Jan, me, and Po Thang to pose with our fish, which would yield lots of sashimi material for Kazoo and Moto, with plenty left to share with the Mexicans on the dock. I just wanted to head for the dive ship and check out our vase. As soon as we could gracefully depart, we did, leaving Kazoo and Moto to the dirty work of fish cleaning.

Out of ear shot of the crowd, Jan said, "Ya know, Hetta, we're gonna have to come up with a story of some kind."

"I know. I've been thinking about that. How about we were anchored somewhere looking at reef fish and somehow the sailfish got tangled in our anchor line, and then the anchor was lost sometime during the melee?"

"Sounds good to me, but we know for sure Kazoo and Moto saw the yellow polypropylene line coming out of that fish's mouth, and our anchor line is white." To make her point she reached over and held up the end of what was left of the severed anchor line.

"I have a feeling they aren't going to be saying much of anything."

Jan cocked her head. "Why do you say that?"

"Because they know I saw what was in *their* panga."

"Abalone? Okay, it's illegal for them to take them, but so what? Who on *Nao de Chino* would even care? I mean, we're talkin' fried abalone steaks for dinner here."

"Abalone, smabalone. They had handheld metal detectors with them. Last I recall, abalone ain't made of metal."

"I've eaten some that tasted like it."

I grinned. "Me too. Not everyone knows how to cook it, but you can bet Rosa will."

"So, what do you think they're looking for?"

"No idea, but I'm planning to find out. They're out all the time by themselves and I now suspect they have a hidden agenda aside from finding a few artifacts from a sunken galleon. Maybe they're here on a secret mission somehow tied to that hundred thousand dollar investment by some folks back in Japan."

"Surely you don't think they were involved in Ishikawa's death, do you?"

I shook my head. "I doubt it. Hell, they might not even know he's dead. Tomorrow night, at dinner, I'm gonna rattle their cage and see what falls out."

"Speaking of what's falling out, if we're gonna get a look at that vase, we'd better haul butt for the boat. Our Japanese buds will be back way too soon."

"I don't think we can risk it yet. Maybe we should rebury the vase in shallow water near Po Thang's beach and get back to it when no one is around."

"Dang, the curiosity is killing me."

"Me, too, but we have to be so careful now. You take Po Thang on a walk at the beach so he won't see me burying the vase. All we need is for him to dive down and get it."

Po Thang, who was dozing after all the excitement, heard his name and perked up. When he saw we were heading for his beach, he rushed to the bow and when we were still twenty feet out, dove in and swam the rest of the way, then disappeared behind a sand dune. Jan sighed and followed him.

We were both exhausted, but I still had to bury the vase. I checked the tide line. Good, low tide. I found a large rock in four feet of water, tied it to the panga with what yellow line didn't get chewed up by the prop, put the panga motor in reverse, and pulled the rock a few feet, creating a hole. I planted the vase in the hole, covered it with sand and returned the rock next to it. Then I went ashore and carefully placed stones above the high water mark, making them look randomly scattered, but actually forming an arrow pointing to my treasure. By the time Po Thang came racing back, I was collapsed on the beach.

Behind every fortune lies a great crime. Honore de Balzac

Behind every great crime lies a whole lot of work. Hetta Coffey

We had our full contingent back on board *Nao de Chino* by Monday evening, with everyone rested and ready to tackle our tough work ahead. Even Jan and I had recovered from our hard weekend of what we hoped was grand larceny.

As expected, Rosa's abalone steaks were melt-in-your mouth delicious, and Jan and I made a contribution of homemade French custard ice cream. Everyone was in good spirits, laughing at our tale of the wild ride behind our sailfish. And, just as I surmised, Kazoo and Moto didn't blink an eye when we blamed the whole thing on our snagged anchor line.

"Oh, by the way Chino," I said casually, nudging Jan with my knee as a signal to watch the Japanese divers for a reaction, "have you heard anything more from Mrs. Ishikawa regarding her husband's disappearance?"

Kazoo only blinked, but Moto's head shot up from the bowl he was holding near his mouth. The chopsticks he was using to shovel rice into his mouth froze in mid-shovel. He stared at Chino as if anticipating his answer, then I caught a movement that was probably a knee-nudge from Kazoo, and Moto went back to his rice shoveling.

Chino swallowed abalone and put down his fork. "I called her this afternoon, to see how she is doing. After the family stayed with us for so long, I felt I owed her at least a courtesy call. She sounded well, but as you know, her English is limited. We mostly communicated through Ishikawa's secretary. Still no news of the missing Airliner, as everyone in the entire world know from so much media coverage, but he was listed as a passenger, so I guess as long as the plane remains missing, she's still hopeful."

Jan and I exchanged a glance. We had discussed often who might have the power to put a dead man's name on the passenger list of a missing airliner.

Moto, looking unsettled, stood and excused himself for the evening.

Kazoo stayed for our ice cream, but took a bowl for Moto when he left.

From their reaction, it looked to me as though they knew who Ishikawa was, but were unaware of his disappearance. What was their connection?

I'm pretty sure Moto was in for a lecture on inscrutability from Kazoo while he ate his ice cream.

"Jan, do you think we can somehow bug Kazoo and Moto?" I asked when we went back in my cabin for our nightly final final wine and gab-fest.

"Our bugging devices are back at the fish camp," she said, talking about them as if everyone had high tech bugs hidden in their lingerie drawer.

"Maybe need to go get 'em?"

"You gonna bug the diver's computers and cabins?"

"I'd like to. Problem is, if they talk to anyone, it'll be in Japanese, so I guess bugging won't help us much, will it?"

"Nope. Same with emails."

"What about research done on the ship's computer? I've seen them use it."

"That's easier. I can maybe look at their search history. But what are we looking for?"

"Damned if I know, but I'm gonna do some cyber-snoopery of my own tonight. Maybe get a clue what they're after. I'm pretty good with Google these days."

"Yeah, well, Google this: Hetta Coffey found dead as dirt in Magdalena Bay after running afoul of a bunch of Japanese gangsters."

"Hey, that's a great idea!"

"You bein' dead as dirt?"

"No. I'll do some homework on old man Fujikawa, maybe find out just who he is. And what he does that puts him in company with Luján."

She finished her wine, gave Po Thang a pat, and went to her own cabin. I fired up my computer, emailed Jenks about our sailfish adventure—mainly because if I didn't and he heard something from Chino, he'd smell a rat—and began my research.

Googling Tadashi Fujikawa got me all kinds of hits, but nothing I could definitively identify as our Tadassan. I knew nothing about him except he was probably elderly, but ageless in that he could be anywhere from seventy to a hundred. He had the wiry frame and thickened, wrinkled skin of many Asian seniors, but pinning an age on them is difficult. He probably practices tai chi or some such.

Next, I entered, **Japanese in Magdalena Bay Baja**.

I already knew something of their history in Baja because Chino recounted his involvement to halt Mitsubishi's plans to build a salt plant in San Ignacio Lagoon, one of the last natural whale birthing grounds in the world. Then, of course, there was my little project last year, involving Tanuki Corporation and the proposed desalination plant, and sea salt by-product. Ishikawa was Tanuki's contact in Japan, but he and Dickless had more planned than salt. And, I saw Japanese vessels daily in the bay, mostly cargo ships picking up seafood in Puerto San Carlos.

What I didn't know was what popped up on my Google search: In 1912 Japan evidently tried to *buy* Mag Bay, and was halted by an amendment, or corollary, to the Monroe Doctrine, prompted by Japan's attempt to buy a port in Mexico. The Lodge Corollary forbade foreign governments from acquiring sufficient territory in the Western Hemisphere so as to put that government in "practical power of control."

Interesting bit of history, but nothing to do with our two divers or Fujikawa.

Another tidbit I found using the same key words was of far more interest: Turns out that following the attack on Pearl Harbor, and probably even before that infamous day, the Japanese navy used Mag Bay as a hideout for submarines. They stayed submerged during the day and surfaced at night, awaiting orders from Japan. The Japanese expected a swift victory, and were poised to take over the United States from several directions, one being Mexico.

But my best find, and one that almost sent me to get Jan until I realized it was one in the morning, was about a Texas Ranger by the name of Van Zandt—Whoa! Didn't we have a county by that name?—who worked as an undercover intelligence officer in Baja during WWII.

I went to the galley for coffee; this was getting way too good to put off until the next day.

When I finally ran out of steam at three, and was forced to shut down my PC out of sheer exhaustion, I'd learned much, much, more and could not wait to share it with Jan.

Well, maybe I could, because it took both Jan and Po Thang to drag me out of bed the next morning, and it wasn't until we took Po Thang to the beach that I got a chance to tell her what I'd found.

Jan listened intently, then said, "Lemme get this straight. This Texas Ranger, who is a *spy* for the United States, hears from *his* network of spies in the Baja that fishing boats spotted Japanese subs in Mag Bay. Then, while some Japanese officers came ashore to make contact with *their* spies, their crew, I'm sure disobeying strict orders, did a little horse trading with the locals?"

"Yup. And this Ranger, Van Zandt, passed this info to an American actress, Rochelle Hudson, who was also a spy for the US, and she relayed it back to Washington."

"Wow, who knew? And who the hell was Rochelle Hudson?"

"I knew you'd ask. You might remember her as Natalie Wood's mama in *Rebel Without a Cause*. She was also the disgraced gal to whom Mae West imparted the immortal wisdom, 'When a girl goes wrong, men go right after her!' "

"Really? I love both those movies. How did she come to be an American spy in Mexico, for cryin' out loud?"

"Her hubby at the time was a Disney exec who doubled as a civilian espionage agent down here. They took several so-called vacations to Baja, looking for any German activities, and somehow hooked up with that ranger to pass on the Japanese sub info."

"So, what happened then?"

"This is where it gets really good. Van Zandt pulled a raid using some Yaqui Indian warriors and blew up two submarines."

Jan's mouth dropped open. "This just keeps getting better and better."

"And, in 1972 someone reported spotting a sunken sub around here, but it was never found again."

"So, our guys might be looking for the wreck? I can see their interest, but why would some Japanese money guys finance *our* expedition just to dive on an old sub wreck?"

I had no answer for that. "I don't know, but I'm going to keep digging. Meanwhile we need to keep an eye on Kazoo and Moto. You check the ship's computer history thing, and I'll do more research."

"So, when do you think we can bring up our vase?"

"Not today. The rest of the dive crew is still within sight. Probably tomorrow, when they dive another sixty-footer. Do you think we could drive to this beach in my pickup? I'd sure like to get that vase into a safe place, and it seems much easier to fetch it by road, rather than bringing it back to the ship by panga, then smuggling it aboard."

"When I was walking Po Thang while you buried the vase, I saw tire tracks all over the desert, but have no idea where they lead. Let's put in the GPS coordinates for this beach, and use Google Earth for a look-see. Maybe we'll spot a road."

I sucked my teeth, Japanese-style. "You very smaht gul, Jan-san."

Paraphrasing an old Kingston Trio song, she said, "You are surprised? I was, after all, educated in your country."

CHAPTER THIRTY-ONE

Google Earth rocks!

There were all kinds of roads leading to Po Thang's beach. The problem is, there were all kinds of roads leading to Po Thang's beach. At least, they looked like roads, but I knew for a fact that many were probably very basic. And unmarked.

As the crow flies, the distance from Lopez Mateos was only about thirty miles. But desert roads in the Baja meander all over the place, so I figured on at least double that. So, best case scenario, the actual drive would take us four hours at an average of twenty miles an hour, and when you add in the times we'd get lost, maybe double that. And we would be completely on our own, as I didn't see one single village along the way.

I called a conference with Jan, told her what I'd learned, and we concluded we might have to make the trip an overnighter.

"I guess we could camp on those dunes behind the beach if we have to. We danged sure can't drive back in the dark. Talk about lost."

"We need a vacation, doncha think? After all, everyone else got a three day weekend, so maybe now it's our turn?"

"Yep, I'll download and print out those Google Earth shots so we maybe have half a chance at not getting lost *too* many times. What are we gonna tell the guys about where we are going?"

"The truth. We're gonna go camping on the dunes."

"Dear CNN: News flash! Breaking news! Hetta Coffey tells the truth."

We planned our beach trip for the weekend, hoping maybe there would be a few cars on those so-called roads, since many Mexicans take their families on outings.

Meanwhile, I was hot on my end of our snoopery, and Jan on hers. We met each evening after dinner to compare notes, as that was about the only time we had alone. Our days were a jumble of dives, along with all manner of other expedition projects.

The expedition finances were not getting any better. Chino flat turned down my offer of ten grand, as well as Jenks's twenty, because there would be no way to recoup our investment. Little did he know I had my own financial recovery plan well under way.

Chino called a meeting to let everyone know where we stood, because the paid crew would have to make other plans before too long unless we got more money.

"According to our expedition accountant," he nodded at Jan, "we've got six weeks, maximum. This is, of course, disappointing, but we do have six weeks and that is good. I, Jan, and Hetta will remain on the job until I have to return to the fish camp, but our efforts will be restricted by time."

I was watching the Japanese divers closely for a reaction. Kazoo frowned and poor Moto's face fell. Of the two, I'd rather play poker with Moto. Neither, however, asked a question, so I did.

"How much will we need to continue until September, as we originally planned?" I already knew the number, but just in case our divers did have a pipeline to more Japanese funds, I wanted them to know how many yen we needed. I'd told Jan to pad the estimate, just in case.

"Jan?"

"Okay, if we're frugal, which we already are, but maybe we can cut a few more corners here and there, like maybe reduce Hetta's rations, another fifty-grand'll get us there with no problem, *if* we don't have any major equipment failures."

Fabio gave me an evil grin. "I'll limit the wine."

"And I," I growled, "will lead the mutiny."

It was the night before Jan and I went off to get the vase that I stumbled across this little unsubstantiated tidbit on an Internet post: *'In 1943, a Japanese vessel, disguised as the fishing boat Tama Maru, carrying $250,000 in gold bullion and Japanese gold coins, was enroute to Mexico with plans to take over the country. It was lost and never recovered.'*

Say what? I did a quick calculation, using the price per pound of gold in 1943, and today's price, and came up with almost nine million dollars. What if this account was in fact true, and our dive buddies had information that the gold was near or in Magdalena Bay?

This was getting mo' bettah! And potentially very dangerous for someone, namely one Hetta Coffey, who might get into the middle of the whole deal.

One Hetta Coffey who might allegedly want that alleged gold!

But, first thefts first: My vase.

We packed sleeping bags, food, beer, a tent, bug spray, more bug spray, firewood, matches, water, and a GPS so we at least knew where we were going, if not how to get there.

Let me just say right here that I hate, hate, hate, camping.

And Jan's idea of camping was in a luxury RV.

Po Thang, however, was probably gonna love this trip, including sleeping on damp sand—as opposed to the nice, soft sandy dunes where I knew for a fact scorpions lurked. Jan had caved in once to Chino's pleas to spend just one night on the dunes, and when they broke camp the next day several scorpions were snuggled up under their tent. Remembering that incident, Jan insisted we take enough blankets to make a pallet in the bed of the pickup.

Chino was surprised we'd even consider this kind of outing, but then again, he was used to us doing the unexpected. He did give us a flare gun to shoot off in case we got in trouble, since they could probably see it from the *Nao de Chino.* We also took a handheld radio for backup.

As expected, the thirty mile trip from the highway into Puerto San Carlos from Constitución ended up being nearly sixty, with several dead ends, wrong turns, returns to what was the main goat path, as opposed to the road under a foot of water, and the like. We left the boat at first light on the off chance that we just might make it to Po Thang's beach, get the vase and beat feet back to a nice civilized hotel for the night, but by the time we wandered over all hell and back, it was two in the afternoon before we finally arrived.

Just in case we had some kind of emergency during the night and had to leave, we decided to retrieve the vase before dark, but first we pitched camp. While Jan piled blankets into the pickup bed, I made a fire site...or tried. Every time I piled the sticks into a nice teepee, Po Thang grabbed one and took off with it. I finally gave up and threw a small branch for him, each time a little further away, so I could get my fire pit done.

We made a sandwich, had a cold beer, and suited up in dry suits to get the vase, even though the water was around seventy-eight. A breeze had come up, and the last thing we needed was hypothermia. I grabbed the shovel, my mask and snorkel, waded out to my rock marker, and soon discovered that digging with a shovel in four feet of water ain't all that easy.

Po Thang paddled around us, wanting to play. I finally gave up on the shovel, and Jan and I took turns diving down and digging with our hands. The sand fell back into the hole repeatedly, and we soon regretted not bringing air tanks.

Finally, when I tried another dive, Po Thang swam under me and latched onto something that wouldn't budge. I had to go up for air, but I was really worried, because the stupid dog wouldn't let go of his find, and I was afraid he was going to drown himself. Jan and I hovered on the surface, watching him struggle, but when he finally came up, he had the end of a yellow polypropylene rope in his mouth.

Following a hard-fought tug of war, and what came close to Po Thang requiring dentures, we wrested the dog-slimed rope away from him, and pulled it straight as far as it would reach, which was just short of the waterline. Thanks to my dog, we now had a method for dragging our vase onto the beach, but we were worn out, so I drove a piece of driftwood into the sand and tied off the line. By this time we were so tired, all we wanted was a fresh water rinse down, warm clothes, and a beer.

Po Thang remained in the water, circling our dive site, while we sipped ice cold Tecate, and watched him. Every so often he'd dive under and bring us a nice shiny shell, and if we didn't move fast enough, a saltwater shower.

"Ya know, Hetta, that dawg has some kind of personality disorder. And, he isn't gonna dry out before we bed down."

"Seems like a touch of underwater OCD. Anyhow, I'm gonna make him sleep inside the pickup cab. I'll clean him, and it, up when we get back to Lopez Mateos tomorrow. You recovered enough to take a look at the vase?"

"Maybe after one more beer. We have some daylight left. Wet dawg alert!"

Po Thang made a beeline for us, his latest find clenched between his teeth, water cascading from his matted fur. We quickly held a blanket up in front of us to ward off his shake. This time however, instead of returning to the water, he sighed and plopped down near the fire. Even nutso dogs have a limit, I guess.

"He looks so sweet, laying there. Let's cook up some hot dogs and make a bunch of extras for him. After all, look at all the gifts he brought us." Jan reached over into the pile of shells and picked one up. "Even a nice bottle cap."

I laughed. "Never look a gift dawg in the mouth."

She handed me the cap and I held it up to the fading light to see if I could make out a brand. In this part of Baja, debris washes up from as far away as the Pacific Rim and it wasn't all that unusual to find foreign garbage.

My breath caught in my chest. "Oh. My. God. Jan, I think this is a Spanish coin."

"Gold?"

"Naw, I think it's silver." I grabbed a handful of sand and began rubbing the coin, but it was fairly well encrusted. However, I could make out what looked like a crest, and judging by the irregular edges, my guess was we had a coin of some age, and maybe value.

Jan grabbed it and squinted. "Chino can tell us what it is, but where did Po Thang get it?"

We both looked out at the water, but it was too dark and cold to go back in, and Po Thang was done for the day.

Needless to say, between the hard truck bed, coyote howls, a damp fog that rolled in, and the anticipation of finding more silver coins, didn't make for a good night's rest. Even before first light we were up and making a fire for coffee, using the truck's headlights for illumination.

"We need hot food, because we have to get that vase out first thing, and I'm going back in to see if I can spot more coins."

Jan went to the truck and came back with two large cans of chicken noodle soup, which we heated in a sauce pan. I think it was the best breakfast I ever had.

It took another hour before we were able to dislodge the unbelievably heavy basket, net, and vase out of the water and almost onto shore.

Jan grunted and gave it a heave, sliding our steal the last foot. "Dammit, it's a stinkin' vase, why's it so danged heavy?"

"Wet sand weighs a lot. Betcha this damned thing is over fifty pounds and if you add the drag of the water and the soft sand it's still in, we've had quite a fight on our hands. Oh, well, it's done. I'll get some tools so we can cut off the net and get that sand out. I'll feel much better when that vase is safely in my truck. I wish I could back the Ranger down here so we don't have to carry the vase up the dune, but I'm afraid we'll get stuck."

Inside the pickup I found a bag of plastic spoons we brought along for scooping out sand. I didn't want to chance using metal, so the process would be slow, but safer.

"You start mucking it out while I scoop water into a bucket. I'm thinking we should transport it in seawater, because who knows what could happen if it dries out too soon after four hundred years on the bottom. As soon as we can see the base, I want to check it for markings."

"Uh, they'll be in Chinese, Hetta."

"I know, but on *Antiques Roadshow* they say if it's got marks, it can be identified as to year and maker. Did you see recently in the news where a Ming vase someone was using for a doorstop fetched over a million bucks at auction?"

"I'll spoon faster."

I was on the way back, lugging the overflowing pail, when Jan screamed, scaring the living hell out of both me and Po Thang.

My big ferocious dog, instead of running to defend Jan, tucked tail and headed to me for comfort, then trailed behind me as I ran toward Jan. She was still sitting in the edge of the water and I thought she'd been nailed by a stingray.

"What? Are you all right?"

She pointed to a pile next to her.

A pile of wet sand. And silver coins.

Po Thang, recovering from his fright, dashed in and grabbed a mouthful of silver.

"Crap! Don't let him swallow them! We'll be here for another day waiting for him to poop."

Jan, giggling, threw herself over the pile and pushed Po Thang, who now considered the whole thing a game, away. He gave her a friendly growl, trotted over to *his* treasure pile, and deposited the coins on top of the shell collection. He made one more pass at Jan, but by that time I was there to help fend him off.

Miffed, he went back to diving and even brought up a few more coins while Jan and I took turns carefully scraping sand from the vase, adding water, and scraping more sand and then putting the coins into another bucket. As we soon discovered, there was more silver than dirt in that vase, but the sand was so hard packed it was almost like concrete.

We were not able to totally empty the vase because our spoons were not long or strong enough, but we did dig out more than half the contents. I stuffed a towel into the mouth, and because it was so much lighter, we were able to lug it to the pickup, even with the added weight of the water we added to the bucket for protection.

I had a five gallon pail in the truck, so we wrapped a blanket around the vase, put it into the larger bucket, and made a few trips to the tideline to fill it. This bucket had a lid, so at least we wouldn't slosh all the water out as we made our way back over the rough road.

We checked the vase out before we wrapped it and saw it was, indeed, marked on the bottom, and amazingly undamaged. I guess, since I'd never seen one before. Anyhow, no thanks to us, there were no visible chips or cracks.

The design was what I expected, with some dragons and the like, but even to an amateur like me, I could see it was quality.

Ka-ching! Ka-ching! Ka-ching!

CHAPTER THIRTY-TWO

While I herded my pickup over tooth-rattling washboard tracks, Jan inspected our coins between stops. There were multiple stops.

On the way out to the beach the day before, we left a trail of small yellow plastic ties on bushes, and around rocks, so finding our way back would be easier. Jan, newly ecologically correct, what with her whale camp experience, insisted we gather each one, even though some of the bushes were heavily decorated with shredded plastic grocery bags. She wanted to snag those, too, but in the name of saving time, I promised, after we were rich, I'd hire and send in a cleanup crew.

The coins were mostly the same, about the size of an American quarter, but not as heavy, probably because they were pure silver, with irregular edges. They were embossed with what looked like two crowned columns and writing that looked to be Latin.

I'd seen the beautiful gold coins from the *Atocha*, and even considered buying one once in a moment of GOTTA HAVE ME ONE OF THOSE. These babies were fairly homely by comparison, but these coins were *our* coins, and once polished, they had to have some value. We were gleeful, and itching to get to a computer, and our best friend, Mr. Google, but first we had to stash our loot, and my pickup, at Granny Yee's house, then get back to the boat.

Grandmothers are supposed to be sweet little things who bake stuff and are totally predictable. Granny Yee, while sweet, little, and a fabulous cook, has been known to go off on a lark.

For example, when I first heard of her, I had this mental picture of a little old gray haired lady dressed in black, clutching rosary beads. What Jan and I soon learned was she was living with a man ten years her junior whom she'd met online. This, of course, didn't sit all that well with Chino, and when he told us this lamentable (in his opinion) tale, that's when Jan found out her *amor*, Chino, was twelve years younger than she.

Not only that, because of a family tradition of early motherhood, Chino, who is twenty-six, has a grandmother who is fifty-eight. Even worse, his mother is only forty-two! Jan is thirty-eight. Needless to say, this age thing is a major source of annoyance to Jan, one I take every opportunity to exploit when I need to get even with her about something.

But back to Grans Yee. We arrived at her house to find she had hopped a plane for Texas to spend a month with my Aunt Lillian, with hopes of meeting a new man. And since my aunt found all of hers at Veteran's Administration hospitals, maybe I should have contacted the President of the United States and warned him of the possible pillage of patients from the

Texas Veterans Alcohol and Drug Dependence Rehabilitation Programs.

However, with Abuela Yee off on a manhunt, it was easy to hide our treasure inside her house, in a place no one would look while she was gone: her bathroom. While the house was always full of relatives, her personal quarters were off-limits, and no one dared break that rule. Well, except me, but desperate times and all.

A trip to the hardware store and the local *yunke* yard—both owned, of course, by Chino's cousins—yielded materials required for a short term fix for where to hide my treasures.

In her bathroom, I turned off the valve to the toilet and removed the water tank lid and the flushing and refill hardware. From past experience I knew I'd break a couple of parts in the process, but the replacement kit I bought would solve that problem later.

Abuela Yee is partial to baby blue, but that particular color wasn't to be found at the junk yard. I did, however, find a slightly cracked yellow toilet tank lid. I stashed the coins and vase in her toilet tank, filled it with seawater, replaced the blue lid with the yellow one, and superglued it down. I figured I'd have to break that lid when I retrieved the booty, so I put the blue one, and the replacement kit, away safely under her bed.

Just in case someone besides me had the nerve to breach the inner sanctum, I covered the toilet top with a baby blue bath towel, then replaced the statue of Our Lady of Guadalupe nestled in a bouquet of blue plastic flowers.

Jan, my lookout while I re-plumbed the bathroom, sat guard on the porch, hanging onto Po Thang's leash. Grannie's goat, Preciosa, was in her enclosure, but by her agitated bleats and stomping hooves, it was obvious she dearly wanted a piece of Po Thang. Po Thang knew it, and cowered behind Jan. Being a Sunday, all the kids, extra relatives, and fish stand employees were elsewhere, so we had the place to ourselves.

We locked up the house and gate and walked down to the wharf, where our panga waited. That walk took the very last of our energy reserves, and all three of us fell asleep in the panga on the thirty-minute boat ride out to *Nao de Chino*.

We boarded just as Rosa was pounding her spatula on the dinner bell, and were the first to the table. I was so hungry it was halfway through the meal when I noticed Kazoo and Moto were missing. Since Sunday was a king of kickback and do your own thing day, that wasn't all that unusual, but I asked Chino where they went.

"Out for more abalone."

Jan and I shared a sidelong glance, and I wondered if those might be "gold abalone" and how we could find out where they were diving.

Tired as we were, we met in my cabin after dinner to start our search for information on both the coins and the vase. We downloaded photos of our finds into our PCs and split our research. I took the coins, Jan, the vase.

It didn't take long to identify the coins as early Mexican. In fact, this series was minted in Mexico City between 1536 and 1542. They were fashioned by hand with a set of die punches sent over from Spain in order to make "cobs"—coins fashioned from irregularly shaped blanks cut from the end of a bar of silver, and stamped by a worker bee using only a hammer, the dies, and an anvil. The original cobs were meant to be shipped to Spain, and remelted to make regular Spanish coins. The word, cob, is thought to be derived from the Spanish, *cabo de barra*, or end of the bar.

My eyes were closing as I read, and I realized I was re-reading some things three or four times without retaining their meaning.

"Jan, I'm done in. At least before I crash and burn I know our coins are the real deal, if not their value. That means the vase is probably authentic Ming, as well. How are you doing on your end?"

"I'm toast. Evidently coins are easier than vases, because there were so damned many of them. I found a few on eBay that look kinda like ours, but they're all reproductions. I'm too sleepy to do more tonight." She closed her PC, stood, and gave Po Thang a pat. "Night, you two."

After Jan left I crawled into my bunk and the next thing I knew it was first light. I let Po Thang out to head for his pee pad while I headed for mine, and on the way back I heard a noise outside. Peering out a porthole, I watched while Kazoo and Moto unloaded equipment and what I hoped were bags of abalone from their panga.

Po Thang returned, and whined for his morning dog greenie—supposedly the equal to human toothpaste in biscuit form—and I groused, "When do those guys sleep, for crying out loud?"

Which got me to thinking about where they go all the time, and more importantly, how to find out what they are up to besides glomming onto sushi makings.

CHAPTER THIRTY-THREE

Monday was a no-dive day on the ship, so we calibrated equipment, repacked rebreathers with CO_2 absorbent, recharged air tanks, and did routine ship and panga maintenance.

Jan and I used disposable rebreather cartridges, or scrubbers, most of the time, which are good for about two hours, but they were not practical for the larger units utilized by the "real" divers. During my Monday inventory, I found we were burning through our stores of CO_2 absorbent at an alarming rate, so I went online and ordered a big batch. I also added more pre-packed cartridges for Jan and me, as we seemed to be diving more.

Rosa fixed a tray for us to take to my cabin for lunch, so Jan and I could once again fire up our PCs and get back on the trail of Spanish silver coins and Ming vases. I made an information file, copied and pasted important info on our coins into it, opening two windows to switch back and forth, comparing our photos with those I found on the Internet.

Our coins, referred to as Charles and Johanna cobs, were technically not cobs. Why? I think the Spaniards did this just to confuse me almost five hundred years later, but probably because cobs were crude, and these coins showed more sophistication, so maybe were not destined for a Spanish meltdown like the true cobs were. CAROLVS ET IOHANA REGES, legible on one side of the coin, told me they were minted during the reign of King Charles—or Carlos— and his mother, Johanna. A shield, divided into four parts, was marked with an M, for Mexico, and the Leon and Castile herald (lion and castle) were inside the shield, the castle in the upper left and lower right quadrants, and a lion in the lower left and upper right.

On the reverse side were two crowned columns—the Pillars of Hercules—which, if I remembered my Ancient History 101 correctly, graced both sides of the Strait of Gibraltar, and served as a warning to GO NO FURTHER. Huh? If no one was supposed to navigate past the Strait of Gibraltar, why were these pillars depicted on coins minted over five thousand miles west of that strait connecting the Atlantic Ocean to the Mediterranean Sea? This sent me off, as I am wont to do, in search of a reason and found that the Holy Emperor of Spain, King Carlos (or maybe his mum or minions) had a sense of ironic humor. Not only were the pillars on his royal shield, they added the words, *Plus Ultra*, meaning *further beyond*.

Take that, you wimpy ancients!

I shared that bit of fun with Jan, who needed a laugh because her research was giving her a giant headache. "Okay, Hetta, here's what I've got. Our vase is either worth forty-nine dollars and fifty cents, or several million."

"Can you narrow that down a tad?"

"Not without more time. There were thousands of vases made, all of them called Ming."

"That Ming was one busy dude."

She grinned. "It was a dynasty, not one guy. Actually lasted for two-hundred and seventy-five years, evidently most of it making porcelain."

"Luckily the Mexicans only made these particular coins for about six years, but the info is still somewhat sketchy. I narrowed the ones we photographed as four reale coins, a little larger and slightly heavier than an American half-dollar, and worth around five or six hundred bucks."

"And we have how many?"

"We don't know yet. I did a rough count of a hundred, but the vase is still half full. Let's say we have two hundred, multiplied by five hundred dollars is a hundred thousand smackaroos."

"Holy crap!"

"But get this, if we have an eight reale in there, only three, count 'em, *three*, are known to exist."

"Wow. What are those worth?"

"Only one I could find sold for two-hundred and seventy thousand dollars, whaddya think about that?"

"Uh, we're gonna need a bigger boat?"

After our lunch break, I was called to First Mate duty.

As we did each Monday, Fabio and I inspected our ship, starting on the bridge and working our way into the engine room. Let me just start by saying Fabio is gorgeous and I'd considered inspecting *him* on occasion, but after I met his equally gorgeous wife, Fluff, I got over it.

There are many things that can go wrong on a boat. On a ship? Far, far, more.

Fabio, a stickler for safety, had a checklist two pages long, and that was only the Monday list. I'd learned more about boat maintenance in the past few weeks than I ever did on *Raymond Johnson*, mainly because I'd lazily relied on Jenks when he was around.

There are also things that tell you when the brown stuff is about to hit the prop. Gauges abound, and alarms that scare the you-know-what out of you when you haven't been watching your gauges close enough.

Oh, and there are holes in the hull. Lots and lots of them. Water and steam are generated by many sources, and they are supposed to go back out. When they don't, sensors hopefully pick up the problem and alarms go off.

So, kind of like going around your house with a box of matches, or a cigarette, to test your smoke alarms, we spent a couple of hours each Monday testing those on the ship.

On a vessel the size and age of *Nao de Chino*, water intrusion is a fact of life. Water sloshes in the bilge at all times, because there are leaks around packing glands and goodness knows what else, that are expected. Newer boats have dryer bilges, but not ours. Also, for some reason our shower water drains into the bilge. Why? Maybe it was just a Japanese design thing Chino didn't have the money to replumb. The first time I re-reddened my hair, Fabio noticed the bilge pump was on, looked overboard, saw a stream of red, and thought someone had been murdered onboard. He now insists I go with Jan to the Estética Unisex Yee in town for a touch up, which is fine with me. We keep it in the family, and while I'm there I get a mani/pedi and an eyebrow redo. For a couple of grunts on a dive boat, Jan and I keep pretty well shipshape.

So, when we got underway on Monday, and even after our meticulous inspection the bilge alarm went off, Fabio shut down the engines and Chino dropped the anchor, even though we were a mile offshore, because that is what you do when you lose power.

Fabio, Enrique and I rushed into the engine room to find the source of excess water in the bilge, but there was none. One by one we checked the bilge pumps and found a smaller one was stuck open, probably by debris that washed into it. A quick cleaning, and it worked, thereby shutting down that shrieking alarm.

Fabio, however, wasn't satisfied with that quick fix, and insisted on a new unit being installed, and that I help with the job. This First Mate thing stinks. There is nothing I hate worse than working in bilge water. No matter how clean a boat is, how well maintained, the bilge is always a stinky mix of salt water and oil, but the fact that our shower water dumped into this one made it even worse.

I ripped off a pair of yellow rubber gloves from under the sink in Rosa's galley to save myself from what I perceived as death-by-other-people's-cooties, and reluctantly returned to the bowels of the ship to help Enrique remove the old pump, run wires for the new one, and test to make sure the alarm works. My revenge on Fabio was holding the float switch into open position, sounding the alarm with no fair warning to the bridge.

Fabio was likely going to make me walk the plank for that little stunt.

Right after he changed his shorts.

244

CHAPTER THIRTY-FOUR

Jan was crunching numbers in Chino's office, which was less an office than a desk with a couple of drawers, when I emerged, freshly showered, from bilge duty. Po Thang was curled under her feet, gave me a sleepy eye, and went back for his tenth nap of the day.

"How are we doing?" I asked.

She sighed. "Broker by the day."

I looked around, saw no one and whispered, "Then we'd best get busy finding some money."

"That's for sure."

"Speaking of finding stuff, I see Sho and Gun are gone again. Did you see which way they went?"

Jan looked puzzled for a second, then laughed. "I get it. Shogun. And of course I did, you think you're playing with kids here?"

"Think we can pick them up on radar?"

"We can try." She looked around. "Where's Fabio?"

"He should be in the laundry room about now, washing his skivvies."

"That was a mean trick. Scared the crap outta me, too, but I wasn't sitting right next to the alarm horn like he was."

"*Moi*? It was purely an oversight."

"Sure it was. Let's take a peek at the radar screen."

There were several vessels, some of them possibly pangas, scattered inside and outside the bay, but it was impossible to pick out Kazoo and Moto's boat.

"Crap. Okay, Hetta, I guess one day, when they take off, we gotta follow 'em."

"I have a better idea. Let's take Po Thang to his beach and I'll tell you what I have in mind. I'll need your expertise."

"You need accounting help?"

"No, your other profession. You know, the one as a call girl?"

Po Thang had heard his name, sprang to attention, and scrambled out onto the open deck, where he impatiently ran in circles. He jumped into the panga the moment we hooked on the cable to lower it over the side.

As the electric winch slowly let out the cable, I speculated, "I wonder what Po Thang would do if we just lowered him a few feet and left him dangling? He reminds me of RJ. He'd sit in the car, in the garage, for hours, hoping to go somewhere."

"I miss that."

"Well, then, you can sit in my pickup for hours anytime you want."

"You're running a mean streak today, you know that?"

"Bilge water poisoning."

As always, fifteen feet from the beach, Po Thang launched himself into the water, and by the time we beached the panga, he was dog paddling around, diving for shells. We sat watching him carefully, ready to run when he headed our way with a goodly coat of salty water to share.

"Wet dawg alert!" Jan yelled, and pushed herself to standing. I jumped to my feet, we scrambled up the dune a bit, and waited until he shook at least twice. He shot us wimps a disdainful glare, threw his soggy tail into the air, trotted over to his shell pile, and spit out another silver coin.

Po Thang had just secured himself at least three trips ashore a day.

Unfortunately for my dog, we had a veterinarian on board. When I told Chino I had to take Po Thang ashore more often, he insisted on subjecting the poor pooch to the indignity of taking both a stool and urine specimen, and then declared people food off limits.

To make it up to my pup, I smuggled food from the dining room and gave it to him in bites every time he brought us a coin. We soon had a large stash of silver, but Po Thang actually got an upset stomach. Life imitates lies.

We were also keeping a close watch on Kazoo and Moto, whose daily late afternoon dive trips were as predictable as Rosa's dinner bell. They left at four, and were always back for the bell at six thirty. I calculated the speed of the panga, time elapsed, and everything we knew, but they could still cover a large area.

It was time to send in Jana Hari.

We were waiting for them when they came back, and gave them a hand with their gear. Jan, even though there was a slight breeze cooling the air, wore the tiniest bikini she had and was flaunting her wares in their faces. They pulled off the wet suits, and handed them to me without a single glance in my direction.

I sluiced the suits with fresh water, squirting some into Po Thang's mouth in a game he loved. So, between Jan vamping for our divers, and Po Thang racing around barking, there was enough pandemonium for me to do my job.

The next afternoon, Jan and I left before Kazoo and Moto did, and were hidden out of sight, waiting for the men to pass on their way out of the bay. Jan had a waterproof chart, and I brought the GPS tracker sent by Craig, my vet friend in Arizona, and meant for Po Thang.

"You think it'll work?" Jan asked as I fiddled with the remote.

"Dunno. That chip was meant to be implanted right under the skin, and I stuck it into the thickest part of the dive suit."

"Moto's got a tracker on his crotch?"

"Yep."

"Eeeeew. Thank goodness it ain't a crotch cam."

"Oh, I don't—here they come!"

I turned on the tracker, and got a jumble of numbers until a ping sounded and it steadied out.

"We gonna tail 'em?"

"Not unless we have to. The range on this thing is five miles, so if the battery peters out, so to speak, before they stop, we'll have to do the whole thing again tomorrow, from farther out."

Po Thang looked their way and whined. "Can it, Po Thang, they can't hear you."

"He's miffed because we didn't head directly for his beach."

"He'll get over it."

After a few minutes the panga slowed, then finally stopped, still within range of the tracker. "Okay, Jan, I think they're there. Write down these coordinates."

She did, then we plotted it on the chart. Just as we thought, they were off a beach not too far outside the entrance, and to the south. "Bingo."

I shut down the tracker unit, which also deactivated the chip. We wanted to do this several days in a row before making our own foray to the site, just to be sure they were going to the same area each day, and I didn't know how long the chip's activation period was.

We returned to *Nao de Chino* before dinner and deposited ten more coins to our stash. We hadn't gotten back to Granny Yee's house yet to retrieve the vase and the rest of the coins, but that day was coming soon, as her last email said she was disappointed in those Texas men; they were all old and sick.

Turns out something was missed in translation. Grans Yee thought the VA was a single's bar teaming with eligible *hombres*.

CHAPTER THIRTY-FIVE

Jan and I pulled up Google Earth, zeroed in on the GPS coordinates we took down that afternoon, and found out Kazoo and Moto stopped their panga fifty or so feet offshore, just outside a cove on the Pacific side of Isla Margarita. Our chart showed the depth at around forty feet.

"Abalone?"

I nodded. "Looks like the right territory. They live on rocks."

"We gonna go out there?"

"Is there a cow in Texas?"

On Sunday, while Chino and the other Mexicans went off to church, Jan and I bided our time on Po Thang's beach, keeping an eye out for the Japanese divers to return from their dive.

Po Thang was running out of coins to fetch, but his shell pile was growing quite large.

Jan raised the binoculars. "Let the games begin."

We hugged shore, keeping *Nao de Chino* between us and the guys' panga, raced out the entrance and toward the GPS coordinates. We'd tracked them twice more, and they always went to the same place, so now we wanted to see what they were doing.

The cove had no beach, just straight, intimidating, rock walls on three sides. And even though it was a calm day, the surge inside the cove was pretty scary. We anchored offshore, suited up, and tied Po Thang on a short leash when I spotted a couple of sea lions. Last thing I needed was him splashing around with sea lions and being mistaken for one by a shark. Shark? I couldn't dwell on that for long if I wanted to keep a clean dive suit.

"Ya know, Hetta, of all the harebrained things we've done, this one has to take the cake. Forty feet, by ourselves, in the Pacific Ocean?"

"We've done it several times now."

"Inside the bay, in calm water." As if to make her point, the surge made the panga swap ends and hit the end of the anchor line with a snap, jerking us smartly.

"Maybe it'll be calmer underwater?" *Sure, and I've got this bridge....*

"I doubt it. Let's make a deal. We both wear safety tethers attached to the anchor line." She gave the line a tug and declared us soundly hooked.

"Deal. No matter what, we can't be more than fifteen feet from the anchor line so we can pull ourselves back to it, at least. Our rebreathers are good for two hours, and if we have to we can come up fast, no problem at this depth. Got the underwater camera?"

"Yep, and the doggie cam is on. This way our relatives can have one last look at us going over the side so they can play the video for all our friends at our celebration of life?"

"Don't be ridiculous. We don't *have* any other friends," I declared and rolled backward into the water before I lost my nerve.

The surge terrified me. I held onto the anchor line like my life depended on it, which it probably did. Churned by the heaving currents, the water was murky, further upping my fear factor. I almost called off the dive, but Jan went by me and I couldn't let her go alone.

We went down fast, which was fine with me. As long as I concentrated on that line, making sure my hands were firmly attached, I felt somewhat secure. As we went deeper, the surge lessened some but was still way over my comfort level. However, I knew if all else failed I had enough in my auxiliary tank to make it back safely to the surface.

And while I recognized all this stuff on an intellectual level, my brain evidently wasn't relaying the information to my heart, which was in overdrive trying to escape my chest. I was burning air at what was probably ten times the normal rate.

Jan stopped suddenly and I ran into her, almost dislodging my grip on the anchor line. She turned, wide-eyed, or at least I think so, what with that big mask and all.

"What?" I hooted. I didn't really hoot, but I knew that's what it sounded like.

She hooted back and pointed at the pile of rocks rising from the sand bottom. I expected to see something large and toothy, but realized I was looking at what resembled a ship's hull.

And no wonder we were anchored so well, as our anchor line disappeared into a large open gash in the wreck, and was rubbing against what looked like a jagged piece of metal. So far the line was still intact, but I didn't know for how long.

I tapped Jan and jerked my thumb toward the surface and she gave me the a-okay sign, her thumb and index finger forming a circle. We had to get back to our panga, like yesterday, before that line severed. We were in the process of over-handing ourselves to the surface as fast as we could when the line jerked violently in our hands, then went suddenly slack.

Jan lost her grip, but managed to grab one of my fins. We dangled together for a moment or two before she realized her tether was still attached to the line and used it to regrip our lifeline.

By the time we reached the surface and pulled ourselves over the gunwale and into the panga, we were totally exhausted from both fear and being buffeted around by the surge. Po Thang was barking fiercely, and when I looked up I saw we were swiftly drifting toward a rock outcropping, and the breakers pounding it.

Without taking time to remove my breathing apparatus, I started the outboard and motored straight out to sea.

It was at least fifteen minutes before my heart settled down, and Jan and I could laugh at having cheated death once again.

"Looked it right in the face," I brayed.

"Speaking of faces, your's is uncommonly white."

"That's because any color I had in my body drained into my wet suit."

"You two lost *another* anchor?" Chino said at dinner that evening.

"Lost is such a harsh word."

Chino grinned at me. "What word would you use to describe cutting two anchor lines in less than two months?"

"Uh, temporarily misplaced?" One thing for sure, both anchors were incriminating evidence that we were somewhere we were not supposed to be. "You can dock my pay."

"You aren't getting paid."

"See, problem solved."

He shook his head and laughed, as did others at the table. Well, almost all the others; Kazoo and Moto's inscrutable faces twitched slightly right at the lip line.

We discussed Monday morning's maintenance schedule and I asked everyone to leave a list of supplies they thought we might need. I added five new anchors to the list.

Back in my cabin after dinner, Jan and I went once again on a cyber hunt, this time for shipwrecks in the area. Several were listed, but none where we found this one. Or rather, Kazoo and Moto found it.

Fortified with wine, we got up the nerve to watch what we knew would be both fascinating and frightening video of the afternoon's dive.

Before I hit PLAY, I told Jan, "You do know that watching this isn't going to do much in the way of getting a good night's sleep, doncha? That was, without a doubt, my very last dive. Ever!"

"Hey, I'm with you. I'm cleanin' out that suit and putting it in moth balls."

We clinked glasses and I hit the PLAY button.

First thing I noticed was the time, with seconds and minutes in the top left corner of what looked like nothing but a big blue blur. Then Jan's head loomed into the view finder as she grabbed the white anchor line. The sound was what one would expect underwater, except for what was probably me hyperventilating in the background.

Just watching this rerun of the dive tied my stomach in knots. "We're gonna need more wine," I groaned.

Po Thang, who had pushed his head between us, seemed to be watching the video, and gave a woof which probably meant, "See, I knew you idiots should have taken me along."

Jan fetched a new bottle and returned just as the wreck appeared. I froze the frame, slowed it, and we watched as the hull grew larger with each freeze frame. It was much clearer in the video than I remembered in real time, but in my fright, my eyes might have glazed over.

"Look at that," Jan exclaimed. "It's broke almost in half."

"I'd say. What kind of ship do you think it is? Looks to me like that hull is steel."

"I agree, just kind of the way the edges are jagged. I'm surprised there isn't more stuff growing on it. Must be that surge keeps it cleaned off or something."

"Or maybe it's been buried in the sand, and a storm uncovered it?"

I advanced the video a few frames, hoping we'd filmed more before all hell broke loose. Or more like *we* broke loose.

I stopped it again and pointed at the screen. "See that tower laying sideways? I get a feeling this was a fishing boat of some kind."

Jan squinted. "I think you're right. That looks like what they call a tuna tower. From up there they can spot schools of tuna."

"Okay, I'm gonna let it roll. Get ready to hang onto your tummy."

As we expected, everything went wonky when that line let go. The next clear identifiable shot was of my swim fin, and butt.

"Ya know, Hetta, that suit doesn't do much for your rear."

"Hey! Things look much larger underwater."

Early the next morning I loaded Po Thang's doggie cam videos into the computer, mainly for amusement. Watching me and Jan being stupid is always good for a chuckle.

What I saw, however, was anything but amusing. I found Jan working in Chino's office and dragged her back to my cabin.

"You are not effing going to believe this."

"What?"

"You'll see."

I replayed the doggie cam footage, which was pretty ho-hum, except for the two of us rolling out of the panga. I thought we looked pretty professional. Po Thang must have decided on a nap, because for the next ten minutes, which I fast forwarded through, the camera captured nothing but floorboards and paws.

The image suddenly rocked as Po Thang sprang to his feet, and lunged for the top of a gunwale. He couldn't get his head completely over the side because of the way he was tied, but it didn't matter; a large fin was clearly visible, circling the boat.

His barks grew more frenzied as he fought against his restraints, but luckily they held. Then, as the boat rocked violently, Jan and I surfaced like two watermelon seeds spit out by old man Neptune, and we launched ourselves over the side, and into the panga. The camera zeroed in on me as I flopped in, evidently saw we were drifting quickly into the rocks, started the outboard, and threw it into reverse.

And clearly behind us, was that fin. The camera jumped as I turned the boat, put it into forward gear and opened up the throttle.

Jan pointed to the monitor. "Say, did we just nick that shark with our prop?"

"I don't know, but one thing for sure, we spoiled his whole day."

We went on deck and inspected the prop for bits of shark, and while we were there Fabio came outside. "What's wrong?"

"Uh, nothing, just checking the prop. You know, safety first." I gave him a salute.

He leaned over and ran his finger along the prop. "Looks to me like you hit something."

"I certainly hope to hell I did."

Jan dissolved into giggles. Fabio looked confused and left.

CHAPTER THIRTY-SIX

Instead of bilge duty that Monday morning following the sunken ship adventure, Fabio assigned me to replace the prop on our 60hp Johnson and, for good measure, made me inspect all the other pangas and outboards. My penance for dinging a shark.

Jan and I had a new plan for snooping, one that did not involve large predators, wild rides on anchor lines, or, hopefully, butt shots.

Two hours before Kazoo and Moto took off for their daily late afternoon outing—and we knew when that was, for the Japanese are nothing if not punctual—we zipped down to the south bay for a hike across Magdalena Island.

Jan and I had climbed around on this island before, when we were spying on Lujàn, and uncovered his plot for baby whale in a can. Hmmm, am I detecting a pattern here?

Anyhow, it wasn't all that hard of a trek that time, even though the volcanic gravel in places is treacherous. Thanks to Google Earth, we knew it was only about two miles across the part of the island we wanted to traverse, but that's as the crow flies. In Baja, you have to follow arroyo bottoms, or hope for four-legged animal paths. At least we had the GPS, and the shipwreck's coordinates, so if we got lost, we could at least work our way in the right direction.

We also took Po Thang, who is great at finding paths, probably because they have marvelous smells such as coyote piss, rabbit poop, and the occasional rattlesnake skin. I always hope he doesn't find the whole rattler. Chino gave him snake aversion training back at the fish camp, but he hadn't been put to the test in real life.

I strapped on his doggie cam harness and his backpack, which by now alerted him he was destined to be tethered to the boat instead of allowed to jump into the water the minute we neared shore. He took it without too much grumbling because he also knew for sure he was going with us.

Jan and I took small backpacks, so between the three of us we had over a gallon of water, cellphones that might or might not work, our own camcorder, binoculars, dog treats, people treats, sunscreen, bug repellent, a couple of printouts from Google Earth, more dog treats, more people treats, and everything we'd need, except maybe a handy 9mm. Snakes, ya know.

Because we meandered all over hell and back, once again leaving little yellow plastic markers so our return would be much faster, the trip took over two hours. Kazoo and Moto were already anchored at the wreck, and underwater, by the time we arrived, so we set up camp, gave Po Thang water and treats, and looked for the best place to watch them without plunging to our deaths over a bluff.

Jan had the binoculars and I was manning the camcorder as we waited for them to surface. We were stretched out on some very uncomfortable, sharp-edged lava gravel, a hundred or so feet up on a bluff, so we didn't have the best view, but then again, they couldn't see us when they came up. We couldn't linger overly long waiting for them to surface though, because even if it remained light until after almost eight we'd be missed by six-thirty, for sure. I figured on the trip back we could cut our walking time in half by following our markers.

At last, as I was counting the minutes, Jan gave my foot a light kick. "They're ready for their close-up, Ms. DeMille."

I leaned over the bluff, zeroed in on the divers as they swam for their panga, and hit RECORD. I couldn't see all that well because of the distance, but I knew the camera would do a better job on replay. The men heaved nets into their panga, followed them, brought up the anchor, and motored away.

Not one single stinking shark nosed around *them*. They owed me.

We made it back to the boat in the nick of time for dinner, but not in time to grab a shower. We were covered in dust, as was Po Thang, so we rinsed off the best we could on deck and hurried down to chow. Everyone was already at the table, and we dug in, but I noticed our Japanese pals were giving Jan and me strange looks all during the meal. They didn't talk much unless directly addressed, but that was their norm.

After dinner, Jan and I went back out to raise the panga and give it a wash, and while we were at it, shampooed Po Thang. Now, even wet, he probably smelled better than us, so the next order of business was the shower. With all this going on, there wasn't much time for our evening glass or two of wine in my cabin, so Jan turned in early and I was left with a wet dog and an empty glass. I'd vowed to stop drinking alone, and that a dog didn't count.

I emailed Jenks, and turned in myself. The next thing I knew it was five a.m. and I was wide awake. Po Thang snored softly on his top bunk, and didn't bat an eye when I went to the head. He is not an early bird dog.

Hooking the minicam to my PC, I downloaded our footage of Kazoo and Moto the day before, kind of hoping for a shark, but no luck. They surfaced, hefted their dive bags into the panga, then left the cove. Nothing new or exciting there.

I ran it back and started over, frame by frame, looking for anything unusual. Kazoo actually got into the panga first, pulled those dive bags over the gunwale, with a boost from below by Moto, who remained in the water.

"*Boor*-ing, Po Thang," I declared. "Wanna go pee or something? I need coffee."

He gave me a one-eyed glare and buried his head in his paws. Too early still.

As I was returning with my coffee, I met Jan in the companionway. She, too, woke early, so I invited her into my cabin for a look at our handiwork. She arrived with coffee, which garnered a slight head raise from sleepy head, and we reran the footage.

"Stop!" Jan yelled, startling Po Thang wide awake.

"What? What did you see?"

"Look at that first dive bag. Notice anything weird?"

I zoomed in on the mesh bag. "Oh, crap. No wonder they were giving us looks at dinner. That's our anchor they've got there. It's no surprise it took two of them to bring in those bags."

"Yeah, why?"

"Because the anchor is heavy?"

"Yep. But what about the other bag?"

Once again I zoomed in and this time we realized the second bag must have been much, much heavier. Even with the two of them, they barely got it over the gunwale, and Kazoo jumped back to clear his feet from the bag's path as it fell.

I stopped the action once again and we stared at the screen.

"Can you zoom in more?"

"I can try." I fiddled up and down arrows on the screen, but all I did was make it blurry. Then I un-zoomed (technical term) one click at a time, until it cleared.

Jan sucked in a surprised breath, and my heart rate doubled. "Hetta, do those look like gold bars to you?"

"Oh, my ears and whiskers, Alice. I do believe they do."

CHAPTER THIRTY-SEVEN

The best defense is an offense, they say.

When you need a good cover story, the best thing is to launch an offensive.

We were all seated at breakfast when I launched.

"You know, Kazoo, you might have warned us about that abalone hole of yours."

He looked as totally confused as I wanted him. "*Desho*?" he grunted, which is the Japanese equivalent to, "Huh?"

In a scolding schoolmarm voice I said, "Jan and I wanted some more abalone shells, so we went out there where we thought you got them, and the surge was so awful, we never even got to look for any. And, on top of that, our anchor got tangled in the rocks and that's why we lost it."

Kazoo's mouth dropped open, but nothing came out.

Chino rallied to his rescue. "You're saying it's *their* fault that you lost your anchor?"

Jan jumped in with a profound, "Well, duh!"

Fabio let go with a guffaw, and everyone but Kazoo and Moto joined in.

Kazoo did manage to clamp his lips into a very Japanese sign of disapproval, but he still looked at a loss. I waited for him to say he found our anchor, but he didn't.

Moto, evidently a little faster on the uptake, said, "Oh. I believe we found your anchor yesterday. We did not realize it was yours. And you are correct, as that dive area is very dangerous."

Kazoo recovered, and I gotta give him credit, his defense tactic was brilliant. He adopted my own scolding tone and shook his finger at me. "Yes, it is very dangerous. And you, as a novice, should never have attempted to dive there."

Which, of course, stirred up Chino, who gave us a lecture on safety.

Jan interrupted his angry spiel. "Chino, honey, you are so right," she cooed. "Hetta and I have decided we are never, ever, gonna dive again, period."

Caught off guard by this uncharacteristically easy capitulation, he said a lame, "Well, then, good."

Fabio eyed us and shook his head. "*Gringas!*"

We made a great show of scrubbing our dry suits, rebreathers, and other dive gear. After they were sun-dried, we packed everything in canvas bags, declared it all retired, then took both bags down into the engine room, to the gear storage bin.

"Think they believed we never dove on the wreck?" Jan whispered when we were back up on the aft deck, reattaching the formerly lost anchor to our panga.

"Who knows? What I want to know is where they're stashing the gold?"

"If it is gold. We don't know for sure. But if it is, don't you wonder if that's why they are really here. And just who sent them?"

"Yep, I've been thinking about that. If they came here on a mission of their own, financed by someone in Japan, that someone wants that gold. So why, if they knew where it was all along, didn't they just come and get it? Why use the expedition for cover?"

"Because they can't just waltz in and go treasure hunting without the blessing of the Mexican government? Chino has a permit. Perfect cover."

"Yes, but this plan of theirs was hatched, in my opinion, long before Chino was permitted."

"You said yourself the Japanese sometimes plan a hundred years in advance."

"They do, but let's say they did have this, whatever this is, in mind since...since when?"

"Maybe since they gave Chino this ship?"

To make a long story short, Tanuki Corporation, whose employee was my contact for that feasibility study I was hired to do for a desalination plant in Magdalena Bay, were embarrassed when it turned out that their employee, the now beheaded and missing Ishikawa, had a scheme to use the desal project as a cover for his more lucrative whale in a can thing.

As I summarized the events as a way of maybe understanding what was going on *now*, it went like this: "So, Tanuki's man in Mexico (and Ishikawa's co-schemer), Ricardo Dickless Lujàn, got busted when we outed their plans, and as a way of saving face, and earning that GET OUT OF JAIL card for Dickless, they gave the *Tanuki Maru*—which was eventually destined to snag baby whales—to Chino for a research vessel."

"Sounds right so far. Chino, who is well respected both in the global scientific community, and locally, was convinced, especially after we dredged up that astrolabe during the hurricane, that his ancestor's galleon sank and deposited other valuable historical artifacts in and around Magdalena Bay, and someone in Mexico city agreed."

I picked it up. "So, Chino renames the *Tanuki Maru* the *Nao de Chino*, but he doesn't really have the money to launch an expedition, so he applies for a grant from Mexico City and gets a lousy twenty-five grand, which won't even fill the fuel tanks, much less outfit a dive team."

"Well, we did get a government discount on the fuel. Only cost us fifteen grand to top 'em off."

"Like I said, no way he could swing this little expedition. Sooo, enter, or re-enter, as it were, Ishikawa-san. With, I might add, a hundred grand bankroll. Coincidence? I think not, dear Watson. And by the way, I suspect the fifty he offered you was on his own dime."

"I should've taken the deal. I mean, since he was dead and all when I got to his room anyhow."

"You are such a sentimentalist."

"I got it from you, Hetta-san."

I shot her a digit. "And, said dead dude is then spirited away by our favorite villain, Dickless, and his band of merry dicks. Only to later be fortuitously reported as a passenger on a missing airliner halfway around the world."

"I've been thinking about that. Bad as I hate to say it, you and I both know that everyone on that plane is gone. Really gone. Even if they find the wreckage, anyone onboard will never be found. Sad, but so very convenient for whoever wanted Ishikawa dead, but accounted for."

"Someone, I might add, with the power to fake a name on that passenger manifest."

She stood and gave Po Thang a head scratch. "And maybe plant two men on our boat? Men who might be carting gold bars somewhere for someone. I just don't think they're freelancing. Way too much coincidence there, as well."

"Okay, first things first. The gold, if that's what it is. Let's find their stash. It's gotta be between here and the dive site."

"My guess is it's here, on the boat. You still got those keys for all the cabins?"

"Is there a bouffant do in Dallas?"

From the bridge, we closely watched Kazoo and Moto's return each day. They couldn't see us, and anyone entering the bridge would be led to believe we were bird watching, since I placed an Audubon Society book nearby.

After each dive, the two brought heavy bags onboard, removed abalone and lobster from those bags as cover, then washed the bags down. They were pretty slick, but because we knew what to look for, we could tell the bags were not altogether empty.

Unfortunately we couldn't exactly follow them to see where they took those bags, and we had to wait a few days to make our raid on Kazoo and Moto's quarters. As luck would have it, Fabio remained aboard that Sunday, but it was manageable because he was only one man, and we were two very determined and underhanded broads.

Since the two Japanese men had been less than warm and fuzzy towards us all week, we left the ship at the same time as the others to put them off guard. Of course, we didn't go all that far, and watched the ship with our binocs. When we saw them leave, we doubled back.

Fabio was surprised to see us return so soon, but we told him everything in town was closed until noon, so we'd decided to come back and make brownies. Fabio has a soft spot for double fudge with walnuts.

Jan's job was to keep a close eye on Fabio's whereabouts while I executed a little B&E job on Kazoo and Moto's quarters. I guess, since I had a key, it wasn't technically breaking and entering, but breaching the privacy of a fellow shipmate's quarters is morally a big no-no.

Luckily, my morals were breached many moons ago.

Jan and I both had handheld VHF radios with us, just in case she needed to alert me of anyone approaching the boat, or Fabio leaving the upper decks.

I hit Kazoo's digs first, as he seemed to be the one in charge of the two-man team, and literally struck gold two minutes after entering the small cabin. Since we were all responsible for cleaning our quarters and changing our bedding, he must have felt confident enough to store the bars in such obvious spots. He had removed the stuffing from the mattresses on both bunks and stacked the bullion into them. A rolled up futon resting in the corner explained where he slept.

When I pulled a bar through a zippered opening, I was surprised at its heft. Measuring about only two by six inches, and maybe two inches thick, it still weighed a good ten pounds or more.

Not at all resembling the Swiss bars I lusted over on the Internet, these looked as though they'd been poured into a crude mold, but there was no doubt at all they were the real deal.

I did a quick count through the thin cotton fabric and figured they were stacked five high, the length of a six-foot bunk. I'd do the math later, but that was one honkin' stash. It was amazing the bunks hadn't collapsed under the load. I was leaving for Moto's cabin when I spotted Kazoo's PC, open, with the screen saver—cherry blossom time in the old homeland—lit up. I jiggled the mouse, hoping for something like an email from his boss, but everything was in Kanji.

Disappointed, I was turning to leave when the screensaver page changed, and a black and white photo of what looked to be a young Japanese soldier popped up. It would have been hard to date the photograph, had it not been for the background. He was posed, looking solemn, as they did in those days, in front of two banners: the Rising Sun, and the Swastika.

The radio crackled, jolting me from my shock. "We have company."

That was all the warning I needed. Carefully relocking the door, I sprinted down the companionway to my own cabin, hid my precious stash of keys, and went up to join the cookie baking.

When I rushed into the galley, I saw Jan standing stock still, her big blue eyes bugging out of a white face. Fabio, next to her, didn't look much better. Po Thang, held firmly by his collar by both Fabio and Jan, was squirming to get free, and growling.

"Wha...oh, hell!" I cleverly blurted as I realized that Kazoo, Moto, and of all people, Ricardo Dickless Lujàn, were in the galley.

They had guns.

I didn't.

Damn.

CHAPTER THIRTY-EIGHT

As I stared dumbly at the gathering of goons, goon *Numero Uno* spoke. "So, we meet again, Miss Coffey," Lujàn said. He sounded, to my shocked self, like the villain in a grade-B movie.

"Much to my dismay. You practice that line a lot, Dickless?"

His face colored, but Kazoo and Moto seemed confused by our comments, for they looked at each other.

Moto, always the one to break silence, asked, "You are acquainted?"

"Why, we're old buds. Matter of fact, last time I saw Dickless here, he was carting away Ishikawa-san's headless body."

"Shut up!" Lujàn shouted, and pointed his gun—looked like a Glock—directly at me. Then, as an afterthought, he changed the barrel's direction, toward Po Thang.

I shut up.

Kazoo and Moto marched Jan, Po Thang, and me to my cabin, and jammed the door shut from the outside with something sturdy. I know because I put my considerable weight against it and it wouldn't budge.

I ran for the computer to get out an email or two before someone thought to shut down the system. Too late. I was rummaging through the desk drawer for my *banda ancha* thumbdrive as Jan plopped down into one of my two chairs and declared, "Well, shit."

"I couldn't have said it better, except I gave up the "s" word. By the way, you owe the cuss jar ten dollars."

"Make it a hundred. Shit, shit, shit—"

"Less cussin' and more doin'." I tossed her my cellphone. "Here, turn this on and see if we have any bars at all."

I found my *banda ancha* thumbdrive and plugged it into the computer.

"Is that broad band thingy gonna work out here?"

"If you get any bars on that phone, it will. Thank the stars I paid for six months service right before I decided to come here."

We were both quiet for a few minutes. I had my fingers on both hands crossed as I watched my hard drive light blinking. I willed it to bring up the Internet, and my Yahoo account.

"Hetta! I got two bars."

"Move over by the porthole, and open it."

"Okey-dokey." She struggled with the stubborn porthole and it finally creaked open. Holding the phone near the opening, she watched the screen. "Three...four! I got four bars."

I picked up the computer and moved next to her. "Bingo!"

I started furiously composing a message to Jenks, Craig in Arizona, and Nacho—who was going to be royally pissed that I didn't have time to bcc his—when I heard a noise outside and just managed to push the computer under a pillow before the door swung open. Jan, who was trying to call Chino, stuffed the cell into her shorts pocket.

The door swung open and Fabio stood there, his hands tied in front of him. Lujàn was behind him with his gun barrel nudging Fabio's neck.

With a savage snarl he must have picked up from Animal Planet, Po Thang propelled himself from the top bunk, sailing over Jan's head and almost making it to Lujàn, who slammed the door. Poor Po Thang caromed backward with a yelp, but when I checked him for injuries, it seemed only his pride was hurt.

Jan and I cuddled him while he continued to growl at the door.

"Get control of your dog or I will shoot him," lily-livered Dickless squalled from the safety of the other side.

"Uh, him, who? Fabio, or Po Thang?"

"I believe he means both of us, Hetta," Fabio said. He always makes my name sound like Aayy-eee-tah.

"Hold on a moment, I'll put on his collar and leash."

"Make it fast," Lujàn warned.

"Get the harness and his doggie cam," I whispered to Jan. She helped me strap Po Thang in. The minicam, to the uninitiated, looks like a large dog tag.

"Okay, he's on a leash now," I yelled.

The door opened and, as instructed by Dickless, Fabio grabbed Po Thang's collar with both tied hands. He looked down, gave me a look of surprise and a small lip twitch. Lujàn, still standing behind him, missed both.

Dickless motioned Fabio out the door and when I tried to follow, Lujàn stopped me with a harsh, "Stay!"

I jumped back just as the heavy door took a swing at my nose. I was a little luckier than Po Thang had been, but it was close. "Well, Sh—"

"Double that. What do you think they're up to?"

"I dunno, but it can't be good."

"When Lujàn is involved, it never is. Why the hell didn't we off him? What were we waiting for?"'

"An opportunity that didn't send us to a Mexican jail forever?"

"Oh, yeah, that. I—"

"Jan? Jan? Is that you?" Chino called from Jan's pocket.

I decided to forget the email for the moment and zeroed in on Po Thang's doggie cam. "Keep Chino on the phone. Maybe I can learn something from the camera."

Jan talked softly with Chino in the background while I tried to see and hear everything the camera picked up. At first I saw nothing but furniture legs, stair treads, and then the bottom of the refrigerator as Po Thang strained towards it, only to be jerked back.

"Not now," I heard Fabio say. "We have to go see *all* of those men on the deck."

"Jan, Fabio says there are more men on deck."

She nodded and relayed the information to Chino.

"¡*Cállate!*" Lujàn ordered.

"Lujàn told Fabio to shut up."

They went out on deck, and now I saw more legs. Lots more legs.

"Sit, Po Thang, sit," I whispered the commands, sending ESP in his direction. Then I saw Fabio reach his hands down in the best sit signal he could muster with both hands tied together. Po Thang sat, and I could now see as far up as the men's hands. No one said anything for a minute, as though waiting for someone. Po Thang, never long on patience, must have raised his head to glare at Fabio, for the camera swung up and captured three faces. Kazoo, Moto, and Lava Lava.

"Jan, Lava Lava is up there!"

Jan started to tell Chino, but then stopped and look flustered. "Uh, how is it we know Lava Lava?" she whispered.

She had a point. How did we explain knowing him without some serious 'splainin' to do? I shook my head and shrugged.

"Uh," she said into the phone, "there's a large mean looking dude with missing fingers on deck."

Po Thang broke all his "down!" training and put his paws on Fabio's side, giving me a great view of the gathering of goons.

Near the edge of the screen, I watched as our old buddy from the resort, Tadassan Fujikawa, walked to the group and bowed, then singled out Kazoo, executed a deeper bow, then pulled him in for a hug, and a fond pat on the cheek, saying, "*Ichiban no mago.*"

He then gave Moto a similar greeting.

I signaled Jan to muffle the phone into a pillow. "Uh-oh, the plot sickens. Tadassan is here."

"Who? Oh, yeah, the old man. We don't know him either, remember? What's he saying?" Jan demanded.

"I don't know, exactly, but he seems to know both Kazoo and Moto. Not just know them, but *really* know them. I heard him call Kazoo *ichinban* something or other. I know for sure that means number one. Remember those Ichiban Kirin beer tee shirts I brought back from Japan?"

Into the phone she said, "And, Chino, there's also this old Japanese dude that we've never seen before in our lives, but he called Kazoo number one somethin' or other."

I threw out my arms and looked to heaven for help. She pulled her shoulders up around her ears and raised her palms in a *What do you want from me?* gesture.

The camera began going in circles as Po Thang, what with no food in the offing, and getting no attention either, settled down for a nap. He finally curled up, and all I could see was deck and fur, but at least I could hear what was going on, even if it was a little muffled. For all the good it did me, as the three Japanese spoke among themselves for a few minutes, until Lujàn interrupted them. "We must go."

Po Thang heard "go" and woke up. He looked up at Fabio and I could clearly see Lujàn was talking quietly with one of his goons. Louder, he said, "Put the captain and the dog into the panga with Mr. Fujikawa and Dojo."

"Jan, Lava Lava's real name is Dojo."

Into the phone she said, "Lava Lava's real name is Dojo," then realized her mistake. "Scratch that."

I needed a new Watson.

To Fujikawa, Dickless was saying, "My man will drop the captain at the town wharf so he can take our message to Doctor Yee, then ferry you to your car. You may keep the dog as further insurance."

Fujikawa gave Lujàn a slight bow. "Yes, you are right, you must meet with the ship." He walked toward Po Thang, who sprang to attention, but didn't growl.

I soon saw why. The old man bent over and offered him what looked to be one of Jan's brownies. Po Thang took it, and over his crunching, I heard Mr. Fujikawa tell Fabio, "Here is the message you will deliver. The dog and women will be released upon my orders. For now, however, I shall retain this dog, and the women will remain on board the ship. You will be told later where you can collect them. If any one of you tell anyone, call anyone, or alert anyone at all, they will die. Am I clear?"

"Yes," Fabio said in a soft voice that belied an underlying anger I knew from experience was there.

Then Fujikawa added, "And, *Señor* Lujàn, I am entrusting you to not only do what you were told, but also to protect my grandsons with your life. *Your life.* Do I make myself clear?"

"Kazoo and Moto are Fujikawa's grandsons," I told Jan, and she relayed that information to Chino, even though she professed not to know who Fujikawa was. Chino had to be getting thoroughly confused by now.

I closely watched Lujan's reaction to that menacing warning from the old man. A throat spasm gave away the gulp he tried to cover up as he registered the threat. He managed to choke out, "You have my word of honor, Mr. Fujikawa."

I laughed out loud. Lujàn's word of honor? Dickless wouldn't know Honor if it came alive and bit him on the ass.

Po Thang jumped easily into the panga, looked up at Fabio, then back at *Nao de Chino*, and whined. Fabio gave him a reassuring pat and my dog buried his nose under Fabio's arm. Not great for recording happenings, but it melted my heart that he felt safe with our captain.

Just before the outboard motor noise drowned out the sound, I heard Lujàn order someone to, "Check on those women. You have no idea how treacherous they are."

"Oh, you have no idea, you rotten skunk," I yelled.

CHAPTER THIRTY-NINE

We barely had time to turn off the cellphone and shut down the computer before I heard a scuffling sound at the door.

"Jan, look scared."

"I *am* scared."

"Well, look it."

The door flew open and Kazoo suspiciously surveyed the cabin, gave us a lookover, and zeroed in on the open porthole. Glancing at the two of us, then back to the porthole, I guess he decided we were too big to get through, then grabbed my computer, and left without a word.

"Dammit all to hell! At least we still have the cellphone."

Nao de Chino's big diesels roared to life, and a couple of minutes later anchor chain clunked over the bow roller, link by link, around the windlass gypsy, and then dropped loudly into its chain locker.

Jan held up the cellphone. "We won't have a signal for long, I'd bet. Two to one we're headed out to sea, and we'll be losing bars in a hurry."

"Call Chino back while we still can. Tell him we're weighing anchor, so ask him to hide near the pier and wait for Fabio, then try to see where those creeps are taking my dog."

"Aye, aye, sir."

"Sorry. I get bossy when I'm upset."

"Hetta, you're always bossy. But it's okay, cuz you sound like you're in charge, and right now, you are. Aren't you? So, boss, what's next?"

"Danged if I know. One thing for sure, though—we need to get the hell off this tub."

Jan looked at the porthole, then pointedly at my rear end. "I could probably do it. You? Not so much."

"Wanna bet?" I showed her my can of olive oil. Jan started giggling. "Oh, man, please tell me we still have the minicam."

"I'm glad to amuse." I rummaged around in my closet, brought out a pair of sweats, pulled out the drawstring, and stretched it across the opening. "Eighteen inches or so. I think I can do it."

"Well, then, I'm going first, cuz when you get stuck in there I can't get out either." She put her head out the porthole and looked down. "About a ten foot drop. Also dooable. There is one itsy bitsy problem, though."

"What?"

"You can't swim worth a damn."

She was right. The boat was doing a good ten knots, which, in a half-hour would put us five miles off shore, and I could probably, on a good day with the assist of a strong in-coming tide in my favor, swim a quarter of a mile. For all the time I've spent in the water, I've just never mastered the swimming thing. In fresh water I sink like a rock. In the Sea of Cortez, I float easily, but the salinity in the Pacific is much less. And then there is the water temperature.

Mulling over our lousy options, I came up with one that was somewhat less iffy.

"Standby. I'll be right back." I opened a hatch hidden behind my clothes in the hanging locker, went down a wobbly spiral staircase and came back with two canvas bags. Another trip down, and I had snagged two rebreather canisters.

While Jan continued talking with Chino—Fabio had still not arrived at the dock in Lopez Mateos—I unpacked our drysuits, goggles, rebreathers, and swim fins. "They don't know about my secret passage. This gear is our key to getting the hell off this boat."

Jan frowned. "Are you sure? Hold on. Chino wants to know if we think he and some cousins should overpower those goons when they arrive, and rescue Po Thang and Fabio?"

"I don't think so. If he doesn't hear from the old man, Dickless might just go ahead and toss us overboard, which I'm sure he's gonna do later anyhow."

"Chino? No, just try to figure out where they go after they drop Fabio. They might be driving a black Lincoln Navigator. Uh, just a guess." She listened for a minute, nodded and then said, "Hello? Hello? Crap, we've lost him."

"Just a guess? You just *guessed* they might be driving a black Lincoln Navigator? If we live through this mess, you're gonna have some 'splainin' to do. But for now, let's prepare to abandon ship."

"It's getting dark, Hetta. If I go out first, do you think we'll find each other? And in the movies don't people get pulled under the ship by the churning propwash or something?"

"Not if the boat is barely moving."

"How are we gonna slow it down? And even if we can, won't they see us when we jump off?"

"Oh, me thinks I'll make sure they're going to be *way* too busy."

I told her what I had in mind and she clapped her hands like a little girl. "Brilliant. Uh, I think. You won't be in danger down there, will you?

"Nope. Piece of cake," I said with a whole lot more confidence than I felt. I was lucky if I didn't end up boiled like a lobster at Fisherman's wharf.

"And we have to swim all that way back to shore. You think you can make it, even with the suit and fins?"

"I'm sure of it. I've discovered over the last few weeks that panic is what tries to drown me. If I get really tired I'll float, using my floatation vest to keep me above water, and if I start to freak, I'll activate my rebreather. One thing for sure, if we stay on this ship and it keeps going, they're gonna toss us to the sharks somewhere along the line. I'd rather we toss ourselves to the sharks. Uh, that didn't come out quite right. You know what I mean."

"Okay, then, let's get 'er done."

"As soon as I'm suited up, I'll fetch rope from below, so once we do get clear of the ship, we'll be able to tether ourselves together. I'm also gonna need you to help me play one length out behind me as I go down into the engine room, just in case I need a guide line to find my way back."

I shimmied into my lightweight Lycra suit, which made it much easier to wiggle into the drysuit, slipped into the closet and through the hatch onto the landing of those tiny spiral stairs, which were obviously designed with a tiny Japanese Chief Engineer in mind. I'd been through the Japanese size thing before, in Tokyo; I was politely directed to the GIANT section in a department store when I was looking for clothing.

My dive booties were perfect for keeping traction on the metal stair treads, but with such tiny passages, I hoped I didn't snag on a bolt or something and tear a hole in either them, or my suit. The stairway led to another metal door, and another loud creak as I opened it. I stood stock still, straining to hear human sounds above the now louder engine noises coming from outside a third hatch.

My headlamp illuminated a small, pitch-black storage room packed with all manner of gear, including rope of various lengths and diameters. The climb back up those stairs trailing two fifty foot lengths of one inch line, which I estimated weighed at least fifty pounds, once again had me vowing to work out more, but weeks of both diving and working on the ship had made me much stronger.

Rambette!

Back in our cabin, I saw Jan was suited up and had our ditching gear stacked by the porthole.

"Bless Captain Bligh's little heart for insisting each cabin be equipped with emergency lighting sources in case the ship lost power during the night. I've only got this one headlamp, and I'll need it right now. Strap on the arm strobe, and stick the flashlight into your waterproof bag. I see you've packed the gear, so the minute I get back, we're going to be the first rats off this ship, okay?"

"I'll be waiting. I added our cellphone into my watertight pouch, so with any luck we'll get a signal when we get closer to shore, and we can call for help. "

"I'll have to use my rebreather gear here onboard, so just tie my fins with yours, and we'll put then on in the water." I tied the two ropes I'd found below together and handed an end to Jan. "Tie this off on the bunk and feed it out as I go, okay? Oh, and lock our cabin door from inside. If anyone tries to come in, stall them, then bop 'em one if they get in somehow. If all else fails we'll go for plan P."

"Plan P?"

"The one where we panic and leap off a moving ship, get sucked into the props and ground into pink slime."

"I think I like Plan A better."

"Then so it shall be."

I looped one end of the safety line around my waist, then Jan helped me put on my rebreather. Its bulk was going to make my trip back down those narrow stairs, and through passages built for small people, much more difficult, but I couldn't do what I had to do without it.

Because I had to use the headlamp until I got through that third hatch, I slid my facemask up my arm and cinched it tight. Some light made it down the stairs from my cabin, but with the outdoor light fading fast, I asked Jan to turn on my desk lamp and shine it into my closet.

Jan played out the line as I retraced my way through the storage locker. Now came the big test.

Before dousing my headlamp, I cranked the handle over and tried prying the hatch open enough to let a tad of engine room light shine through. Doing combat with yet another cranky metal hatch that surrendered inch by stubborn inch, I managed to snake my head out for a peek. Next time I'm First Mate on a ship, I'll dole out WD40 by the case.

The airtight hatch was smaller than the other two had been, but when I didn't see anyone in the engine room, I squeezed out and made tracks for the chain locker, where I knew a large, and I do mean giant, pair of bolt cutters lived in case we ever needed to cut the anchor chain. I could barely lift them, but struggled my way to the huge generator and left them there.

The electrician's tool box was right where I left it when I helped install and rewire the bilge pump. I took out some wire cutters and scuttled around the engine room, snipping all the wires leading to all the bilge pumps, especially the alarm connection.

The next task was one I wasn't so sure about. Making my way to the automated Halon fire extinguishing system, I traced what I thought was the wire to the bridge alarm. It was too big to snip with my wire cutters, so I lugged the getting-heavier-by-the-minute bolt cutters over.

By now, I was sweating sheets both inside and outside my suit in that hot engine room. Constantly wiping salty sweat from my eyes, I regretted not bringing a bandana or something for a headband.

Now came the fun part. I mentally reversed the kind of check and safety list all savvy boaters live by in order to prevent major damage their boat.

Every boat generator has an overheat alarm, so I disabled this one by severing its wiring, and also removed a thermostat which automatically shuts down a genset when it overheats. I then worked at loosening the stainless steel hose clamps securing the exhaust hose. They were (*Gee, thanks, Fabio, for running such a tight ship*) so secure I couldn't do anything with my sweat-slicked hands. Once again, I hauled those bolt cutters over, and sliced, with a great deal of difficulty, a hole in the exhaust hose.

Immediately, boiling hot water shot into the air, barely missing me. I knew there was nothing more I could do to the generator without ending up like an overcooked spaghetti noodle so I moved on to the next task at hand.

Backing away, I inserted and clamped down on my mouthpiece and took a couple of breaths of refreshingly cool air, before slipping on my mask. Which fogged immediately. Unzipping an arm pocket, I took out a small bottle of defogger solution, rubbed it onto the glass, and put it back on. I could see!

Unfortunately, the heat, and now steam, had me sweating to the point where salty perspiration filled the mask. I pinched my mask's purge valve and dumped it as I made my way to the big honking engines.

With great trepidation, I approached them, looked them over and found the thermostat sensor. Not really knowing what I was doing, I just started cutting any wire I saw, then jammed the blades of the bolt cutter into the exhaust hose. A satisfying geyser shot out, so I once again jumped out of the way, scurried to the other engine and repeated the same operation.

The bilge was rapidly filling with water, and just as I reached the storage room door, engine exhaust number one blew an even larger geyser that reached the overhead piping. As an afterthought, I found what I thought was a pipe leading from our eight-hundred gallon fresh water tank, and cut it.

It was time to boogie. I considered closing the door to the storage room, then decided to leave it open, just in case Jan and I had to come back down into the engine room and try to escape via another route.

Unfortunately that route entailed hand-to-hand combat with a bunch of goons, but on the upside, maybe I'd get to whack Dickless.

That didn't quite sound right.

CHAPTER FORTY

Jan was waiting impatiently, clearly worried about my well-being when steam rose through the hatch. She pulled me from the steamy closet, and slammed the hatch shut. I gave Jan a thumbs-up, pulled off my mask and hood, and spit out my mouthpiece. Cool night air from the open porthole felt like a little slice of heaven on my face and wet hair, but inside that suit I was still boiling.

"Hetta, you don't look so good. Here let me unzip that suit for you." She jumped back as about a gallon of water spewed out. "Maybe you should have peed in the sink like I did after you left."

"Eeeew. I hope you filled our water bottles first. And for your info, I did not pee in my suit. I think I'll use that sink real quick though, before we jump."

"I want to see this, Shortstuff. It's worth—what was that?"

There was a sickening, growling sound, and the boat veered wildly to port and listed sufficiently to tilt the deck and throw both of us against the bulkhead near the porthole. The ship righted itself somewhat, but then the other engine quit and we lost steerage and turned broadside to the small seas. As we rapidly slowed, I noticed a pronounced list to port.

"Okay, Jan-san, sorry to ruin your voyeuristic treat of the day, but now I don't have time to use that sink. Get out that handy knife of yours and cut my safety line so's we have maybe ten feet left. Then, out you go!"

As she cut the line, she said, "No, I changed my mind. You first. I may have to shove your big butt out, so while you were gone, I olive oiled the porthole."

"Great, all I need is some Parmesan cheese. I'm already boiled and salted.

The cabin lights dimmed.

I grabbed our dive bags, and a couple of personal things off the bed, which I stuck into my dive suit and zipped it up.

When my head and shoulders cleared the porthole I realized the upper deck lights were still on, but we were leaning with our side of the ship at about a twenty percent list, which was in our favor. We'd be hard to spot from the deck, even if they weren't blinded by their lights. There was, however, just enough ambient light on the surface to make me remind myself it was only a ten foot fall. It looked like a hundred. I couldn't back out now anyway, for with a mighty heave, Jan pushed my butt, and I was spit out like a watermelon seed. This watermelon seed spitting out thing was becoming way too common.

I did my best to roll, and not land on my face, which I didn't, but I hit the water hard enough on my side to knock the air out of me. Jan came cannonballing down not fifteen feet away and swam over to me.

Gasping for air, I managed to ingest half of a small wave before Jan grabbed my arm and began side-towing me away from the boat. "Float on your back, Hetta, I've got you."

I tried, but without my fins to give me a boost, I sank like that proverbial rock and panic set in. Conjuring up all the self control I own, I fought off every fight or flight instinct in my body, and let her jerk me back to the surface. As she towed me, she said, calmly, "We're gonna get away from the ship, and then we'll put on your mask and fins. You'll be safe. Use your rebreather if you have to, okay?"

I nodded and coughed up seawater, then opened my eyes and looked back up at the ship.

Moto was standing on deck, looking straight down at us. He leaned over and picked something up. My heart seized, thinking it was an automatic weapon.

Then, as the ship listed slightly more, he grabbed the railing with one hand, bowed deeply, and tossed Po Thang's raft over the side. He then turned and disappeared from sight just as the last deck lights went out.

I told Jan about the float, we put on our fins and masks, and with my fins on, I was Michael Phelps personified. At least in my own imagination. The truth was, I was still having to work to stay above water, but if I treaded hard enough, I got the job done.

We finned over to the float, which was dark blue and not easily seen if anyone on deck had looked over the side. Once we had a grip on the float we both paddled rapidly away and were soon out of eyesight from the ship.

Strange, torturous, noises cut through the still evening, and then a full moon blessedly rose from behind the Baja mountains, illuminating *Nao de Chino*, and her alarming angle of list.

"Holy crap, Hetta, what did you do to Chino's boat?"

"I allowed us to escape, that's what. What an ingrate. I probably saved your life."

"Oh, yeah, but then I saved you."

"Might I remind you we are floating out in the Pacific Ocean in the dead of night? Somehow that does not constitute *saved* in my book."

We were quiet for a few minutes as we changed direction and kicked our way toward shore, now that we knew where it was.

"I didn't mean to sink it, you know. I only wanted her dead in the water so someone could get the gold and grab the bad guys. I hope Moto saves himself. He did us a huge favor, you know."

"You think they'll send out a Mayday?"

"Probably not. My guess is they'll try to get as much gold as they can and escape in pangas. From what I overheard when they were all on deck, there's a ship out here somewhere they're supposed to meet. If they call anyone, it'll be them."

"So what did you do when you went into the engine room? Whatever it was, it sure worked."

"Maybe a little too well. I cut the lines to all the warning alarms, then put holes into the exhaust hoses and cut power to all bilge pumps. Well, except the manual bilge pump, but it wouldn't do much against all that water coming in, even if they could get to it. I'm guessing a few hundred gallons of water flooded out the engine room and for some reason the ship is listing to port."

"Why do you think that's happening?"

"I don't know, but—Oh my God."

"What?"

"I need to concentrate for a minute." Jan said okay and I ran calculations in my head to support a theory doing its best to bloom there. We paddled along toward shore while my brain crunched numbers.

"Okay, Jan, I need you to store these numbers under all that blond hair. Let's say one of those gold bars in Kazoo's cabin weighs roughly twelve and a half pounds."

"Okay."

"And I did a rough count of what he had in his cabin, and came up with around…twelve hundred of them? Can that be right? The bunk is about three by six feet and the bars are six inches by two inches, and about one and a half inches deep. They were stacked six deep."

"TMI, Hetta. Stand by." Jan's mental calculator went into overdrive, working on Too Much Information.

I was redoing my own numbers and when we were done we agreed that twelve hundred bars was about right. "Okay, then, here's what probably happened, and if so, that ship is doomed. If one bar weighs a little over twelve pounds, that makes a total of over fifteen thousand pounds. Moto might have an equal amount in his cabin, so when we veered to port, maybe the load shifted. We're talking about thirty-thousand pounds of gold suddenly moving to one side of the ship, and along with all that water in the bilge, it's sayonara, *Nao de Chino*."

"Oh, dear. Chino will be broken hearted."

"Hey, I'm heart broken too. All that gold, lost again."

We paddled in silence once again, until Jan asked, "Think it's okay to turn on a flashlight now so I can see the GPS."

"Do we really want to know how far we are from shore?"

"Probably not. Let's take a break, climb up onto the raft, and see which way we drift."

"Sounds good to me." I hadn't wanted to admit how winded I was getting, but Jan must have picked up on my fatigue.

The minute we stopped churning water, we heard a hum.

"You hear that?" we said at the same time.

It was growing louder.

Jan cocked her head. "That's an outboard motor. What do you think, friend or foe?"

CHAPTER FORTY-ONE

As we held onto our raft, floating and listening, we realized the boat we heard was coming closer to us, but not all that fast. The outboard spluttered some, and had the sound of so many overworked models in Mexico. "Think it's someone from *Nao de Chino* coming after us?" Jan whispered.

"Naw, sounds like a clunker. Besides, I doubt anyone but Moto even knows we're gone. He's not going to tell anyone, since he threw us this raft. We locked our cabin from the inside, and besides, what would they care if we went down with the ship? I think that's an old panga we hear, and it's coming from the direction of Mag Bay."

"Just in case, though, put on your mask and let's use our rebreathers to hide under the float, okay?"

"Good idea." I slipped on the mask, inserted my mouthpiece, let go of the raft and sank rapidly towards the bottom. I managed to grab the safety line we'd tied between us, and jerked Jan under, as well.

She evidently grabbed onto the raft and somehow pulled me back to the surface. Shoving her mask onto her head and spitting out her mouthpiece, she whispered, "Geez, Hetta, you just gotta stop packing in the tacos. What's with you? Smuggling gold?" Then her eyes widened. "Oh, hell, you are, aren't you? How much do you have on you?"

I spit out my own mouthpiece. "Five bars. Oh, and some silver coins."

"Well, for cryin' out loud, drop your weights!"

She helped me release my weight belt and it fell swiftly downward. I suddenly felt much lighter, but I was still too heavily laden with gold to reach ideal buoyancy.

Jan pulled a tube from my vest and pushed a button on the buoyancy compensator. "Let go of the raft. Let's see how you do now."

I didn't sink. "Good, now we need you to reach neutral. Keep adjusting it until we can float just under the raft until that panga goes...oh, hell, I think he's headed for us. Dive! Dive!"

I fiddled with the control on my buoyancy vest until I was able to hover four feet under the raft, and Jan and I held hands as we waited. Sure enough, the unmistakable underwater sound of an outboard grew more distinct. We couldn't be certain how far away it was until, in the moonlit water, I spotted telltale white water stirred by the props. I squeezed Jan's hand and pointed to the whirling water. She squeezed back.

We floated, waiting anxiously until the bottom of the panga glided up to the raft, and nudged it.

A hand reached into the water and pulled on the tether line that was still attached to us. We quickly untied ourselves, and as soon as I was free, I swam to the other end of the panga and sneaked a peek above water. The skiff, an old beat up model not unlike my *Se Vende*, was definitely not one of the newer pangas from *Nao de Chino*.

When the boater started hauling our float into his boat, I had to stop him. I propelled myself out of the water, grabbed the gunwale, and threw my weight onto it, throwing the unsuspecting man overboard. He came up spluttering and flailing, and it was obvious he couldn't swim a lick. Takes one to know one.

Jan surfaced, clambered into the panga and pulled the man back in. It was easy, as he looked to weigh ninety pounds soaking wet, which he was.

The man was terrified, and cringed in the bow as he coughed up water. If he'd ever seen *The Creature from the Black Lagoon*, he probably thought he was living it.

Jan pulled off her mask and hood, and when he saw she was a woman, he relaxed visibly. Mexican men always underestimate us *Gringas*.

Speaking to him softly in Spanish, Jan assured him we were not only not going to harm him, we were grateful that he came along to save us.

I hadn't realized how fluent she'd become in Spanish, but then again, she lived with a Mexican and worked in a fish camp. As they talked, I tried to heft myself into the panga, but couldn't make it.

"Hey, a little help here?"

"You know, I'm thinking of throwing you the raft and leaving you out here. Your greed has finally reached an all time stupidity level. You could have drowned both of us."

"Oh, come on. We're safe now, and r-i-c-h." I wasn't taking any chances of the man not speaking English.

"How r-i-c-h?"

"At today's rate? One m-i-l-l-i-o-n t-h-r-e-e."

She held out her hand. "Well, welcome aboard, sailor."

As we motored back to port, Jan checked the cellphone, but we still weren't getting more than one bar, and decided to save the battery time for when we got closer.

The old Mexican seemed fascinated with the two *gringas* he'd pulled from the sea, and when Jan fibbed she was engaged—which sounds so much more respectable than shacking up with—to Chino, he beamed. Seems he was somehow related. What a surprise.

"I wonder how he spotted us?"

Jan asked him. "He says he can hear a fish fart out here. He's been fishing these waters for over seventy years, and notices anything different. When he saw the raft, he came over to check it out."

"Lucky for us." We were putting along at the speed of grass growing, but it was obvious the old motor couldn't go any faster. "I wish this thing could speed up. We've got to rescue Po Thang."

"Where do you think they took him?"

"My guess? That house in Constitución. Where the black Lincoln Navigator you never saw might be by now."

"Maybe Chino will kinda forget about that."

"Fat chance." I looked out to sea, but there was no sign of *Nao de Chino*. "I think she's gone."

Jan followed my gaze. "I hate to say it, but I agree."

"I hope that surfeit of skunks went down with her."

"Except for Moto. I like him."

"He did the right thing. My guess is Dickless was planning on grabbing the gold, tossing Kazoo, Moto, and the two of us into the drink, and never meeting that ship Fujikawa was talking about."

"Maybe Moto and Kazoo figured that out somehow. Otherwise, why would Moto, who was most likely sent by his grandfather to retrieve the gold, throw us a raft? He had to know we'd sic the authorities on them."

"Fujikawa is just another of Luján's victims."

When the old man heard Luján's name, his head snapped up and he spat over the side. Another fan, I surmised?

I didn't have a chance to ask him, because we heard another panga, and it was headed straight for us at a high rate of speed. In the moonlight I thought I recognized it.

"Jan, I'm almost sure that's Kazoo and Moto's panga!"

Jan quickly explained there were bad men in that boat who would harm us. The old fisherman waved us down into the bottom of the panga, and covered us with nets, then pulled the raft over us.

A wake rocked the boat and we heard the outboards grow quieter as they slowed and came alongside. The fisherman talked with them for a minute or two, told them he'd found the raft floating a mile back, but no, he hadn't seen any people. We could barely hear him under that raft, but he sounded perfectly calm, not giving away any fear he might be feeling after we told him to be careful.

Evidently satisfied with the fisherman's story, someone hit the throttle on the other boat and roared away.

We pushed out from under the nets and raft, and peeked over the gunwale, just in time to positively identify the big panga with twin outboards from *Nao de Chino*.

Jan asked the fisherman what they wanted. He told us they said they were looking for some fishermen who fell off a panga, but he didn't believe one word of it, since he had evidence they were lying right here on his very boat. And, he spat into the water in the direction of the departing panga, and added we were right; bad men were in that boat.

Actually, what he said was, "*Ese hijo de puta rata*, Luján."

My sentiments, exactly.

CHAPTER FORTY-TWO

Luján, that "son of a whore rat bastard" according to our old fisherman, had roared off toward Puerto San Carlos, and according him, he had three others with him, all Mexican. So where were Kazoo and Moto? Since Dickless was looking for survivors, maybe they escaped *Nao de Chino*?

Jan once again checked the cellphone, and got three bars. "Give it a shot," I said.

She hit redial and smiled. "Ringing!"

"Yee haw!"

The old fisherman gave me a toothless grin. Boy, was he going to have a tale to tell around the cantina.

"Chino? Battery running low. We are safe in a panga. Go get Po Thang."

She hung up. "He heard me and was saying something about Puerto San Carlos, but the phone battery just petered out. Dang it, we can't catch a break."

"Are you kidding me? We just escaped a sinking ship."

"Hetta, you sank it."

"Oh, yeah. Well, we're safe, and we have g-o-l-d. Now all we need is Po Thang."

Jan explained to our rescuer that some other bad men had kidnapped my dog and we needed to get to port immediately. He asked why we didn't say so before, and opened up the throttle.

Sigh.

It was nearing midnight by the time we reached Lopez Mateos, but Fabio waited for us at the pier in Granny Yee's van. Chino had told him we were in a panga on the way to port, so they reasoned that's where we'd end up.

When we told him *Nao de Chino* most likely went down, he became furious. "That is the very last hay! That *pendejo*, Luján, he sank my ship? I will kill him." Then he evidently described, in Spanish, how he planned to do in Dickless. I caught the word, *huevos*, and figured Fabio was going to remove Lujan's in some very unpleasant manner. Our fisherman grinned widely with approval and clapped his leathery hands. His night was just getting better and better.

"Fabio, it's last straw, not hay," I told him, to change the subject from who actually sank his ship.

He glared at me. "Why are you still wearing a dive suit?"

"Uh, I don't have anything on under it," I lied. "Want me to take it off?"

"No! Let us go back to Abuela's house so you can get clothes. And your pickup. Chino has been tracking some mysterious black Lincoln Navigator. He sent a cousin to follow the panga with your dog in it, and it went to Puerto San Carlos, and then they got into the car and were driving south the last time I talked to him. That was thirty minutes ago."

We thanked the old man and he asked me to marry him.

I think.

Abuela Yee was back home from Texas.

And she had a new toilet.

The one we left there? With silver coins and a vase in it?

She had it thrown into the bay. Said her nephew, the *yunke* dealer, wouldn't even take it, because some idiot had glued the tank top on.

When we left she was chatting online with a guy down in La Paz. She said he was younger than her, and not sick like all those men in Texas. That VA place was the worst singles meet and greet she'd ever encountered. She did tell us, however, that Aunt Lillian found a new vic…uh, boyfriend.

Jan borrowed granny's cellphone. We called Chino, found out he was still trailing the Navigator, and was entering the outskirts of Constitución.

"Should we tell him where to go?"

"No, ask him to stay on them and maybe we can beat them to the house. I wonder if there's a way to slow Fujikawa down?"

Jan held up a finger. "Chino, can you call your cousin, that cop in Constitución, and ask him to have the Navigator pulled over? I know it's Mexico, but maybe a cop is actually awake at this time of night."

To me she said, "Chino says he'll do what he can. Why couldn't we just ask that cop to stop Fujikawa and spring Po Thang? We get the dog, and game over."

"Because I have information I want to give to Tadassan personally, not the least of which is that his grandsons are not only missing, but maybe drowned. And then, when Fujikawa later learns the *honorable* Dickless is safe and sound, Luján might finally face his day of reckoning. And when the Japanese mob is involved, that ain't going to be a pretty day. Oh, yeah, we're heading straight for that house."

I gave Fabio the slip by running a red light, then cutting through our love hotel. This fight was personal for me and Jan, and we didn't want anyone else in danger. We'd had enough of that. By the time Chino and Fabio got together and found us, we planned to have the whole thing under control. Hey, it could happen.

Chino called us on Granny Yee's cell and told us the Navigator had pulled into a gas station, so I told him to forget about trying to raise a cop. What I didn't say was that the delay gave us the time we needed to set our trap.

The rusty bus across the street from Lujan's lair gave us cover once again. And, as before, his house was lit up, but when I peeked through the gates, it looked as though no one was around. I was trying to figure out how to scale the wall when the gates started sliding open. Evidently someone had opened them remotely from a block or so away.

We scooted through, and around back, just as headlights swept into the drive. From behind a bush, I saw it was a large SUV, not the Navigator.

"Jan, turn off the phone. We can't have Chino calling again now."

"Roger."

Doors on the SUV flew open, Luján and the other dicks stepped out, and went into the house. Luján was not a happy *pendejo*. He was deriding his minions, cursing a blue streak, and I swear, somewhere in his diatribe, I heard my name.

The black Navigator roared down the block and turned into the drive a little too fast and, way too late, Lava Lava saw the SUV. He hit the Dicklessmobile with a satisfying Wham! The alarms on both cars went off, and dogs all over the neighborhood sounded off, as well. The airbags exploded in the Navigator, and the back doors sprang open.

Unfortunately, Po Thang vaulted from the car and headed straight for me.

I was really glad to see him, but timing is everything.

So they say.

Mine is almost always a mite off.

Fujikawa was unharmed, Lava Lava had a bump on his head, and they, along with Jan and me, were being held at gunpoint in the living room.

It was obvious by the actions of our captors that they were pissed off, but not exactly sure what they were going to do about it. I helped things along by recanting for Fujikawa my version of the night's events, leaving out some minor details, like I was the one who sank the ship. For some reason Dickless didn't object to my tale, probably because he was curious as to my side of events. Or because he was going to kill us anyhow?

As I recounted Moto's act of defiance by tossing us a life raft, two of Luján's men exchanged surprised glances, but the significance of later seeing it on the old fisherman's boat evidently didn't register on the boss.

Po Thang had obviously grown fond of the old man, who blinked back a tear when hearing of Moto. He put his head into Fujikawa's lap for an ear rub, and I'm not sure who was comforting who. Whom.

Undaunted by the gun barrel pointed our way, the old Japanese man hissed at Luján, "You have lost the ship, the gold, and both of my grandsons? How could this happen? We trusted you."

"That'll learn you, dern you," I growled. I still hadn't completely forgiven him for taking my dog. And then stealing his affections.

Dickless's face went reddish, and he yelled, "You shut up, Hetta Coffey. I am certain you had more to do with the loss of that ship than you admit. And by the way, how did you find my house?"

"I followed a trail of crap. And you might not believe it, but yours stinks."

Fujikawa grunted approval. Lava Lava actually smiled. Jan drew in a sharp breath, no doubt expecting the top of my head to disappear.

I tried catching Lava Lava's eye to bring his attention to something very important I'd spotted. When the big guy looked my way, I held my index finger horizontally in a "Bang! You're dead" gesture and indicated the gun-toting Mexican punk. Lava Lava didn't have an index finger, but his eyes followed where mine pointed. A look of realization crossed his face, and gave me a blink and an almost imperceptible nod.

I nodded back, then shouted, "Hey, Dickless! One, two, THREE!"

Lava Lava mowed down all three Mexican henchmen, including the one holding the gun, while I tackled Luján. Jeez, the little *hijo de puta rata* was solid. However, I had surprise on my side, and Jan for back up. If you're going to get into a brawl, make sure your best friend is an old rodeo hand. Preferably a hawg wrestler.

We threw the rat pack into a bathroom and I was wedging a chair under the door handle when Chino, with Fabio on his heels, crashed through the door.

"Ya know, Chino," Jan said, "I think it was unlocked."

He opened his arms wide, "Preciosa, you are safe!" He grabbed her in a bear hug and gave her a long kiss.

Jan went all starry-eyed, and I wondered when she was going to realize he'd just called her by Abuela's pet goat's name.

Fabio, on the other hand, was not so pleasant. Turns out the love hotel's night clerk, alerted when I flew through the driveway and out the back, recognized Abuela Yee's van following me, and closed the barrier in front of and behind the van. They wouldn't let him leave until he paid for three porno flicks he'd watched during a previous stay. As he told the story, Fabio gave me a suspicious look.

Poor Mr. Fujikawa, once he got over the shock of what Lava Lava and I did, was despondent. "What have I done? I only wanted to recover the gold for Japan, and I have caused the deaths of Ishikawa and my grandsons." He looked around the room, probably for a sword to fall upon, so I tried distracting him.

"Tadassan, we don't know Kazoo and Moto are dead. Ishikawa? I can pretty well confirm he's gone. Do you know who killed him?"

He shook his head. "I now suspect it was the pig, Luján."

"I think I can help you out with that. But what did Ishikawa do to warrant such violence?"

"I do not know, but I was to meet with Ishikawa the day after the luau. He said maybe we were making a mistake, but he would explain later. There was no later. He disappeared and our friends back in Japan feared him dead, but we were not certain."

"Oh, he is," Jan chirped. "We saw him the night of the luau. He was beheaded. And Hetta took pictures."

"What luau?" Chino asked. "Beheaded? Ishikawa? I thought he was on that Malaysian airliner."

"Jan, I think you'd better take Chino outside. You got some 'splainin' to do."

CHAPTER FORTY-THREE

We left Luján and his men in the tender care of Lava Lava. Actually, I was now calling him Dojo, since we were best buds. We forged a bond following our joint flying tackle takedown, which he gave me full credit for. He said I was a velly smaht gul to realize the bore size of that gun was way too small for a real 9mm Glock, and was most likely an air pistol.

Fujikawa made some calls before we left, and three guys with missing fingers showed up at the house. And to make absolutely sure Dickless wasn't going to have a nice night, I borrowed Dojo's Smart Phone, accessed my email account, and forwarded to him an email I'd sent to myself after the luau. Yep, the one with those damning pictures attached. I'd wiped then from My Photos in my computer, but not before sending myself that email.

I also LIKED Dojo on Facebook. You never know when you're gonna need a friend like him.

Fabio wanted to stay around and join the Japanese dudes in the fun, but we talked him out of it.

Since Po Thang was unwelcome at Abuela Yee's, I went to Rosa's to see if, by some wild chance, I could get some food and sleep before dawn, when we had agreed to go look for any sign of *Nao de Chino*.

Rosa made me some scrambled eggs as she sobbed over the loss of both our ship and her job.

My eggs were a mite on the salty side.

It was a somber group that left the Puerto San Carlos pier at dawn.

One of Chino's cousins had located the dual-engined panga Luján used to escape the stricken *Nao de Chino* so Jan, Chino, Fabio, Po Thang, and I took that one, while Dojo, Fujikawa, and a rather mean looking, short-fingered Japanese man rode with Chino's cousin.

Using the GPS doggie tracker I'd zipped into my waterproof pouch before we jumped ship, when I was still hoping to later locate the *Nao de Chino* and all that gold, I led the search party. We soon got a reading for the chip in Moto's crotch. Well, not in *his* crotch, but his drysuit's crotch. I picked up the signal two miles past the entrance to the bay, but when we zeroed in, we found nothing but an oil slick and some debris.

Fujikawa sobbed inconsolably, so Jan and I changed pangas and held his hands, telling him how brave and generous Moto was to try saving our lives, which he probably would have had the old fisherman not come along to pick us up.

"Tadassan, can you tell me how you knew about the gold your grandsons found?" I asked. Jan shot me a dirty look for intruding on his grief, but, hey, I wanted to hear the story. I also wanted to know if they'd recovered all that bullion from the wreck site.

He told a tale straight out of a Clive Cussler novel.

"It was 1943, and I was a seventeen-year-old sailor in the Japanese navy. I was young and foolish, and actually believed we could win a war against what Admiral Yamamoto called a sleeping giant." He sighed deeply and dabbed tears with the hand I'd let go of.

"That was you in the photograph on Kazoo's screen saver?"

"How did you see it? He should never have taken such a chance."

Since I wasn't about to tell the man I was skulking around, spying on his kin, I was glad Jan diverted him with a shoulder pat. "He loved you and wanted a reminder."

The old man nodded. I did the math and realized he was ninety-three years old, and looked every minute of it in his grief. We waited for him to continue. As we did so, a large air bubble rose to the surface and rocked our pangas.

When we settled out, I prompted Fujikawa. "I lived in Japan, and can understand how your people believed they would win. They are very, uh, patriotic." I actually consider Japan, because of its homogeneous population, the most intolerant, racist place I'd ever lived, but figured this was not the time to debate social mores.

"Yes, and we were more so back then. One would say, in today's terms, fanatical. The military had a plan to buy Mexico, or at least Magdalena Bay, so when we won the war, we would be in place to invade the American mainland, and Mexico as well. Baja would be easy, as we brought enough gold to pay off every official with any influence.

"But what we had not counted on," he gave a slight smile, "were the Texas Rangers."

Chino, who had been listening with fascination, asked, "The baseball team?"

"Van Zandt," I said. "He was a former Texas Ranger, and an American spy during WWII."

Fujikawa nodded. "We learned his name later, after he blew up our ship. There are some in Japan who consider him a great war hero. He was, of course, not *our* war hero, but his bravery is unmistakable."

"Many in Texas never believed him when he said he blew up some Japanese vessels. He said he sank two submarines, but didn't mention a war ship."

"We were disguised as a fishing vessel."

"So the rumor is true? You were on the *Tama Maru*?"

He looked startled. "You know about that?"

"Found something on the Internet, but again, it was considered a rumor. So, why did it take seventy years for someone to come looking for the gold?"

"I'm sure they did, but without any success. I was the only survivor, and considered the ship lost for all time. I have lived long, but when I was told my time is almost up, I decided to try and regain the gold for my country. We hired Ishikawa, because of his ties to the Baja, to track down the wreck. The problem was, I could not recall where the *Tama Maru* went down."

"But you finally did?"

He raised his shoulders. "I had mistakenly thought we were near Scammon's Lagoon, not Magdalena Bay. Remember, I was only a deckhand. We all knew of our secret mission, but not every detail."

Jan chimed in. "So, you sent Ishikawa to Chino's fish camp to see if he could locate the wreck site."

"Yes. But, in the meanwhile, we had a team researching documentation during that era, and found

Van Zandt's story, so Ishikawa surmised we were searching in the wrong area."

"So he hooked up with his former partner in crime, Ricardo Luján."

Chino's cousin spat and said, "*Hijo de Puta*, Luján!"

Everyone in the panga nodded in agreement.

I suppose Dickless should not consider ever running for man of the year.

"And, it unfortunately cost him his life. And ultimately, the lives of my grandsons." He teared up again.

"But how did Luján locate the wreck?"

"I underwent hypnosis. I had drifted in a lifeboat for days before I ended up on a beach, but I vividly recalled the topography of where the ship went down. I was able to literally have a map maker and artist recreate the location, and the rest was a matter of divers scouring the coast."

"Mexican divers?"

"No, we sent our own divers in on cargo vessels, and it did not take long for them to locate the wreck. We arranged for my grandsons to retrieve the gold under the cover of Chino's expedition, and the plan was to have the *Nao de Chino* rendezvous with our own ship, transfer the gold, then leave the research vessel adrift. Kazuto and Mototada insisted we report the *Nao'*s location so it could be saved."

Jan said, "But Lujan double crossed all of you. He was going to take the ship, and the gold, and throw your grandsons overboard. The dirty skunk wasn't counting on Hetta, though."

I shot her a warning look. Judging by the company the old man kept, I sure as hell didn't want an apparent Japanese crime boss knowing I sank the *Nao de Chino*, and drowned his grandsons.

Luckily, at that moment, my GPS pinged.

"Jan! Moto's crotch is on the move!"

CHAPTER FORTY-FOUR

Jan yelled at Chino, "Moto's crotch is moving!"

He leaned toward us. "What?"

"Moto. His crotch is moving away. We have to follow it."

Chino looked confused, once again, by his seemingly demented Preciosa. "I have no idea what you are talking about."

"Hetta chipped Moto's crotch, and now it's moving. Oh, never mind, just follow us."

"And turn on your fishfinder," I added. The old panga we were on didn't have one, but Chino's panga was state of the art.

As we motored slowly, following a now zigzagging pattern, Chino reported painting two moving targets about fifteen feet under us. We followed for ten minutes, keeping up easily. They were headed directly to the ship wreck site.

"This cannot be random, like a fish swallowed Moto's suit or something. Mr. Fujikawa, I think your grandsons are swimming down there, and are afraid to surface, thinking Luján is up here in their panga."

His face lit up, and I saw that seventeen-year-old sailor. "We must alert them. How?"

"Stop the panga, I have an idea." I rummaged in my pocket, found a dog treat and threw it overboard. After looking at me for approval, Po Thang followed, splashing us all in the process. He paddled around on the surface for a minute, then dove. He was down so long I began to worry, and when he finally surfaced, I could tell he was frustrated to come up empty-mouthed, but the dog treat either sank too deep, or disintegrated.

Undaunted, he dove again, and this time he came up accompanied by two very tired, but happy divers.

EPILOGUE

Jan and I both had a lot of 'splainin' to do.

But first we had to find that toilet Abuela Yee had one of the cousins toss overboard into the bay. Her generation of Mexicans still don't get the green thing, and use large bodies of water as garbage dumps. Luckily Jan knew where they dumped most of the time, and it was only twenty feet deep.

Po Thang zeroed in on it pretty fast and we dragged the toilet to shore, retrieved the vase, and I reluctantly turned it over to Chino, along with the gold bars I'd snatched from Kazoo's cabin and managed to save from the *Nao de Chino*. As Jan said, it was the least I could do after sinking the man's ship. And since this gold wasn't from a galleon, he could sell the bars and get a new research vessel.

I hate it when I do something noble.

After losing my summer job due to me sinking my work place, I went back to Guaymas and took the *Raymond Johnson* to La Paz, where it was hot as hell, but my air conditioner worked just fine. Once we were settled in at Marina de la Paz, Po Thang and I drove back north, to spend the rest of the summer at the fish camp.

My new summer job entails cleaning fish and patting handmade tortillas into perfect rounds. I'm getting pretty good at both, and am considering opening a taco stand.

Chino came back from Santa Rosalia one day with a newspaper in hand and gave it to me. The article, on page three, was headlined: BAJA REAL ESTATE BROKER FOUND BEHEADED, FOUL PLAY SUSPECTED.

Jan, who was reading over my shoulder, snorted. "Ya think?"

It went on to identify the victim as Ricardo Luján, but that was about it. Everyone in Mexico knows when someone gets his head removed, it is at the hands of a cartel. And, everyone in Mexico also suspects it is because the victim either had it coming, or was, at the very least, involved in the drug trade. And besides, some folks just need killin'.

On another front, Chino's cousins reported spotting a mysterious submarine that surfaced one night near where the *Nao de Chino* sank, so we figured the Japanese were retrieving their gold. Not that anyone who knows what actually took place that night wants to talk about it for fear of losing fingers, or worse. And since Jan is the only person who knows I sank Chino's boat, I keep a sharp knife handy, just in case she even thinks about ratting me out.

The missing airliner Ishikawa was reportedly aboard has never been found. However, before Dickless went headless he told Fujikawa's fingerless buds where in the Baja desert they'd dumped Ishikawa's body.

Fujikawa must have confessed the sad truth of her husband's demise to his widow, for Chino received a small box of ashes to scatter in the lagoon where Ishikawa learned to commune with whales instead of canning them.

We received news from Japan that Mr. Fujikawa went to that place where Japanese mobsters go to meet up with the many they had a hand in sending there ahead of time. He probably got better treatment here on earth, as he was buried with full military honors and, in my vivid imagination, many three-fingered salutes.

Jan and I, as a reminder of our summer adventure, now wear silver coins around our necks, as I managed to hang onto twenty of them I'd stuffed into my drysuit before we bailed out of *Nao de Chino*. We're still looking for a fence for the other eighteen. Chino was suspicious of their origins, but I told him I bought them on eBay.

And then there is Nacho. He never returned my calls, but one day when I left my bi-monthly meeting at the mine, a camera identical to the one I'd handed off to the panga driver the day Po Thang was returned to me was in the driver's seat in my pickup.

I soon discovered it couldn't be my lost camera, because the lone photograph I downloaded into Jan's computer was taken earlier on that day I got my dog back, and before I handed over my own camera. The photo showed a man, and Po Thang, sitting cozily side by side on the balcony of what I recognized as the resort where this whole mess started. It was shot from behind, and captured a Kodak moment, which I would call it if it didn't show my age. The man and dog, their heads nestled together ear to ear, were the picture of contentment. Just by the back of his head, I recognized Nacho.

Photo shopped across the bottom of the picture was a message: DON'T EVER CALL ME AGAIN!

Jenks, who is due in any day for a one month stay at the fish camp, is bringing me a new laptop, as mine now resides with the fishes. I'm on pins and needles awaiting his return. He says he's heard some disturbing rumors, and that I might have some 'splainin' to do.

Fabio returned to Ensenada right after *Nao de Chino* sank. His annoyance at being the captain of a ship lost at sea was tempered somewhat by Chino paying his entire salary for the summer, and a promise of his part of the cannon loot once they were raised. His parting words to me were, "Do not ever call me again."

Am I starting to detect a pattern here?

Hasta luego!

About the Author

Raised in the jungles of Haiti and Thailand, with returns to Texas in-between, Jinx followed her father's steel-toed footsteps into the Construction and Engineering industry in hopes of building dams. Finding all the good rivers taken, she traveled the world defacing other landscapes with mega-projects in Alaska, Japan, New Zealand, Puerto Rico and Mexico.

Like the protagonist in her mystery series, Hetta Coffey, Jinx was a woman with a yacht—and she's not afraid to use it—when she met her husband, Robert "Mad Dog" Schwartz. They opted to become cash-poor cruisers rather than continue chasing the rat, sailed under the Golden Gate Bridge, turned left, and headed for Mexico. They now divide their time between Arizona and Mexico's Sea of Cortez.

Her other books include a YA fictography of her childhood in Haiti (*Land of Mountains*), an adventure in the Sea of Cortez (*Troubled Sea*) and an epic novel of the thirty years leading to the fall of the Alamo (*The Texicans*).

From the author

Thank you for taking time to read my book. If you enjoyed it, consider telling your friends about Hetta, or posting a short review on Amazon. Word of mouth is an author's best friend, and is much appreciated.

I have editors, but boo-boos do manage to creep into a book, no matter how many people look at it before publication, and if there are errors, they are all on me. Should you come upon one of these culprits, please let me know and I shall smite it with my mighty keyboard!

You can email me at jinxschwartz@yahoo.com

And if you want to be alerted when I have a free, discounted, or new book, you can go to http://jinxschwartz.com and sign up for my newsletter. I promised not to deluge you with pictures of puppies and kittens.

Also, you can find me on Facebook at https://www.facebook.com/jinxschwartz That puppy and kitten thing? No promises on FB posts :-)

Made in the USA
San Bernardino, CA
03 December 2015